#BLESSED

By T M Creedy

For the real Dave and Vicki – thanks for the material.

CHAPTER ONE

Vicki Campbell-Roberts@luckyladysoblessed
Happy Birthday to my darling husband! #birthday #partytime #cake #besthusband #bestcouple #couple goals #strong #kingandqueen #family #fatherandson #growoldtogether #owntheworld #grindhardstayhumble #haveitall #blessed

Katie
April

Of course I noticed him. Who wouldn't? With those melted chocolate eyes, dark hair, tall, lean footballers' body, and slightly shy smile. He had a quirky way of dressing too, which set him apart from the usual t-shirt and board shorts bloke in the street or your typical arrogant suit-wanker on their lunch break. Oh he was noticeable enough – classic tall, dark and handsome.

    I lived in a smallish seaside town that still didn't feel like home, even after almost twenty years. After meeting Adam, the man I was to marry, as a teenager I'd washed up here, leaving everything and everyone in my old life behind because I would have done anything to be with him. His life and future were here, he had decided, and therefore so was mine. I landed a minimum wage job in a high street book shop, for a nationally recognised chain. You know the one – books, magazines, cards and wrapping paper – that sort of thing. It wasn't my dream profession or anything and could certainly not be described as a career by any means, but I had been here so long now I couldn't imagine what it would be like to work anywhere else. I didn't have much in the way of ambition, and Adam always told me it was the best I could hope for anyway, what with me leaving school with hardly any qualifications. He didn't like me pointing out that it was his fault I had flunked most of my exams as I had been in the back of his Ford Cortina most nights when I should have been revising. It didn't pay very much, even as one of their longest serving employees, but it was OK for now while I figured out what to do in the bitter aftermath of our divorce.

I'd reached the dizzy heights of team supervisor and the regional manager had recently been hinting that I could even aspire to become "Management" if I was prepared to put the work in. He said this with total seriousness, with his professional but fair face on, as if working in "Management" was an especially juicy dangly carrot waving in front of my face and distracting me from the frequent soul-beatings of stocking shelves and having to be nice to the customers. Team supervisor was good enough for me. At least it meant that I didn't have to work weekends anymore.

I worked with some good people and we were a happy team, like a family. A family of fuck-ups, but still family. We had a good laugh and looked out for each other. On one of the frequent, cringe-worthy team-bonding days out that Head office insisted on we were charged with coming up with a Mission Statement for our respective teams. Everyone else put forward senior management approved missives about customer service, and best organisational practice. Ours came from an especially awful car-chasey, rogue-cop, the-bad-guys-always-wear-black movie flop in which the rogue cop's partner (the one who always dies first in these films) says "I got your back, dawg" a lot, so our team motto is "I got your back, dawg" to be said as often as possible in the day and always in an extremely bad New York drawl. We failed on the Mission Statement task but, hey, we failed as a team.

Before I found out his name, he was just called "Him"– everyone knew who I meant. I'd seen Him a couple of times browsing the sports magazines. Technically we're supposed to discourage this practice but realistically we all know we'll never stop people from thumbing through the new books and flicking over this month's Vogue or Woman's Weekly – it's ingrained in people to do, and the number of people I've seen SMELL a new book or magazine! So many customers do it without realising, and without knowing they're being pointed to and laughed at by the shop staff. They just pick up a book, open it up to the middle and have a good old sniff. Darren, who works in the warehouse, reckons the printers are using some kind of mind altering, mood lifting chemicals in the ink to encourage people to buy more, a bit like those taste enhancers they put in Pringles which mean you can't stop eating them.

So I walked past Him one day when he was having his browse and smiled as I do to all the customers. (It's more of an 'it's OK - I won't ask you to leave if you're not going to buy anything' smile rather than an actual 'Please, please ask me if you need help in any way - I really have nothing better to do' smile). And he smiled back. Properly, like he was saying hello, which normal customers NEVER do; they either want something or they have a difficult question or otherwise they just want to be left alone to their browsing but they never, ever smile at you like you're a real person.

He was there again the next day and this time he smiled AND started a conversation.

"Hi."

"Oh……..ummmmmm…..hi."

"Nice day today"

"Yes," I said. "Warm for this time of year."

"Very." he said "Looks like we might get a proper summer this year."

"That'd be good." I said, before walking past him with my box of replenishment stock for the Pens section.

Later I had one of those Baby in Dirty Dancing moments – the one where she can't believe she said something as dumb as 'I carried a watermelon'. I should have said something witty and funny back instead of 'That'd be good' but, to be honest, for our whole fifteen second interaction I was wondering what the hell he was talking to me for. Maybe he thought he knew me from somewhere but couldn't remember where, and was doing that British good manners thing of being polite until he recalled my name, or maybe he was one of those people who feel sorry for anyone working in retail and is made to wear a purple polyester blouse as their uniform. Maybe he made a point of being friendly to society's low down on the food chain population, and said hello and please and thank you to everyone – homeless people, waitresses, leaflet distributors, ice cream sellers and street sweepers. Not enough people do this, you know. Maybe he was just brought up nicely and had good manners.

And so this became our pattern, our norm. He popped up every day, sometimes twice a day, either by the magazines or skimming through books in the Business section, and sometimes in the Arts section, where he would be seemingly engrossed in books about photography and design. We always smiled at each other now and said "Hi, how are you?" like we were friends, and this did not go unnoticed by my co-workers. There was much elbow-nudging, eyebrow-wiggling and smirking in my direction whenever he was spotted lurking by the bookshelves trying to catch my eye, but it was all good natured banter.

But it also did not go unnoticed that he wore a wedding ring.

CHAPTER TWO

Vicki Campbell-Roberts@luckyladysoblessed
Best day ever with these ones!! XXX #beach days #swim #sand #sun #familyfirst #barbeque #husbandandwife #sunglasses #Tom Ford #bikini #Heidi Klein #sobeautiful #beachbody #beachhair #goldencouple #luxelife #couple goals #lovealways #kisses
#happiness #ladyhaveitall #grindhardstayhumble #blessed

Katie
May

It might have been a Tuesday when it happened. Probably was a Tuesday; Tuesday's are the worst day of the week, even worse than Mondays because you feel like you've been at work a week already but it's only TUESDAY and you have days and days until the weekend. I saw Him striding towards me, moving in a purposeful manner and waving a magazine at me.

'Hiya, I know this is a pain but would you be able to keep this aside for me? It's the last copy and I've just realised I've come out without my wallet and I'm due at a meeting in five minutes so I could pop in later and pay for it……if that's OK?'

He handed me the magazine, Match, the footballer's bible.

'Sure, no problem.' I said. 'I'll just put your name on it and leave it here behind the till. If I'm not here when you come in later someone else will be able to ring it up for you.'

'Thanks so much.' he smiled widely 'that's really helpful. The name's Dave.'

'OK. Dave.' I returned his smile. 'We'll see you later.', and he rushed out of the shop, but stopped to turn and smile at me again from the door.

'Thanks, Katie!' he shouted.

How the hell did he know my name? I stood thinking, puzzled for about five seconds, then remembered - oh yeah, staff name badge. Katie – Happy to Help! Yep, that's me.

Now I had his name – Dave. Dave, Dave, Dave, Dave. Not the most noble of names but I was willing to overlook it. 'Common.' my mother would have said. 'Nothing good was ever done by a Dave. David Cameron, David Hasselhoff, David Beckham.' She would have reeled off the Dave's she didn't like.

'David Bowie, Dave Grohl, Davy Jones from the Monkees.' I would have countered. I agreed with her about David Beckham though. I held a lot of conversations with my mother in my head. She never stopped telling me what a mess I'd made of my life.

Dave returned just before closing to pay for his Match magazine. I was just starting the end of day duties and was at the till when he walked in.

'Thanks for that. I was worried I'd miss out – got to keep up with the footy. It's the last game of the season soon!' he grinned.

'What team are you then?' I asked, not out of any genuine interest but it was a good way to keep him talking. I liked his voice. It was low and gentle, and he was well spoken, intelligent, not like some blokes who can't string two words together.

'City, of course! I'm City till I die, me!' he said passionately. OK, maybe not so intelligent then.

'Oh right. I'm Spurs. Well, they're my husbands' team really. Ex-husband I mean. But you sign up as a fan for life when you marry into his family.' I trailed off. That was the limit of my football talk exhausted.

He groaned.

'Aw not Spurs? They've had a bad run again this season. See, what they need to do is to sell off some of their mid-fielders and………' He must have seen the glazed horror in my eyes because he stopped talking and laughed. 'Not the world's biggest football fan then?' he teased.

'No,' I blushed and laughed too. 'I always used to switch off when my ex was talking football. Part of the reason we split up, probably.'

He leaned up against the counter showing no sign of wanting to leave, even though we had all but closed the shop doors.

'So what are you doing now? Are you finishing up for the day?'

'Yeah, just got to cash up and that's another day done.' I shrugged. 'Another day done - another day closer to death!' It was something my chronically depressed Gran used to say when I was little and it's always been a running joke in my family.

Dave threw back his head and roared with laughter.

'My Grandad used to say that! He wasn't joking either but it always made me and my brothers' laugh.'

'Maybe it's an old person thing?' I said. 'Something to do with growing up during the war and not expecting to survive another night's bombing.'

'Live for the day – that's what I say.' he was still smiling. 'Will you be going for a drink after work tonight?' he asked.

'Not tonight. Got things to do at home. I'm not much of a socialiser anyway.' I don't know why I said this. It made me sound like a right boring Billy-no-mates. His smile faltered just a little.

'OK. Well. Have a good one.' he said, before picking up his magazine and then with a final "Bye" he was gone.

It didn't occur to me until later that night that maybe, just maybe, he might have been asking me out.

'Go for it.' Mel said. 'If he asks you again you say yes – got it?' Mel was on my team at work and was known for her blunt talking and sometimes brutal honesty. She was a bit prickly with the customers and more than once I'd had to rescue some poor sod from her sharp tongue but she was good as gold with a big heart and fiercely loyal to her friends.

'But he's married.' I sighed.

'You don't know that for a fact.' Mel said. 'He could be separated, or widowed! You might be the first person since his wife died that he's built up enough courage to ask out and you turned him down flat and now he won't have the balls to try again.'

'I didn't turn him down flat. I didn't know he was asking me out! And anyway, it could just be my imagination. Maybe he was just being polite. And since when does he have a dead wife?' I busied myself by giving the greetings cards display a good tidy. 'I'm not even sure I'd even want to go for a drink. I haven't been out on a date since I split with Adam and I really can't be arsed with all that awkward early getting-to-know-each-other chit-chat. I'm too old for that sort of thing.'

Mel snorted.

'Too old? I've got more than thirty years on you and, let me tell you, if a man that good looking asked me for a drink I'd be straight in there like a shot. He'd be warming my bed before he's even finished his pint!'

I giggled. Mel has such a wonderfully youthful outlook on life, she dresses like she's still in her twenties rather than her sixties. She's made a point of growing old disgracefully and I want to be like her when I grow up.

'Well, if he comes in today why don't you ask him out for yourself then?' I asked her cheekily.

'I would – if he wasn't so clearly making eyes at you! Life's short enough and you can't really think you're going to be on your own for the rest of it? You deserve some happiness after Adam so take it where you can find it.' She reached out and gripped my hand. 'I'm serious luv. Just go and have some fun, why don't you?'

'Thanks Mel.' I gave her hand a squeeze. 'But I don't think he's really interested in me; you know - like that. He's just being friendly, that's all.'

'Whatever.' Mel said, in the way of someone who always knows better. 'I'm on your back dawg.'

'Got your back Mel. Got your back.'

The next time I saw Dave I was staring into space. I'd gone to the bank during my lunch break to get a statement, and I was looking miserably at my balance at the bottom of the page when his voice behind me startled me out of my suicidal thoughts.

'You look far away.' Dave appeared next to me. 'Everything OK?'

'Hmmmm? I wish I was far away. Actually I was wondering how the fuck I'm supposed to live on THAT until next pay day.' I waved the paper statement at him. 'Living on a single wage is harder than I thought. Hi, by the way, sorry to moan at you. And for saying bad words.' I said, acutely aware that he probably did not want to hear about my financial woes.

'No worries. I'm a good listener if you need to vent. And I can swear better than anybody so your bad word didn't even register.' God, he was just so sweet! 'I've got time now if you want to grab a coffee?' He raised his eyebrows and gestured towards the door.

'Um – Are you sure?' I said weakly. I hoped he didn't think I was one of those sad, needy single woman who's pathetically grateful for any attention – because I'm not. I don't need charity. But I did need coffee.

'Yeah, course, let's go. I know a place round the corner.' He touched my shoulder briefly and we walked together in the direction he pointed to. I felt a bit awkward and shy in his company but he filled the silence with his cheery chatter. 'I'm on lunch now so I've got until two. I work just a few doors down from you actually, at the EYE 4 Design Company. Do you know it? I'm their main graphic designer but also their number one salesman. Actually, there's just me and the boss, so I'm the number one everything.' he laughed. 'That's why I like looking at the Art and Design books at your shop so much, if you were wondering. Been there seven years now so I pretty much run the place.'

He manoeuvred himself so he was walking on my left, closest to the road. A gentlemanly act, I thought. We came to the café and he reached out and opened the door for me. Another gentlemanly act. Hmmmm, the boy had manners.

'Grab a seat and I'll get the coffees. What would you like? He moved towards to counter.

'Latte, please. Loads of sugar.' I said, trying to sit as gracefully as possible on one of the big, squashy sofas. 'Wait – I've got money.' as I dug into my bag for my purse.

'No, this is on me.' he insisted, making me feel bad and needy again. He returned with our drinks and sat down next to me.

'Cheers.' he said, clinking our mugs together.

'Cheers.' I replied. 'And thanks.'

'We got on so well!' I enthusiastically updated Mel at work later as we were stocking up the fiction section. 'He's just so easy to talk to and we've loads in common. We were laughing and joking like we've known each other for years. And he's got such lovely manners. He was all pleases' and thank yous' to the café staff and one of the waitresses accidentally dropped a cup so he went over to help her pick up the broken bits. But the best thing was that he was genuinely interested in what I was saying. He really listened, you know? And asked questions in the right places.' I was rabbiting on I know but Mel listened to me patiently, occasionally making positive noises at my glowing minute by minute report of Dave and our coffee together.

'And did you ask him about his wife?' Mel cut in, when I stopped for air.

'No.' I don't know why I felt so defensive all of a sudden. 'That didn't come up in the conversation. But he's got a young son, Josh, and he talked about him a lot. He's five.'

'So now what?' asked Mel 'Did he ask you out proper?'

'No, but we swapped mobile numbers.' I said 'So at the very least, I've made a new friend, haven't I?' I grinned up at her.

'Ah that's nice luvvy…..' I knew Mel and she was building up to say something further 'Just be careful – I don't want to see you getting hurt again so soon after Adam.'

'But you were the one telling me to go for it!' I spluttered. 'You told me to go have some fun!'

'I know I did, and you still should.' Mel soothed. 'But if he's got a wife and kiddie you need to ask yourself what's he playing at. He could be one of them love rats with girls all over town.'

'He isn't like that. It was just an innocent cup of coffee.' I'd convinced myself, but I could tell Mel still had her doubts.

He sent me a text later that same afternoon.

Hi. Just seeing if this is the right number?

Did he think I'd fobbed him off with a fake number then?

Hi – Yes, right number ☺ I sent back.

Good. I enjoyed our coffee today. Maybe we can do it again sometime ☺

Oh God. How do I reply?

Yes, I'd like that. My turn to pay next time though ☺
Cool.

Back home alone in my tiny studio flat that night I thought back over what we'd talked about at lunchtime. I liked the idea of a new friend. Apart from my work colleagues I'd deliberately cut myself off from the friends that Adam and I had gathered during our fifteen-year marriage - it being too painful to watch them choose sides. Eighteen months ago Adam had decided that we'd got married too young, too soon, and that he needed to leave so we could salvage what was left of our friendship.

'We'll just end up hating each other of we stay together.' he told me. 'It's not you, it's me.' Yep – he'd actually said those very words.

He'd packed and left soon after, emptying all of the savings in our joint account and flying to Thailand with a girl he'd met online four months earlier. He may as well have saved his breath and just said 'Katie, may I introduce you to my early mid-life crisis?' After that there was no friendship left to save.

I had been so broken by it all that I'd shut myself away, wounded and grieving, and it was only the routine of getting up and going to work each day that saved me from laying down and willing myself to stop breathing. I couldn't afford the rent on our lovely little two-bed house on my own meagre salary so I had to move somewhere smaller and cheaper, and I was lucky to have found this apartment. Yes, it was only a studio but it was a little jewel of a place. It was close to town. I had my own parking space. And although it wasn't exactly spacious, it was bright. Light poured in all day long from the big windows on both sides. It had recently been renovated and my landlady, Jackie, had done an amazing job of making the best use of the small space. It had a new kitchenette and bathroom suite in a neutral modern style, cream carpets in the lounge/bedroom area and Jackie had even bought new furniture for it, a big plus as most of the rental places I had seen so far had been furnished with a dead granny's old cast-offs and unwanted bits of broken furniture. Jackie had provided a bedroom set in pale wood, a cream damask-covered couch with big, puffy cushions and a clever folding dining table set that either seated four people or could be folded away into next to nothing to create more space. It was cosy and homely, and I had brought new pictures and colourful accessories to make it my own. Slowly, I got used to this new way of life that had been thrust upon me without warning and sometimes I even believed I was content.

Coming home to a quiet, empty house that was too quiet, too empty was the hardest part of all, so not long after I moved in I went to our local animal shelter and came back with a pair of guinea pigs, named Monkey and Rocket, and a whole bunch of associated things that pets require – cages, water bottles, hay and straw, and special cereal. Adam hadn't wanted pets, said they were too much of a tie, so I identified with them. They were as unloved and unwanted as I felt and I knew I could give them a safe and happy forever home. They repaid me tenfold daily, making me laugh with their funny little faces and happy popcorn jumps. It was wonderful to come home to someone who was so pleased to see me (even if it was just because I could open the fridge and they couldn't), it was wonderful to open my front door and feel the life of them, giving the flat a heart and soul.

Settling back into my comfy sofa with a glass of red wine and a packet of Malteasers, Monkey and Rocket happily snuffling into their hay in the cage on the floor next to me, I tried to concentrate on the new crime thriller series just starting on the BBC. My phone buzzed with a new text and Dave's name flashed up on the screen.

How you doing?

He's texting me again – in the evening - is this normal for a new friendship? I wondered if I should ignore it, and keep our communication strictly to daylight hours and work time, but I felt guilty, like I was making a big deal out of nothing. I fired off a reply, quickly, before I thought about it too much.

Well, I have wine and chocolate so it's all good!

Good to know. Fancy another coffee tomorrow?

Tomorrow? That was quick.

OK, sure. Same place?

Yes. Can you do 1.00?

I was fairly sure I could manipulate the staff lunch breaks to allow me to leave just before one o'clock. It would mean jiggling a few other people about from their usual break time but it was high time I put myself first for a change.

Meet you there at 1.00?

He sent me back a winking emoji.

Even though two cups of coffee would only be around a fiver, I literally had to empty the piggybank I threw my coppers in, to scrape together enough cash to pay for them. It was so hard living on my wage alone. We had been doing really well with our savings before Adam decided to help himself to the lot; there was almost enough for a deposit on a house. Even though we hadn't been rich by any means, I had never before been in the position of having to scrimp on basic necessities. Now I was lucky if I had thirty quid a week left to spend on feeding myself, after paying the rent and the bills, running a car and trying to keep the tax man happy. I couldn't really afford to buy all the hay and food the guinea pigs needed every week but I wouldn't be without them now, so I made sure they had the best things to eat, even if that meant another night of beans on toast for me. I prioritised buying wine over buying food anyway, taking full advantage of the Co-op's half price offers, never paying more than five pounds for a bottle of Spanish red.

Arriving at the café the next day ten minutes early I was pleased I had got there first. I would have time to get the drinks in and claim the best couch, the big, saggy leather one with all the cushions. I sent Dave a text asking what he wanted to drink.

Hot chocolate please. With cream and chocolate sprinkles. And chocolate sauce. And some biscuits.

I had just about enough money if I stuck to a plain flat white for myself, so I ordered his pudding of a drink and sweet-talked the barista into giving us a couple of the complimentary biscuit accompaniments. Sinking down onto the leather cushions, I fidgeted around, trying to get comfortable. I'm a "curl-up-like-a-cat" person. I like tucking my legs under me and leaning sideways onto the arm of the couch, curled up into a ball and hugging one of the decorative cushions to my tummy, cleverly disguising any bulgy bits.

Dave bowled in minutes later bringing with him the smell of sunshine and his own citrusy aftershave. It was a heady combination and I felt a flicker of excitement deep in my belly.

'Here's your kiddie drink.' I held out his chocolate and cream mess. 'Do you need a bib? Or maybe a curly straw?' He laughed and stuck out his tongue at me.

'You're the one who needs a straw.'

'Why?'

'Because you suck!'

I walked right into that one.

'Child.' I scoffed, unable to stop the smile from showing on my face. 'You argue like a ten-year-old.'

We chatted easily and somehow got onto the subject of travel and holidays. I had told him about the world trip, like a grown up gap year, Adam and I had taken over ten years ago now. We had planned each stage meticulously, budgeting for backpacker places and beach shacks as our accommodation so our money would last us a full two years. Only, a few months into this trip of a lifetime, Adam had got bored of the travellers' lifestyle much sooner than I had. Our savings, which we had both worked so hard for, now went on five star hotels and domestic flights instead of the local buses and trains we were supposed to get and within eight months of leaving dreary, rainy England we were back again. Adam had slipped seamlessly back into his job as a housing officer for the council while I had to practically beg for my old job at the book shop back, accepting all the worst shifts and monotonously working my way up the retail ladder again.

Dave was talking about following the next football world cup and that led us onto places we had always wanted to go. Top of my list was Italy. I had a thing for classical architecture and the history and beauty of the place called to me. I doubted very much I would ever get there now. I couldn't even afford a bus across town let alone be able to fly to an expensive European country. I may have well have wished to be blasted into space.

'You'll get there one day.' Dave said encouragingly. 'Why do you stay in that job if money's such a struggle?'
It was hard to explain to someone just how hard it had hit me when Adam had, rather one-sidedly, declared our marriage was over. I'd sunk to rock bottom, drowning in grief, and lacking the energy or self-belief to launch myself up again. He had talked down to me, dismissing my ideas and my hopes and my dreams as nonsense for so many years that he had me convinced I was nothing without him. For a long time, I believed I wasn't capable of looking after myself. That I needed someone to care for me, and carry me through life. So it was a small but satisfying victory over Adam that I was proving him wrong now. I wasn't winning, but I was just about managing, and it was small, painful baby steps that

had got me this far. Getting my head around finding a better job was one step too far for me at the moment.

The hour was up before we knew it and we both groaned at the thought of having to cut short our conversation and go back to work,

'I feel so comfortable with you.' Dave laid his head on my shoulder briefly. 'Let's just stay here and not go back.'

'Unfortunately, as we're supposed to be responsible adults, that wouldn't be the grown up thing to do.'

I gave him a shove and he slumped sideways onto the couch. Pulling an exaggerated "don't want to" face, he stuck his thumb in his mouth and shook his head, like a toddler on the edge of a tantrum.

'Come on.' I whacked him gently on the leg. 'If you're a good boy I'll buy you some sweeties.'

That evening he sent me a text, quite late and just as I was going to bed.

Can you put up with my company again tomorrow?

Three days in a row?

Why? What do you have in mind?

I really couldn't afford to keep buying expensive coffee and treats every day.

It's Friday! That calls for a celebration – we could do lunch?

Now I don't know what to say. Does he mean a lunch-lunch or does he mean a date-lunch?

Lunch sounds good.   Do you want to meet somewhere?

We could try that new Thai place next to the cinema complex?

OK so this was definitely a date-lunch. He's suggesting a proper lunch at a restaurant instead of grabbing a takeaway sandwich and sitting in the park. I hope he's paying. I text him back.

Thai is my favourite. What time? I'll meet you there.

2.00? Late lunch. My treat.

Good. I wanted to text back and say 'It's a date!' but it felt all wrong and he might think I was weird.

Cool. See you then.

Was I too old to still say the word cool?

I sank back into the couch and finished my glass of wine, then got up and poured another. I have a date tomorrow, I thought. I have a date with someone I barely know and who wears a wedding ring. Tomorrow I will ask him about his wife, I promised myself. I will ask him to be honest with me and if he does turn out to be still married, then I will walk away with grace and dignity. I have no desire to be 'the other woman' for anyone.

Wait a minute – what am I thinking? It's just a friendly lunch with no ulterior motive. He probably gets bored in his lunch breaks and, since we work practically next door to each other, he thinks of me as a good lunch buddy. He's not planning on seducing me between the prawn crackers and the Pad Thai!

Another text lit up my screen.

> **Night xx**

Kisses.   Oh shit.

CHAPTER THREE

The next morning, I dressed more carefully than usual. Not that I could do much to improve my uniform. My plain black work skirt wasn't too bad so I thought I could take a nice top and change into it at lunchtime, instead of the usual purple horror I had to wear. I took a bit more time with my hair, running the straighteners over it and smoothing it down. I'm not one for trowelling on the make-up but I did go as far as applying dark mascara and a slick of eyeliner. My eyes are my best feature I've been told, with long thick lashes and a vivid shade of blue.

I was a bundle of nerves all morning and, unusually, I didn't share my lunch date plans with the others at work, not even Mel. Somehow it just felt too important to share, and too private to talk about, and I didn't want to see the doubt and concern on Mel's face, or invite another lecture. The day crawled past even more slowly than usual but finally it was quarter to two and I quickly ran to the big chemist next door to spritz myself with one of their most expensive designer perfume samples. I was early again and arrived at the restaurant with ten minutes to spare so I waited outside, watching the street for my first sight of him.

Two o'clock came and went, then ten past became quarter past and still he hadn't turned up. I felt sick and so stupid – maybe it was a joke and he was in his office laughing at me, never intending to meet me in the first place. Maybe he'd changed his mind. Maybe he'd had an accident on the way here. I checked my phone but there were no new messages. By twenty past two I'd had enough and my concern turned to anger. Fuck him then! Mortified and ashamed at being stood up I turned to go, glad now that I hadn't mentioned my 'date' to anyone at work.

'Katie! Wait! Where are you going?' He was running up the street to me.

'I thought you weren't coming – you're so late!' My anger turned to relief at seeing him.

'I'm so sorry.' he leaned in and gave me a peck on the cheek 'I was on a phone call at work and it went on for ages. You look great!' He leaned in again and sniffed the air by my neck. 'And you smell amazing.'
He was forgiven as easily as that.

We were seated across from each other in the restaurant at an intimate table for two. Again the conversation flowed easily. We were sharing more and more details of our lives and I found myself talking about things I'd bottled up for years. About how as the third and final child in my family I always felt like I was the tag-along kid, always following my older sisters around and being told by my mum not to ask questions or do anything that required her attention. 'Don't be such a nuisance' were the words that dogged me most of my young years. When I was about nine my eldest sister let slip that I had been an accident and my mum and dad had neither planned nor wanted another baby. From then on the family called me 'Axsy', short for accident, and was meanly used in front of friends and relatives, who would then be confused and require an explanation for the unusual nickname. My mother and sisters would chuckle with amusement and say 'Oh it's so funny this story, she was an accident you see, and we never wanted her!' Cue uproarious laughter from everybody except me. I would hide myself away in my room, or in the rotten, falling down treehouse at the bottom of the garden and plan to escape just as soon as I could get away.

Dave won the worst childhood competition though. He'd had a terrible time when he was little –he grew up poor, living on one of the worst estates in Manchester. His mum had left him and his four brothers when he was nine years old, and with his dad having to work all hours to keep the family housed and fed, it fell to Dave to look after his younger brothers. He'd cook and clean, do all the washing, get them all to school and tried to keep them from killing each other. I was heartbroken for this little lad, especially when he said his mum had promised him she'd come back – only for him because he was her favourite, and he'd held onto that hope for so long. He found out years later that she had told each of the brothers the same thing. That she would come back for them, and them alone. She never did.

'Are you still in contact with her?' I asked, outraged at this woman who'd treated her children so badly.

'Not really. I saw her at my Grandads funeral last year and she sometimes remembers to send a birthday card to Josh. But that's it.' He shrugged it off as if it wasn't a big deal but I could hear the hurt in his voice and knew he must have carried this around with him for most of his life.

'My life seems almost normal compared to yours.' I was almost apologetic. 'I suppose a lot of people have 'youngest child' syndrome. I was lucky. I had a way out when I met my ex-husband. And look at how well that turned out!'

'You've done a lot of travelling though. It wasn't all bad.'

'And now here I am – living alone in a tiny flat with only two guinea pigs for company.' I smiled to show him I wasn't complaining. 'Talk about living the dream!'

'You don't seem to being doing too badly.' he said admiringly. I'd given him the bare bones of my break up with Adam. 'Strong, independent woman that you are.'

'Yes, well, funny how strong you can be when you're forced into it.' It was true, I was a lot stronger now than I ever thought I was capable of.

There was a lull in the conversation as the waiter came to clear our plates. It was now or never, I thought.

'So Dave………Who exactly do you live with?' I asked, shyly, cautiously. He looked confused for a second, then guilty.

'My son Josh.' he paused. A long, long pause. 'And my wife Vicki.' He finished quietly.

'I already knew that.' I told him, even though I hadn't – not for sure. 'I just wanted to know whether you'd be honest with me or if you'd lie because you could. So well done – you passed the first test.' He was silent for a minute.

'Does it matter?' he asked, softly, and looking directly into my eyes.

'No.' I could honestly say that at that very moment it didn't. He kept looking at me, staring into my eyes and I couldn't look away. Something was definitely happening here.

'You have the most beautiful eyes I've ever seen.' he whispered, moving his legs under the table so they were wrapped around mine.

So much for me walking away with grace and dignity.

Vicki Campbell-Roberts@luckyladysoblessed
Date Night with my Love Bear! #Malbec #movies #dinner #greatcouple   #romance   #honeymoonneverends #happiness   #snuggles   #besthusband   #bestfriend #workhardplayhard   #earlynight   #winkwink #hangovertomorrow   #lieinbed   #moresnuggles #grindhardstayhumble #ladyhaveitall #blessed

CHAPTER FOUR

Katie
June

In the following weeks we met every week day. He'd text me six or seven times during the day and I'd run out and meet him as soon as I could get away for lunch. We'd grab something to eat and go to the park, lying on the grass in the sun, or we went back to the same café where we'd had our first coffee together, and sit side by side on one of the puffy couches. Side by side soon relaxed into comfortably slumped against each other, and if we were at the park he'd lie on his side facing me, tickling my bare arms with blades of grass.

It was a golden time of basking in a new relationship. Already so comfortable with each other, we spent the hours talking, laughing and teasing. We found common ground, both admitting that we loved shopping in charity shops, and I discovered that he hated salad cream. Mayonnaise was fine – especially on chips, but salad cream? No way! I told him how I hated all seafood, and couldn't bear to even walk through the fish market. After that, nearly every time we walked past the entrance he would grab my hand and try and drag me in, laughing at the horror and nausea on my face.

He had a way of looking at the world and always seeing beauty. He would point out things to me that he found beautiful – a big old tree, an imaginative shop window display, a happy looking dog. His wide-eyed wonder at the everyday world made me see the beauty in these things too, whereas normally I would have walked past, not noticing the glint of sunshine on the water in the harbour or the shape of the flowers in a garden. I remember thinking that, because of him, it was like I was seeing the world in colour for the first time instead of dull black and white. I was looking life in the eye instead of walking around with my gaze on the ground and missing out on what was happening around me. I floated back into work after these lunch dates with the biggest smile on my face, not caring that some of my workmates disapproved of this new arrangement. They knew by now that Dave had a wife and child, and they also knew there was something building between us.

'It's wrong, and it'll only end in tears.' Mel was probably the most disappointed in me. 'Someone's going to end up being hurt and it won't be him.'

'We're not doing anything wrong, Mel.' I still believed this myself. 'We're meeting in busy public places and having lunch, that's all – it's not as if we're spending all afternoon bonking each other's brains out in a room at the Travelodge, is it? We like each other, and it feels like we've been friends for years. Best friends.'

And it did. He was fast becoming the most important person in my life.

CHAPTER FIVE

I had resisted, so far, meeting him after work for a drink although he kept asking. I knew what would happen if we added alcohol into the mix, there was already an undeniably strong attraction between us and drinking together would dissolve whatever resolve we had left. I was still curious as to why he was doing this. Why was he openly forging a romantic relationship with me, quite brazenly and in full view of our whole town? We hadn't spoken much about his wife, he hadn't mentioned much about his home life at all, apart from little snippets about his son. All he had said was that he was lonely, and had been a bit sad, before he met me.

'I don't think I could get through the day if it wasn't for meeting up with you at lunchtime.' He told me one day. 'I spend all morning wishing the day away, and all the time we're together I keep wishing for time to slow down. I don't want to go back to work - I hate walking away from you, all I want to do is turn back. Meet me tonight after work – please?'

I felt my resistance crumble. Holding up my hands in surrender, I backed down.

'Alright, alright, we'll go for a drink.' I said, before adding 'ONE drink!' in a stern voice.

We met at The Shepherd later that evening. I'd rushed home after work first to change into something a little more socially acceptable than my work uniform, hurriedly fed Monkey and Rocket, and dashed back to the pub where has was waiting for me at a corner table. A bottle of red wine was already open and he poured two large glasses, while I slipped into the booth beside him.

'I thought a bottle would be cheaper than buying by the glass, and there's not much more than two glasses in here anyway.' He passed me my glass and I took a large swig, swallowing almost half a glass in a single gulp. Feeling the alcohol hit my empty stomach I relaxed and concentrated on enjoying being out on a sunny evening.

The pub was quiet so we could talk without having to shout over other peoples' noise. The wine slipped down easily and by the time we'd finished the bottle I had felt serene and happy.

'Fancy another?' he said, pointing at our empty glasses.

'Oh go on then, I'll get them though.' I said, making my way over to the bar. Dave was right – a bottle worked out cheaper than two glasses so I ordered another, choosing a Spanish Rioja that I knew was decent and praying my debit card wouldn't be declined. 'Cheers.' we said, clinking glasses again. Another glass of wine and I was definitely feeling the effects. We hadn't stopped talking and laughing. Almost without noticing, we had slid closer together on the padded bench seat and were leaning into each other, legs entwined under the table. His phone rang. He glanced at the caller display.

'Shit, sorry. I've got to take this.' He answered the call and I couldn't believe it when he proceeded to chat to someone called Razza about their football training the next day, of all things. As if that was an essential call he absolutely needed to take while he was in my company! Feeling neglected, and more than a little bit drunk, I started poking him in the ribs making him gasp and laugh.

'Stop ignoring me!' I said, squealing when he put him hand over my mouth to shut me up. He was still trying to keep his conversation going with Razza and at the same time tickling me with his other hand. I bit his hand, the one covering my mouth, hard.

'Gotta go mate, speak to you tomorrow.' he hurriedly finished his phone call and cut Razza off. 'Ouch! I can't believe you did that! That hurt!' he laughed.

'You were neglecting me!' I said in mock outrage.

'I'd never neglect you. You're unneglectable!' he declared. 'Yes that is a word. He got in there before I could pull him up on his non-words. 'And beautiful and interesting and funny and sexy.' He kissed the tip of my nose. Then he cupped my face and gave me a soft, gentle kiss on my lips. 'I hope you know I'm serious about this – about us' as he stroked the side of my cheek. 'I don't want you to think I'm some kind of player. All I know is that I want to be with you, spend all my time with you, and make you happy again. I want to be the one who takes the sadness out of your eyes.'

'But....' I was lost for words, and lost in his eyes. 'You can't..... You're risking everything. I've got nothing to lose but you have.' I exclaimed. 'Look, I don't care that you're married and I know that sounds bad but it's true. Your marriage is your lookout and your business, not mine. But I'm not looking for complications in my life, and skulking about hiding from your wife is not exactly romantic. This town is too small – you WILL get found out.' I told him.

'It won't be like that.' He promised, and leaned in to kiss me again. 'See, we're out in the open and I'm kissing you and I don't care who sees us. Oh God, why couldn't I have met you before I got married?'

All of a sudden I felt stone cold sober. This was the crossroads – I could stop this right now before too much damage was done or I could continue playing the game.

'I need the loo.' I said, disentangling myself from his embrace, and rushing up the stairs to the Ladies. I smoothed down my hair and looked at my flushed face in the mirror, my eyes sparkling, my cheeks pink from too much wine and too much attention. What do I do? I asked my reflection. I like him, I really, really like him. So do I let this carry on to the next, inevitable stage where it becomes a proper affair and accept that I will be the other woman? The hidden woman, the one who spends Christmas alone because he has obligations to his family and needs to keep the appearances up. The one who spends her nights on high alert, waiting for him to find a spare hour so they can hook up for sex? Or do I do the responsible, grown up thing and send him back to his wife?

The wine I had drunk made my decision for me. Fuck it! I was triumphant. He wanted me, he'd made that clear. Nobody had shown me this much attention in a long, long time.

Let's see how far he's prepared to take this.

Coming back downstairs I looked over at our table. It was empty – he had gone.

He hadn't quite gone. On the bench behind the table, placed where I would see it, was a shoe. His shoe. Just the one. I collapsed with laughter. This was his way of telling me he'd be back, and true enough, he limped back into the pub on the other shoe, seconds later.

'Just nipped out for a quick smoke.' He said, pleased with himself for coming up with this clever message to me. He knew I'd get it. 'Come on – let's go. I'll walk you home.'

It was a clear night after a warm day but there was a sneaky cold breeze licking up and down the street. It was only a ten-minute walk back to my place and our path took us straight past his office. I shivered and Dave said he had a spare jumper at his work and we could drop in and get it if I was cold. He unlocked the door to EYE 4 Design and let us in. It was a large, modern open plan space that smelt of printer ink and paper dust.

'This is me.' he pointed to the large corner desk unit. I took in the big double screen PC and various printer type gadgets. I took in the family photos of him, his wife and his son that took pride of place. They were professional studio shots and showed an adorable dark haired boy giggling uncontrollably at the camera, while his proud parents looked on with undisguised love and affection.

Dave turned me round by my shoulders and kissed me, properly. Hard and passionate. He backed me up against his desk and bent me backwards so I was semi-lying across the top, pressing up hard against my pubic bone and lying almost completely on top of me.

'Are you sure you know what you're getting into?' I whispered seriously. His only answer was to kiss me again.

Later he walked me home. It was clear he wanted to go further than kissing but I just wasn't feeling it – instead I could feel his wife's gaze staring at me from her photo on the wall. Her smug smile making me feel…….. not guilty, not exactly, more like I had just been issued a challenge. It was his son Josh's happy, gappy grin that made me stop and push Dave away. Wrong place for this, I thought. And the harsh light in the office made me feel uncomfortable about taking my clothes off, even though Dave's hands were already under my top, undoing my bra and squeezing my breasts. I sat up, flustered, my back aching from being pressed into the desk's hard surface. I didn't have to say anything; he knew this was not going to be the night. And anyway, I wanted romance. I wanted candlelight and soft music, a comfortable surface. I'm not fussy, it didn't have to be a bed. A fluffy rug on the floor in front of a roaring fire would be perfectly acceptable. He walked me home and I made it clear that he wasn't coming in with me, not then.

Thank you for a wonderful evening.

His texts came through just as I was getting into bed.

I'm walking home, thinking of you x

I held my phone in my hand for ages, wondering if I should reply. Confusion, drink and tiredness fogged my brain and I set the phone down next to my bed and switched off the light. It wouldn't hurt to back off a little now and let him wonder why I didn't text him back. I needed him to know that I had no intention of being an easy lay.

Sleep wouldn't come that night. However hard I tried I couldn't get the thought that I was caught up in something dangerous and life-changing out of my head, and that I should be running as fast as I could in the opposite direction. My phone chirped once more.

> **I want to be with you. I want to hold you in my arms, on a soft fur rug in front of a roaring fire. I can see us in a tiny wooden cabin somewhere, with snow falling down and covering the windows. I can see you looking up at me with those big blue eyes of yours and smiling that beautiful smile. The one you keep only for me. I would lay you down gently on that rug and make love to you until we both cried with ecstasy. When I am with you, there is no one else in this world. There is just you and me. Sleep well. X**

Whoa, did this guy have the ability to see into my mind? Did he know what I was thinking? I'm scared.

CHAPTER SIX

The next day at work I was tired and hungover. I'd just dealt with a staffing crisis as two people had gone sick and I had to ring round our casual staff to see if anyone could fill in at short notice.

'Good, was he?' Leered Darren loudly, and in front of everyone else during the morning tea break, pointing to a faint mark on my neck. Damn, there's no way I could pass that off as a work injury, I thought, checking it out in the mirror in the staffroom. That was definitely stubble rash bordering on a hickey.

'Never you mind.' Was the best I could come back with. I just wasn't in the mood for one of Darren's light-hearted ribbings. I could sense Mel's disapproval, tinged with genuine concern, from across the room. I was going to have to hear her out, even though she had no right to lecture me on my private life, I thought crossly. Thankfully, saved by the bell – just then the phone in the staffroom rang and I answered it.

'Oooh Katie, there's been a delivery for you!' Sang Philippa, who was working on the main tills at the front of the shop. She sounded full of excitement and I knew she couldn't wait to gossip about this to the others later.

'Be right there.' I said coolly, giving nothing away and deliberately making them all think that I'd been called away to deal with another work problem on the shop floor.

When I got downstairs Philippa pointed to the large, colourful box that had been left. **For Katie** it said in big colourful letters on the top. It was huge, at least three-foot-tall, with **'Open this way up'** written on it in black marker.

'A young man left it for you.' She gripped my arm in a painful death grip with glee. 'Lovely looking he was, very polite too. And look! He's buying you presents already. Big presents!' she trilled approvingly.

35

There was no way I could move the box to anywhere more private and by now a small crowd of both staff and shoppers had gathered around it, speculating on what could be inside. I had a mad flash of imagination and pictured Dave jumping out of the box stark naked and with a raging hard-on, shouting 'Ta-Dah!!' That would get a mention in the shopper satisfaction surveys...

Grabbing some scissors from the till area I used them to carefully slice open the packing tape on the top of the box. Pulling back the cardboard, I peered into the void and out floated a unicorn. Well, a unicorn balloon anyway. An actual life-sized (how did I know it was life-sized? Have YOU ever seen a unicorn? No? Well then, how do you know what size they are?) - A beautiful pink and white helium balloon in the shape of a unicorn, then. It had an envelope tied around its neck and another, smaller, box attached to its back. A collective gasp and an 'Ooooooooh' came from the group of onlookers, and then a small round of applause.

'Read us the note!' Somebody yelled.

'What's in the small box?' Shouted another.

'Sorry folks! The note and the box are for my eyes only.' I said, getting a bit annoyed at the lack of privacy and the ostentatious display I was unintentionally providing. The unicorn was floating gently in the air, weighted down by little silver decorations on its hooves. I untied the envelope, opened it and read:

> **I have been so lucky. I have found a mythical and beautiful creature that only exists in legend. It is more stunning than I could have imagined, and I am entranced by its mystery and allure. I can only hope that this enigma finds me worthy and places her trust and faith in me. I cannot wait to spend time in her company again XXX**

My heart twisted with hope and desire. My brain cringed with embarrassment. Mythical creature? Alluring enigma? That was a bit much.

I took the box from the unicorns' back and looked closely at it. It was almost definitely from a jewellers and looked expensive. Opening it slowly, there, resting on a bed of blue velvet, was the most beautiful sliver necklace I had ever seen. I had mentioned to Dave weeks ago how much I loved silver jewellery, especially antique jewellery, and now he had found this. He had probably spent hours looking for something unusual and unique which he thought I would like. The delicate silver twist chain held a heavy pendant which flowed down from the centre of the necklace. It was in the shape of a fairy, exquisitely made in pure silver with its filigree wings outstretched, it was simply breathtakingly stunning. It was almost certainly made in the 1920's when the Cottingley fairy hoax was at its peak, and the gentry went mad for all things fey. There was another note inside the pendant box.

This fairy symbolizes that our lives are forever linked and our love forever strong. Wear it with the love in which it was given.

Oh My God, what the actual fuck?

Now if I was being honest, brutally honest, the first thing I felt when I read that note was disappointment. He had mentioned the 'L' word, twice, while for me, at this point, it had never crossed my mind. What did he mean by 'our love forever strong'? We weren't IN love; we were barely in lust. We had only just met and I was not a believer of love at first sight. So yeah, I was disappointed that he was using such a strong word so lightly and without the respect it was due. And I was scared. I didn't want to play this game anymore.

37

Mel caught up with me as I was trying to manoeuvre the unwieldly empty box and the floating unicorn balloon safely off the shop floor.

'What the hell have you got yourself into?' she hissed at me. 'Accepting presents like this from a married man. It's shameless, that's what it is, shameless!'

I put the box down with a thump. 'Leave it out Mel. I'm not in the mood.'

'Not in the mood? I would have thought you'd be over the moon with such a showy display. A bit vulgar if you ask me....'

'I didn't ask you Mel, and before you carry on judging me any further I've decided to end it. Alright? Happy now?' My voice cracked on the last words and I turned my face away as my self-control vanished, and my face crumpled into tears.

Mel fished in her pocket and handed me a crumpled tissue. Blowing my nose, I took some deep breaths and tried to pull myself together. I'm a really ugly crier, I'm sorry to say, and once I start I find it really hard to stop.

'What's really going on, eh love?' Mel's voice was gentle now, all trace of banshee gone. 'I think you've gone and got yourself mixed up in something you know you shouldn't be.'

'It's just got a bit much.' I stammered, still trying to stop the flow of tears. 'I thought it would just be a bit of fun. I didn't want it to be anything serious.' I passed her the note and then showed her the necklace. She looked at both for a while without saying anything, then handed them both back to me. She pulled her glasses off and started cleaning them with the hem of her work blouse – a habit she had whenever she was thinking hard.

'Well. Looks like he means business. You haven't done the dirty with him yet have you?'

Crossing my fingers behind my back I tried to look affronted.

'NO! We've just been out a couple of times as friends, that's all'

'So where has he got this idea that you're star-crossed lovers then? There was no getting anything past Mel.

'OK, we may have had a bit of a kiss.' I admitted. 'But that's it, I swear. He's never even been inside my house and the rest of the time we've been out in public.'

Mel breathed on her glasses and wiped them again, then put them back on her face and blinked owlishly.

'Looks like he's after more to me. A lot more. All these flowery words about being in love, he's only trying to get into your pants.' She huffed. 'I don't like to be crude but there it is.'

I didn't think this was the time to own up to him getting inside my bra. If Mel thought she was being crude by mentioning my pants God knows what she'd make of us rolling around on top of his desk last night.

'I don't know why he's suddenly decided that it's love.' I mused. 'We barely know each other.'

'Time to get things straight, I think. You need to let him go. It isn't possible for a man and a woman to just be friends. One always wants more than the other one.' With these wise words Mel gently punched the unicorn on its nose. 'You'll do the right thing; I know you will.'

She had such faith in me. I couldn't bear to disappoint her again. My phoned buzzed.

Did you like it? I hope so - you mean the world to me x

I hesitated only briefly over my reply.
We need to talk.

CHAPTER SEVEN

We had agreed to meet at lunchtime as usual at the park, and now we sat on the grass behind a small copse of trees, hidden from view.

'It's all just too much, you're taking things too fast.' I told him. 'I didn't realise you were going to be so intense about this, and I'm sorry, but I can't do it.' I took a deep, shaky breath. 'I don't think we should see each other again.' I could see the hurt and confusion etched onto his face and I nearly cried.

'But...' He shook his head as if to shake off what I was saying. 'I thought we were getting on great, I thought we really had something here.'

'That's just it.' I said angrily. 'It can't be something. It can't be anything. You're not free to offer me that, are you? You shouldn't be making promises you can't deliver Dave— you belong to someone else.' I was sorry to be having this conversation but I was sure it was the right thing to do - not necessarily the easy thing but the right thing. Cruel to be kind and all that. He sat up and hunched over his knees, looking miserable.

'I don't belong to anyone.' He offered weakly 'It's not like that.' He took both of my hands in his and squeezed. 'Please. Don't do this. I'm so unhappy at home and meeting you has been the best thing to happen to me for a long time.'

'I don't understand what it is you want from me.' I said. 'I told you I wasn't looking to get into a serious relationship, and now you're sending me expensive presents and talking about being together forever? I mean - what the fuck?' I had a sense of dread that he was about to tell me he was leaving his wife and son. An unwanted vision of him turning up on my doorstep that night, surrounded by suitcases, and declaring 'I've left her! I'm moving in with you

40

forever.' swam around the back of my mind. It was one thing to hang out together at lunchtimes, having a bit of a flirt, but being a proper couple was quite another. I tried to picture us living together, arguing over the mundane details of who paid the bills and who put the bins out, me doing his laundry, him sitting on his arse watching the game while I hoovered around his feet, him putting up with my moods, me putting up with HIS moods. 'NNooooooo!!!' my brain wailed. It was not a picture of domestic bliss. She was more than welcome to keep him. The thought of me becoming an instant step-mother to Josh frightened me to death. I didn't really like children, I mean, they were OK when they were someone else's but I didn't like them enough to want any of my own – it was the one thing which both Adam and I agreed on fervently. As for being the other woman and responsible for the break-up of his marriage, I'd just been through my own messy divorce, thank you very much, I wasn't in the mood for another!

'I think you'd better tell me about why you're so unhappy at home.' I wasn't the answer to his problems. Starting a new relationship while you're still in another is never going to end in happy ever after. Either way, he was lying to his wife and to himself if he thought he could get away with it forever. I thought if I could get him talking, play at being a marriage counsellor for a bit, he'd get it all out of his system and realise he was being a bit of a dick and that things weren't so bad in his marriage after all.
He sighed.

'Where do I start?' He had still been holding my hands up until this point, and now he dropped them gently, folding his arms across his chest in a classic defensive posture.
'When I first met Vicki, I was at a very low point in my life. I'd just got out of prison....'

'Did you just say PRISON?' I jumped in, shocked. He had never told me about being in prison.

'You have to understand, I was eighteen. On the dole, no prospects and no hope. Where I grew up, you're expected to be a hard man, a bad lad, and you make your money by dealing or stealing. My dad got me my first proper job, in an abattoir, hosing down the pens where they did the initial butchering. I lasted two days before I quit. I preferred the indignity of being on benefits to that hellhole of a place. Anyway, once a few of my mates were going round to this girls' house, one of them was sort of seeing her. She was a bit posh though, her folks were loaded so we thought she was way out of his league, you know? She was having a bit of a party while her parents were out so we got invited along. We all had a few drinks and then she said her dad was a right wine snob and had some good stuff lying around. Turns out he was a bit of a collector, had a proper wine cellar and everything, so we went a bit mad, opening random bottles and taking a swig and then pouring the rest of the bottle down the sink, saying it was corked. We didn't know what the fuck we were talking about – it just seemed funny at the time. So then of course her parents come home, take one look at their ransacked wine cellar and throw us out. I'd hidden a couple of bottles in my coat so I took them with me. How was I to know they were worth a couple of grand?' he grinned. 'Naturally they pressed charges for stealing and I got nine months for burglary. I wasn't prepared for life in the nick, I was young and stupidly naïve, an easy target – and I felt really alone. The prison was quite far away from my dads' house and he found it too difficult to get the time off work to visit. I didn't hear anything from my mum, the whole time I was inside. Only one of my brothers bothered to visit or write – or rather his girlfriend at the time did. She was studying for an NVQ in Childcare and Vicki was on her course, they became friends and so Vicki started writing to me too. When I was released she offered me a place to stay while I got back on my feet, and I never left.' He looked over at me, I was hanging on his every word, but still reeling from the prison thing.

'We were both very young, but Vicki seemed so perfect. She was so sweet and innocent – wanted to be a nanny, wanted to care for me and look after me like no one else had in a very long time, and I guess I fell for that side of her. Her parents were - are – very well off and she'd never wanted for anything in her life. It was like she was charmed and nothing bad had ever happened to her, so nothing bad could ever happen to me if I was with her. I asked her to marry me after six weeks. Her folks weren't happy about having me as a son-in-law, they even made me promise never to mention that I had been in prison to any of their friends and family.'

'Do you get on with them now?' I asked when he paused. The church clock struck two o'clock. We were both supposed to be back at work by now but this was far too important to stop. I knew I'd be in all sorts of trouble with my manager but at that moment I didn't care if I never went back. I needed to know how he had got from being infatuated with his perfect wife to begging me to be with him. He gave a dismissive shrug.

'Yeah, kind of. They tolerate me I suppose. They got better when Josh came along, first grandchild and all that. But that's when things started going wrong for me and Vicki. After Josh she lost all interest in me. I know that sounds really selfish and a lot of new dads feel like that but she had no time for me at all. I was just, - in the way. And she was obsessed with trying to be perfect – the perfect mother, the perfect wife with the perfect family. I know I'd put her on a pedestal but it was like she kept on climbing up a higher and higher, self-made pedestal that I couldn't reach. She honestly believed in her own hype and there was no let-up, ever. We all have to fit in with her vision of a perfect life, and she gives us each our roles to play – like we're characters in a book, or one of those fly-on-the-wall TV shows about Z-list celebrities.' He gave a mirthless laugh. 'Ha! She would LOVE to have her own reality show.' He plucked at the grass absently, lost is his telling of the story. 'She started creating a fictitious life on her social media profiles on Facebook and Instagram, to get more and more followers and likes. It was all fake. Banging on her perfect life – she even talked about starting a blog! And it was all lies, the stuff she was saying, the photos she was posting, it was all carefully staged to make everyone in the world think she had it all. That's one of her favourite hashtags - #lady have it all.' He said this last bit with so much bitterness. 'You should have a look sometime and you'll see what I mean. One time, we were at Gatwick airport, and she kept nagging me to buy one of those lounge passes – you know the ones that cost about twenty quid and give you access to the airline lounges for a couple of hours? As soon as we were in the lounge she starts taking all these selfies and putting them on her Instagram saying she was in business class and she was a successful business woman on her way to a high level conference and it was all total crap! What the selfies didn't show was her fed up husband and our screaming, over-tired son, waiting to catch the EasyJet flight to Lanzarote! We didn't even pay for it; we were too skint – the whole holiday was a present from her parents! And she just got worse. Now she spends all her time updating her profile and her image – she's vain and shallow and her whole life is a complete lie. She's set herself up as some kind of style and fitness icon and everything, EVERYTHING, is about her. And now she wants another baby and I don't. She thinks it will make her look better to her followers if she had another kid to dress up and show off.' He slumped back and lay on the grass with his eyes closed. 'She doesn't give her son enough attention as it is. He's just a prop as far as she's concerned. I worry about Joshie, I really do. Sometimes I think she wouldn't notice if he was on fire. I don't want him to grow up thinking that you have to have all these material possessions to call yourself successful. And I certainly don't want him thinking that looks are all that matter in this world.' He ran out of steam and his flood of vitriolic contempt ebbed away.

I didn't know what to say, she sounded like a complete mare and not someone I could like. It made me feel better about nicking her husband.

I sat there quiet for a couple of minutes, wondering if he would say anymore.

'Do you see now why I want to be with you?' He asked suddenly. 'You don't care about any of that shite, how other people see you or what clothing label you're wearing.' I looked down at my cheap work clothes and raised my eyebrow at him.

'Hashtag purple blouse, hashtag black skirt with grass stains, hashtag rocking the work uniform?' I joked weakly.

'Exactly!' He cried. 'You totally get it! That's why I love being with you so much, you make me laugh my socks off. I haven't met anyone in so long who makes me feel like you do.' He threw his arms around me and hugged me to him. 'Now that you know, what it's like for me, will you change your mind and let me see you again? Please?' I nodded into his chest, breathing in the scent of his aftershave and feeling the muscles in his arms squeeze me tightly. 'Thank you.' He whispered so softly I could barely hear him.

'I still need to think about things though.' I told him. 'I'm still afraid of getting involved, you're still taking a huge risk. What would happen if she found out – about me I mean?' I looked up at him, questioning.

'It's complicated.' He wouldn't quite meet my eye. 'If it wasn't for Josh we'd be divorced by now. But I could never leave Josh and, with her family on her side, if she wanted to she could make sure I'd never have access to him again. Her father has invested heavily in my design business too so it could all just blow up – I'd lose my son and my job.' He leaned his forehead against mine. 'I can't leave her. You need to understand that but you also need to know that I want to be with you. I wouldn't take the risk if it wasn't worth it.'

I heard the words 'I can't leave her' and my brain went 'Yay! Phew!' He stood up and held out his hands to pull me up to my feet, my legs cramping from being sat on the hard ground for so long.

'Come on – we need to get back to work and face the music.'

I was seriously late back. I had four missed calls on my phone, two from the shop manager, and two from Mel. No sooner had I walked into the shop when the manager Mr Butterworth, or Mr Jobsworth as we called him, requested my presence in his office – immediately. I tapped on his door and stuck my head round it.

"You wanted to see me?" I asked lightly, as if nothing was amiss.

"Come in and close the door." He barked. "Sit down!" I sat down, preparing myself for a bollocking, and hoping that would be the end of it.

"Can you explain to me, precisely why, you are almost one hour late back from your lunchbreak?" he intoned in a serious manner.

46

"I'm really sorry." I grovelled apologetically. "I had a bit of an emergency and was unavoidably late. I didn't mean to be and I promise it won't happen again"

"What kind of emergency?"

I had to think quickly. He knew I had no relatives close to me so I couldn't say a family emergency. A veterinary emergency? One of my guinea pigs was sick and I had to get them to the vets immediately, necessitating in a high speed drive to the surgery therefore I was unable to answer my phone? No, he wouldn't accept that.

"Um, it's a bit embarrassing actually" I squirmed in my chair and tried to summon up a blush. "I, um, got my period unexpectedly and I had to go home and change my uniform"

He turned bright red and I swear he almost physically recoiled from me. The good old 'got my period' excuse never fails on a man. They know that they can't ask any more questions after that, in case you go mental and start crying or accusing them of gender discrimination.

"Yes....well......I can see why that would have had an impact on your time-keeping. But" he said. "BUT, that does not explain why you couldn't inform either myself or your team that you were going to be late. A simple phone call would have sufficed and we would not have spent the last hour being concerned for your well-being. One of your team was all for phoning the local hospital in case you'd been in an accident." That would be Mel, I thought, drama llama that she is.

"I'm very sorry Mr Butterworth. I understand how my selfish actions have had a negative impact on my colleagues and will endeavour to work in a more collaborative way in the future." This was exactly the sort of fluffy waffle the management team lapped up.

"Nevertheless" he went on. (What kind of person actually says 'Nevertheless', I ask you?) "This is not the only instance of tardiness. It has not gone unnoticed that you have been frequently late in the last few weeks, five minutes maybe ten, here and there, and your attitude has certainly taken a dip recently." He must have been on a Management Skills course recently because he suddenly changed the tone of his voice to 'Caring' mode. "Is there anything you want to talk to me about? If you're having problems at home still, with your …. husband……"

"EX husband" I clarified.

"Ex-husband." He nodded. "We can offer you some support, if you'd like. I have the number of the Employee Assistance Helpline. Or I could alter your days off for the next few weeks if that would help – have a couple of days' holiday? Get yourself into a better place?"
I resisted the urge to scream at him that anywhere was a better place than this dump.

"Thank you for your concern, but I'm fine." I reassured him. "I really would like to get back to work now."
He started shuffling some papers on his desk. "I am going to have to put this incident on your file I'm afraid. We will review it again when you have your annual appraisal, see if things have improved." He looked disappointed in me. "This does mean I won't be able to recommend you for the Fast Track Management Programme this time, you understand?"
I stifled a smile. I hadn't wanted to be on the Fast Track Management Programme anyway. I'd been working here for more than fifteen years without a promotion so what the hell was fast about the management programme?

"Yes, I understand." I would start applying for new jobs that night.

CHAPTER EIGHT

Later on, glad to be back home, I was half-heartedly updating my CV and browsing local job vacancies on my laptop. Dave's story kept replaying over and over in my mind and I remembered that he had said I should look at his wife's Facebook and Instagram profiles, so I could see what he meant about her being a vain, pretentious little bitch. My words, not his.

Now, I hate social media – absolutely cannot stand it! I'd had a Facebook account once, years ago when it was at the height of its popularity. Once I had caught up with a few people I had been to school with, liked all the pictures of their kids and foreign holidays, and commented on how the boys in my class all looked like their dads now, I'd gotten over it the whole Facebook thing. I ended up blocking most of the people who had tried to 'friend' me. I had absolutely no desire to know these people anymore and I kept getting friend requests from Scott Bolland, the weird- looking, smelly, undersized kid in my class who followed me around for almost four years. He broke into my house once to leave a love letter on my pillow and my dad threw him out, literally picked him up by the scruff of his neck and threw him into the road and broke his arm. Also Elaine, the bossy, fat ginger girl who bullied me mercilessly all through high school was on there – desperately trying to 'friend' everyone so she could post pictures of her fat, ugly ginger kid as if to say 'See? Somebody did have sex with me once!' Bet she had a date with an anonymous donor and a turkey baster. Anyway, I committed Facebook suicide and closed down my account six months after I opened it. As for Instagram or Twitter or Snap Chat or any of those other sites – what could I possibly post that would be of interest to anybody else? Pictures of my reduced-to-clear section at the Co-op dinner? Photos of

Monkey and Rocket, my fur babies, eating carrots? I had nothing to shout about and I just wasn't interested in other people's lives very much so I had no reason to even look at those sites.

They're the home of the vainglorious, the insecure, the delusional and the humble-braggers. They're just a way of silly girls to put up pictures of themselves and fish for compliments – most of them doing that stupid, camel-faced selfie pout that makes them look like they're been punched in the mouth.

I poured myself some dinner (Yes I probably was drinking too much these days but work made me do it) and opened the browser on my laptop. I typed in 'Vicki Roberts' in the search bar and she popped up straight away. I clicked on the first result, the Instagram link.

**Vicki Campbell-Roberts@luckyladysoblessed
543 posts 331 following**

What's with the double-barrelled surname? I wondered. Dave was just plain old David Roberts. Did she tack her married name on the end of her maiden name to try and make her sound more classy? I had a quick horrible thought that maybe she could see who had been looking at her profile. But there was nothing to trace back to me – I was just an observer. I had not signed up to Instagram or entered any of my details so I didn't think she'd be able to see that I had been nosing at her photos. According to Dave, that's what she wanted anyway, for everyone to look at her, to follow and adore her.

Holy Mary Mother of God – he wasn't lying.

I scrolled down page after page of photos. I vaguely remembered what she looked like in the family photos hanging on the wall in Dave's office, but now I could have a proper look at my leisure. I scrutinised her closely. Short - very short - was my first impression. Long, dark, layered hair, HUGE teeth – too many teeth and they stuck out in a rodent like way. Looking closely, I could see one of her eyes drooped slightly lower than the other, giving her a bit of a lopsided squint. All in all, she looked like a squashed squirrel. Oh My God Dave, what the hell were you thinking? She's awful! When you were talking about how perfect she was I had pictured some kind of angelic, vision of loveliness. A blonde haired, pink cheeked, ethereal beauty not this rather ordinary, big arsed midget, posturing– and most definitely selfie pouting like a boss camel – against various backdrops of beaches, formal balls and luxury holiday destinations. I picked some photos at random and read the hashtags she had attached to each one. So many hashtags, sometimes thirty or more and all totally banal, smug and self-congratulating – and, as Dave had warned me, untrue.

There's one from months ago, a close up selfie of her reclining on a bed of crisp white cotton, pouting stupidly at the camera.

Vicki Campbell-Roberts@luckyladysoblessed
Post Photoshoot Nap. #needsleepnow #beautysleep #model #beingfabulousishardwork #greeneyes #goodhairday #onlocation #studio #workhard # loveharder #dontgiveup #grindhardstayhumble #selfie #queenb #ladyhaveitall #blessed

OK – <u>Things I Found Wrong with This Post</u>

One: She doesn't have even have green eyes, they're a sludgy hazel.

Two: She's not a model. She's a part time nanny. Models are generally taller than four-foot high, darling.

Three: Queen B of what exactly? Queen of the humble brag? Queen of playing pretend? Queen of talking utter shite?

Four: Grind hard stay humble? What the fuck was that about? There is nothing, nothing whatsoever, that could be defined as 'humble' about this woman.

Five: Who the hell describes themselves as fabulous? This doesn't work unless you're a gay man, preferably American and as camp as a Boy Scout jamboree.

I hated her instantly. She epitomised everything I loathe about social media. The lies, the bragging, the 'look at me, look at me!' religion that these sites peddle. I couldn't help myself and I scrolled on and on, clicking on each picture and getting angrier at each one. There she was on the beach in a bikini (clearly sucking in her stomach). Every couple of weeks she posted a photo of her hair, in before and after shots. Brown to blonde, blonde to brown, back to blonde again and each time gushing about how she was so glad to be blonde/brown. There she was at the gym, giving fitness advice and showing how you too can look like you've dropped ten pounds if you pose like her in the mirror. There were countless nights out, endless pictures of her food (#smashed avocado!), Selfie after selfie of close ups of her face, always calling herself beautiful, always saying how lucky she was. There were even more pictures of her striking an exaggerated pose in a full length mirror and quoting designer label names so her adoring public would know just how wonderful she looked in expensive clothing. There were, I noticed, no pictures of her with other women. She didn't seem to have any friends, it was always just her, Dave and Josh, occasionally an older couple whom I took to be her parents. And in every single post she had attached the final hashtag #blessed.

How can you hate someone you've never met? I could - she made it easy.

What I wasn't so prepared for was how many photos there were of Dave. Well, her and Dave. He featured in well over half of them and she always referred to him as her 'Love Bear' (pass the sick bag!) or her soulmate or her best friend (and again!). Pictures of Josh were in there, but only ones that had been carefully choreographed. Josh wearing cute little shirts that matched his dads, Josh playing on a beach with a bucket and spade, although the main focus of the photo was his mum perched on the sand in a bikini and tossing her hair around. There were none of the candid, honest moments that you always get with kids. Messy faces covered in ice cream, playing with Lego on the lounge floor, going on the swings at the playground. Everything was posed and arty, and when I looked closely, completely stiff and unnatural. I could see the traces of tears in Josh's eyes where he was no doubt told to sit still and for God's sake don't mess up your clothes! I saw the unhappiness in Dave when he was pictured at yet another black tie event, her hanging off his arm, he was the perfect accessory to her latest designer dress.

She had posted pictures of her parents and referred to Scotland a lot, so I imagined her talking with a squeaky, Scottish accent to accompany her squirrel-like features. She was becoming more like a cartoon caricature than a real person. I found the post that Dave had been talking about, the one in the airport lounge, and read her comments about being a business traveller. She had put a lot of crap about doing it for your family, strong woman in business, blah blah blah blah #blessed. I wondered what the rest of her family and those people who actually knew her thought about her creative licence with the truth. Surely they must know she doesn't work in business. She's a part time nanny who works a couple of hours a day. Don't they wonder how she can afford such a luxury lifestyle on Dave's average salary? Where all the cash for the designer wear and the extravagant holidays came from? It didn't add up, didn't make sense. The woman was delusional at best, mentally ill at worst.

All of my reservations about Dave and me and starting a relationship with a married man, a father, disappeared in an instant. If he was willing to risk everything, risk losing custody of Josh for the chance of some happiness with me, then I would do it. Being married to such a superficial nightmare of a woman must be like another type of prison for him, but this time I would be the one offering him an escape. If he wanted that chance, I would give it. And if she found out? Well, that would wipe the smug smile of her squirrelly little face, wouldn't it?

Vicki Campbell-Roberts@luckyladysoblessed
Back to Black — the brunette returns again!
#brunetteisback #darkhair #longlashes #beauty #esteelauder #tomfordlipstick #feelingsopretty #bardotdress #MACcomsmetics hardworkpaysoff #lifestylegoals #curls #greeneyes #super skinny #date nights #youwantmylooks #grindhardstayhumble #ladyhaveitall #blessed

CHAPTER NINE

Katie
July

I'd been browsing through her Instagram for hours, gnashing my teeth at each new brag and each vain, narcissistic post. I was itching to troll her – to set up a fake account in a false name and start following her, ridiculing her and bringing her down a peg or two or three.   Realising it was getting on for one in the morning, I finally shut down my computer and started getting ready for bed. My eyes were hot and dry, and my bottle of wine had mysteriously emptied itself. Monkey and Rocket were blinking sleepily up at me, wondering why the light was still on, and why they hadn't had their normal bedtime treat of a fresh grape yet. I brushed my teeth and flopped into bed. It was a hot night and I kicked my duvet off, pulling just a thin sheet over me. Switching off the light, I lay in the humid darkness, wide awake and my thoughts racing.

A noise woke me sometime later. I peered, bleary eyed at the bedside clock and saw it was almost quarter to three in the morning.   What had woken me? I wondered, half listening in my half-awake state for another noise. I heard it again – a soft knocking at my front door. I was lucky in that my studio flat had its own entrance, opening on to the strip of garden at the side of the house. Whoever it was knocked again. Willing them to go away, I turned over and pulled the sheet up over my head.

'Katie!' A hissed whisper called out my name. 'Katie, lemme in.' More knocking, louder this time. They'd start waking up my neighbours if this carried on.

'Katie?   Katie?   KATIE!!!!' He wasn't whispering anymore, and the knocking started to shake the front door in its frame. Huffing, I got up. I was only in a vest and pyjama shorts so I wrapped the sheet around me and went to the door. Leaving it on the chain, I opened it a fraction. Dave was standing, swaying dangerously off balance, in the garden, about to throw what looked like half a brick at my window.

'Dave what are you doing, you idiot?' I was raging. He had scared the shit out of me, banging on my door in the middle of the night.

'Katie lemme in, please' He begged. I realised he was so drunk he could barely stand. His clothes were muddied and torn and he had a big graze on his face and a split lip that was oozing blood onto his shirt.

'What the hell happened to you?' I asked. 'You look like you've been in a fight.' I took the chain off the door and opened it, ushering him into my flat. He could barely focus and once he was in the hallway his legs gave way and he slid down the wall and onto the floor.

'Jus...wan...see you.' He garbled. 'Jus wan ta tell you…..please…….don leave……..me.' His head slumped to one side, his mouth open and drooling like the feckin village idiot.

'Come on.' I sighed. 'Get up. You can't stay there. God, you're in a right state aren't you? You're filthy – I'll run you a bath.' I got up and went into the bathroom, fitting the plug and turned on the taps.

'Katie!' His voice from the hall was urgent. 'Jus…..wanna…..say…..' He heaved, once, twice and then vomited copious amounts of yellow bile down his front, which mingled with the blood already there. 'Whoops. Soz….sorry.'
Lovely. What an utter Prince Charming. Fortunately for him I'd always had a strong stomach so a bit of sick didn't faze me much. I poured half a bottle of Radox into the bath, added a couple of capfuls of Dettol for good measure.

'Come on. Bath time, you big stinky muppet.' I manoeuvred him onto the floor of the bathroom. 'Arms up.' I said, like I was talking to a child. He obeyed and I pulled his shirt off over his head and threw the stinking mess into a corner. 'Legs out.' I undid his belt and started trying to get his jeans off his legs.

'Woo, way-hey!' he slurred. 'Having yer way with me, are ya?' I rolled my eyes.

'Because you're just soooo attractive in this state, I can't help myself.' I said, deadpan. I managed to get his jeans off. I refused to take his boxers off though, he could just get into the bath with them on, I thought. With my help he levered himself upright and gripped the side of the bath, then he rolled sideways and crashed straight into the tub onto his back like a humpback whale. A tidal wave of hot scented water flooded the floor of the bathroom and soaked the sheet that was still wrapped around my body. At least that will help disinfect the floor, I thought philosophically. Dave groaned and lay back in the bath. I picked up a soft flannel and began to sponge the blood from his face.

'How did you get this?' I asked, gently.

'Fell over in the car park. Forgot to put my hands out to stop me falling on my face. Fell on my face.' He was sounding a bit more coherent now, and winced as I dabbed blood from his cut lip. I grabbed some shampoo and began washing his hair. He moaned with pleasure as I rinsed the dirt and blood from his scalp.

'I just wanted to see you.' He said, trying to grab one of my hands. 'I needed to see you.' He wasn't forgiven, not yet.
'I'll leave you to soak for a bit.' I gathered up his filthy clothes. 'I'll put these on a quick wash, and then through the tumble dryer so you should have them back clean in an hour or so. Have a go at getting the rest of that mud off you,

yeah?' I checked his jeans pockets before chucking the lot in the wash – hoping no one else in the building would wonder why I was running the washing machine at three in the morning. His phone, keys and wallet I put safely on the kitchen worktop, and I noticed his phone flashing. The screen showed seven missed calls, all, I presumed, from his wife wondering where he was. I put the kettle on and set about making us a cup of tea. Strangely enough, I was flattered that he'd come to me tonight, like he was a hurt child and I was the grown up he needed help from, the one he wanted to look after him. I left him wallowing in the steaming water for ten minutes then knocked softly on the bathroom door.

'You just about done?' I asked. He was still lying prone in the bath, his legs up on the end of the tub, the water lapping around his ears. He was sound asleep.
I pulled the plug and the dirty water swirled away. He'd wake up when he starts to get cold, I reasoned. Sure enough, he jerked awake seconds later, shivering but looking a lot cleaner, and a bit more sober. I held out a towel, my best and biggest, fluffiest towel that was my special occasion's towel for when I treated myself to a bubble bath by candlelight. He stood up shakily, grabbing on to the shower screen for balance, and stepped out of the bath and bundled himself into the towel and into my arms. I rough dried him, and then wrapped round him the soft, fleecy throw that's usually draped over my couch. He lay down on my bed and pulled the sodden boxers off, hidden beneath the blanket. I put them in the dryer ready to be reunited with his other clothing when the washing machine finished and put a cup of tea, a glass of water, and two paracetamol tablets on the bedside table next to him. Cradling my own cup of tea, I sat down on the other side of the bed.

'Well. Where do we start?' I took a sip of tea. 'Do you want to begin by telling me why you've turned up here in this state?' I was calmer, now that he was more with it, and not likely to vomit on me again. He looked so vulnerable, lying naked but for a blanket, on my bed. He opened his mouth to speak but all that came out was a sob. And then another. Then he was crying, properly crying with great heaving wails and hitching breaths. He buried his head in his hands and covered his face. Shit, what should I do? A great big naked man was crying like a baby in my bed. I put my tea down and slid over to him, putting an arm around his shoulders and drawing his head onto my breast. He moved so we were lying down that way, resting his head on me so it was natural for us to cuddle together, my arms around him, and him clinging onto me like he was afraid of being snatched away. His sobs subsided and he lay still, but neither of us made any move to move apart.

'I'm sorry.' He said, quietly and soberly. 'I've made an arse of myself tonight.' I tightened my arms around him. 'Turning up drunk, getting you out of bed.'

'Vomiting on my floor, crying into my pillow.' I added, kissing the top of his head to show him I wasn't angry – not anymore. He cringed.

'I'm so sorry about that. I think maybe it was the shock of falling over, made me get, you know, emotional.' He said the word 'emotional' like it was a sex offender at a play group.

'I think it was probably the amount of beer you drank!' I snort-laughed.

'Beer, wine and brandy.' He added. 'And a joint on the way here.' He laughed as well.

'Dickhead.' I ruffled his hair affectionately. 'No wonder you were in such a mess.'

'I did it because I was afraid I'd lost you.' He lifted his head up and looked at me. 'I thought you'd decided you didn't want to get involved with a loser like me, and with all the baggage that comes along with me, so I drank to forget you.'

'Didn't work too well then.' I said. 'Seeing as you turned up here like a homing pigeon. It did cross my mind, calling the whole thing off. But I don't think you're a loser – well, I didn't before tonight anyway.' He poked a finger into my ribs, right where he knew I was most ticklish. I squirmed away, laughing loudly. 'Look, being serious, I have been thinking about it. There needs to be some ground rules though.' His face filled with hope.

'Does this mean……?'

'Yes. But on two conditions.' I sat up so was looking down at him. 'One – you need to be honest with me at all times. I can accept anything if it's the truth, but if you start lying to me – we're done!' He nodded, started to speak but I silenced him with a finger on his lips. 'And two – if either of us wants to stop, at any time, we're both honest about that too, and we'll let each other go. I don't want anything else from you. I won't ever ask you for anything more – I'm just asking for complete and total honesty.' He threw himself on top of me and pinned me underneath him, his face suffused with pure joy.

'Yes, yes of course!' He rained kisses all over my face and neck. 'Oh my God, thank you so much for this chance. I promise I'll never hurt you – ever. And I'll be honest, all of the time, I swear. You'll get sick of how honest I'm going to be!'

The washing machine beeped to a stop and I wriggled my way free from underneath Dave and got up from the bed. I moved his now clean, vomit and blood free clothes into the tumble dryer, and turned back to face him.

'Well. It looks like we've got about an hour until they're dry. Whatever shall we do now?' I asked, all wide-eyed innocence. He looked at me, his lean, muscled torso rising from the bedcovers and he whipped the blankets off the rest of his body, completely revealing his naked glory. I dropped the soggy sheet that was clinging to me and peeled off my vest, striding back towards him on the bed. 'Ah. I see you've thought of something.'

CHAPTER TEN

It was like our thousandth time, not our first. There was none of that 'should I put my hand there, does he like it like this, where does this bit go?' awkwardness that accompanies first-time sex. It was so familiar, like reuniting with an old lover you had never been able to forget. We were matched, giving and receiving in equal pleasure, and our obvious enjoyment in each other only made us bolder and more adventurous. We lay together, breathless and sated, watching the first light of the new day turning my room golden.

'I haven't had sex like that in years.' He said seriously. 'Really, like, years and years.' Ha! I thought – she's crap in bed then, I win. From the kitchen area I heard his phone buzz with another call, then the 'Ping!' of a voicemail message.

'I need to go soon.' He pulled me to him, running a hand down my thigh and pulling my leg across his body. 'Is it OK if I have a shower?'

'Course.' I understood that he needed to scrub off the smell of sex with another woman before he went home. I tried not to think of him crawling into bed beside her, tried not to picture him putting his arms around her in a familiar embrace. He got up and walked naked into the bathroom, closing the door. The tumble dryer had long since stopped tumbling, so I pulled out his dry, fresh smelling clothes and folded them on the bed, ready for when he got out of the shower. I couldn't resist picking up his phone and swiping the screen. It was locked, but the most recent text message was still scrolling across the top of the screen.

Where are you? You were supposed to be back by 11. Josh won't go to bed until you're home. You know I have an early hair appointment tomorrow you selfish bastard!!!

It was her – the other Kardashian sister. Putting herself first as usual. If I had known his PIN, I would have unlocked his phone and sent her a reply.

Just in the shower after the most amazing sex of my life. Don't wait up.

The shower stopped running and Dave opened the bathroom door, a towel wrapped around his waist. He saw his freshly laundered clothes on my bed, threw a grateful look my way, and started to get dressed. I hadn't bothered putting any clothes on, just wrapped the fleecy throw around me like a sarong. Dave picked up his keys and wallet, gave his phone a brief cursory look and shoved it back in his pocket. I saw him out into the dawn light, where he kissed me hard on the lips and left.

Back inside, I had a quick shower myself and set about tiding things up. There was no point in trying to go back to sleep now, I had to be at work in less than two hours. I picked up my phone to turn off the pre-set alarm for the morning and saw that I had had a text whilst I was in the shower.

Thank you for the most amazing night. I did not want to leave you this morning. I can still picture you, standing there in the moonlight, looking beautiful.

I smiled. I was tired from having almost no sleep, and bruised and sore from our lovemaking, but I had never felt so happy. I took the silver fairy he had given me from its box and fastened it around my neck – it was my good luck talisman now and I would never take it off.

Vicki Campbell-Roberts @luckyladysoblessed
So lucky to be spending my life with this amazing man.
Happy Anniversary baby XXX #anniversary #couplegoals
#truelove #kingandqueen #hug #cuddles #1000years
#soulmate #putaringonit #instadaily #instagood
#grindhardstayhumble #ladyhaveitall #safe #happylife
#familyfirst #bestfriend #blondehairdontcare
#havemorefun #blessed

Katie
August

From then on we saw each other almost every day. We would meet for lunch or coffee, and several times a week he would come to my flat where we would cuddle up on the couch, drinking wine and half-watching movies. He would invent all sorts of excuses not to be at home, telling her he was at his brothers' house, or watching the game and he would rush over to spend the evening with me. We fell into a happy, lazy routine. Every time he left my bed in the early hours, he would whisper 'I don't want to go.' and I would whisper back 'Stay with me.' But he couldn't of course, he had to be there in the morning so Josh wouldn't miss him, or notice he wasn't there. Actually, to be honest, I was glad to have my bed back to myself. It was lovely him being there for a short while, but I found I couldn't get used to sleeping next to someone again after being on my own for so long. Sometimes, I thought he'd never leave and a part of me was relieved when he got up to take a shower, and go home. The whole arrangement was working out perfectly, the nights were spent together were enough and I wasn't bothered that he was going home to his other life. I knew he preferred to be with me.

 With Dave's help and encouragement, I started applying for jobs. I had realised that I had fallen into a routine of always taking the safe option when confronted with any decision, a hangover from the dark days after Adam had left, and I had felt worthless, my confidence at rock bottom. This was how I had ended up in my current job, by playing it safe and thinking I didn't deserve anything better. Now, with Dave to bolster my self-esteem, I started applying for vacancies that I would have previously thought were way out of my reach.

'You have loads of skills that employers are crying out for!' He would say whenever I began to give into the self-doubt, and let the creeping, negative thoughts seep into my brain. 'You have supervisory experience, good knowledge of IT systems, and plenty of transferrable skills.' He offered to take my CV and give it an overhaul, using his graphic design talents to make sure it really stood out. I wrote off to apply for office work, administration roles or receptionist vacancies at large corporate organisations. They had previously unheard of luxuries on offer to their employers – like sick pay, pension schemes and some places even offered Soup Mondays and Fruit Fridays, not to mention that the salaries these places were offering were almost twice as much as I was currently getting in my almost minimum wage retail job. By the time Dave had finished my new, pimped up CV I could barely recognise the person it was describing, he had made me sound so competent and so employable.

I had lost some of the closeness I had previously enjoyed with my team at work, and it was the perfect time to move on. They were divided in their opinion of mine and Dave's relationship, some seeing it as wrong and just asking for trouble. Some thought of me as the scarlet woman, messing about with someone else's man, letting down the sisterhood, whatever that meant.

They saw him when he collected me for our daily lunchbreak, and saw him again when he dropped me back at the shop later with a kiss, and every one of them had an opinion on the matter they were only too keen to share. He was brilliant at getting them on side though – finding common ground with each and every one, learning their kids and grandkids names and asking after them, talking football with the boys, and even discussing the latest E.L James book with Philippa, like it was the greatest literary offering the world had seen since her last pile-of-shite effort. I started signing birthday cards with 'Love from Dave and Katie' and we began to get invites to barbeques and parties as an accepted couple.

The only one Dave couldn't charm was Mel. She would stare gimlet eyed at him and make a cutting remark about cheating husbands and absent fathers, before turning her back on the both of us and flouncing off, barely speaking to me for the rest of the day.

I was still checking his wife's Instagram account for new posts every day, sometimes three or four times a day. It was an addiction - I literally couldn't stop. She was just so awful that each new ridiculous selfie made me want to hunt her down and tell her a few home truths. She wasn't perfect, or some kind of celebrity. She wasn't even that attractive and no one in the real world actually cared what she was doing that day, or wearing, or eating. I felt like telling her that her so called perfect marriage was an illusion, and that her so called perfect husband would do or say anything to get away from her, would lie through his teeth so he could spend his nights with me.

Dave hadn't spoken much about her since his confession in the park that day, and she didn't come up in his conversation other than to moan about her cooking. She was a terrible cook apparently, despite her frequent posts about her food. Bad in the kitchen, bad in bed – the points were certainly racking up in my favour.

It's surprising how much you can learn from someone's social media profile. I learned that her fashion sense was dubious. She favoured in-the-moment, on trend fashion, regardless of whether it suited her or her body shape. Some of her photos suggested that she had a constant battle in keeping her weight down, she had a bit of a belly and the kind of arse that you just know was going to explode into mammoth proportions when she reached middle age.

I liked to think that I was definitely winning at this stage.

CHAPTER ELEVEN

Vicki Campbell-Roberts@luckyladysoblessed
Always go after the life you want. My best times are my nights in with my two men XX
#summer #bestfriend #sunshine #drinks #pizzatime #goodtimes #blondehairdontcare #MACcosmetics #SuperDry #nevergiveup #fatherandson #family time #lovealways #successful #couplegoals #grindhardstayhumble #blessed

Katie
August

Seriously? She posted that crap the morning after one of my nights with Dave, together with a photo of him and her and Josh bundled together on a sofa, presumably in their house. She'd put some cutesy little graphics on their faces to make them all look like bunny rabbits; long ears, whiskers and little black triangle noses. To the rest of the world, it looked like they'd all had a lovely, cosy, fun family night together, when, actually, he was in MY bed doing things that are probably considered illegal in less enlightened parts of the world.

'Just ignore it.' Dave told me, when I showed him the post on my laptop. 'It's an old photo, taken ages ago before you and I even met.' If that was true, then how come in the photo Dave's upper arm showed his latest tattoo? We'd gone to the tattoo parlour together one day, and I'd sat next to him in the tattooist's chair, flicking through the magazines while he got inked with that very design, and tried not to squeak with pain in my presence. I pushed away the flicker of doubt, sure I was just overthinking things. Maybe he was remembering it wrong, got his dates mixed up.

'I don't know why you keep looking.' He was annoyed with me now. 'You know she lives in her own fantasy world, so just let it be. If it winds you up so much stop checking her Instagram posts.' He sighed, and rubbed his eyes. 'Look, you know what it's like for me. I've learned to ignore it most of the time. You and I know the truth, and the truth is I love you.' I leaned into him and he put his arms around me. I rested my head on his shoulder and we stood like that for a long moment, drawing strength and calmness from one another.

'I love you too.' I kissed him. We had been saying this to each other for a while now, although the words still felt strange on my tongue. He always signed off his texts with 'Love you' when he was sober, and 'I love you so much' when he had a few drinks. I felt I had to say it too. It was only polite.

One Saturday I was at home, pottering around, doing nothing very interesting and half thinking I might walk up to the local Antiques and crafts fair, a bi-monthly event which was held in a scruffy church hall not far from my flat
There was a knock at my door, and I paused in my pottering. Not many people knew where I lived, and my front door wasn't that easy to find if you didn't know the layout of the flats in the building. You had to go through a side gate in the garden, off a tiny lane, before following the path round to the double garage doors. My door was tucked in between the garages and the back of the neighbour's fence, so it was unlikely that anyone could have stumbled on it by accident. I thought it must be Jackie, my landlady, but she was scrupulous in phoning ahead to let me know in advance that

she would be popping round, if it was convenient, following the Good Landlords Code to the letter.

The knock sounded again. I put down the clothes I had been folding and went to open it. Dave stood on the other side, a small boy clinging onto him like a baby monkey holding onto his mother for dear life.

'I'm so glad you're home.' Dave hoisted the boy further up on his hip. 'We've had a bit of an accident, haven't we Joshie?' The boy let out a whimper, which built up into a crescendo like wail, and buried his head in his father's neck.

'Um.... Come in.' I opened the door wider and Dave carried Josh into through into the kitchen. 'What on earth's happened?'

'We were on our way to the school, Josh goes to Soccer Stars there on a Saturday morning, but he tripped over and fell into the gutter. He's hurt his knee quite badly. I thought we were closer to you than we were to our place so I hoped you'd have a first aid kit?' He raised his eyebrows questioningly.

'Yes....well...not a proper first aid kit as such but I've got some stuff, cotton wool and wipes and so on.' I looked at the small, hiccupping figure he held and my heart melted. Even in this grubby, bleeding state I could tell he was adorable looking child. He has Dave's dark hair and eyes. I could see nothing of his mother in him, he was a Mini-Dave through and through.

'Put him down on the worktop and let's have a look, shall we?' I went to the bathroom cabinet, found the antiseptic wipes and lucked out, there were a few adhesive sterile dressings lurking in the back. I had no idea where they had come from but they would do marvellously.

Coming back into the kitchen, I saw that Dave had calmed Josh down a bit, and he was sitting on the draining board next to the sink. One knee was badly grazed and had bled quite a bit, staining his little football shorts, and running down into his socks. I started filling the sink with warm water and opened the pack of cotton wool, ready to gently clean him up so we could see how bad the cut to his knee was.

'Do you want to do it?' I asked Dave, feeling that this was a job for Josh's dad, not a stranger.
He grimaced.

'Do you mind doing it? I'm really not good with blood. And I know for a fact that you are.' He said, remembering the night he had bled and vomited on my floor. He smoothed Josh's fine hair back from his face, where it had mingled with the little boys' tears and snot. 'Joshie, this is Daddy's friend, Ka..... Janet.' he told him.

'Janet?' I mouthed, not understanding.

'Janet works at the library, where you go for your storybooks.' he continued, staring at me and putting emphasis on the name 'Janet'. I got it then. Josh was of the age where he didn't understand about keeping secrets. He would, in all probability, go home today and tell his mum how he fell over, and that dad took him to Janet's house to get cleaned up. By giving me this alternative identity Dave was keeping my real name out of the equation. She couldn't possibly have any suspicions about cuddly, mumsy Janet who works in the children's library.

'Hi Josh.' I said softly. 'I'm sorry you hurt yourself. I'm going to give your leg a wash so we can see where it hurts, OK?' Josh whimpered a bit and said in a tiny voice. 'I got my shorts with blood on them.'

'Don't worry about that. They'll be good as new after a wash. Now, let's have a look at that knee. I'm going to be as quick as I can, OK?' I rinsed some cotton wool in the warm water and started gently dabbing the blood away. Josh sucked in his breath and hissed 'ow'.

71

'I know, I know.' I sympathised. 'All footballers take a tumble now and again, don't they? You see them on the telly, rolling on the ground until the man comes on the field with the magic sponge to make them better.' I was talking nonsense, trying to take his mind off what I was doing. The blood on his knee had dried and stiffened, and it was taking a fair bit of wet cotton wool to get down to where the skin had been grazed. There were bits of debris sticking to the cut and I cleaned away the tiny pieces of gravel as gently as I could.

'Tell you what, Dad.' I turned to Dave. 'I've got some hot chocolate in the cupboard. Do you think you could make us some while me and Josh are doing this? What do you think Josh? Do you think you could manage some hot chocolate?' He nodded a small nod and then said shyly.

'Marshmallows too?'

I smiled. 'Let's see what we can find. I'm not sure I have marshmallows but I think I have some squirty cream for the top!'

Dave busied himself finding mugs and heating up some milk in the microwave.

'Not too hot.' I whispered. 'And a little bit of sugar in it, if he's allowed? - to help with the shock.'

'I think I need the sugar for the shock.' Dave said. 'One minute he was walking beside me holding my hand, happy as a lamb, and the next he was on his knees in the road, leg covered in blood and wailing like an air raid siren! I was terrified he'd fallen onto some broken glass.'

'It doesn't look too bad.' The wound was cleaning up nicely and I could see the bleeding had mostly stopped. One of the sticky bandage patches would be fine, if Josh could keep it on long enough for his knee to stay clean. Josh had stopped sobbing completely by now, and was looking around my flat with curiosity.

'Why you have a little house?' he asked innocently.

'Josh, don't ask questions like that - it's rude!' Dave looked at me apologetically.

'No, it's fine.' I laughed. 'I don't mind. I live on my own here Josh, so I only need a little house.' He seemed satisfied with that answer and carried on looking around, finally noticing Monkey and Rocket's cage in the corner.

'What's in there?' He shouted, pointing to the cage.

'Guinea pigs.' I told him. 'I have two. They are called Monkey and Rocket. Would you like to meet them?' He nodded excitedly. 'Just let me put this big plaster on your leg and you're all done. Well done, what a brave Joshie you've been!' He grinned up at me and held out his arms for me to lift him up and off the kitchen worktop. I glanced at Dave, not knowing if I should pick Josh up but he just nodded it was OK. I set Josh on the floor and got him to flex his knee a couple of times, so I could be sure the bandage would stay in place.

'Does that feel OK?' I asked him.

He nodded and said 'Thank you Mrs Janet.' very politely. 'Can I see the giggy pigs now?'

We had a lovely hour or so, drinking the hot chocolate that Dave had made. Josh wanted to keep putting more and more squirty cream on top until his dad said he'd make himself sick. Monkey and Rocket were running around on the floor, playing in the houses and tunnels we had made for them out of cereal boxes and newspapers. I taught Josh how to hold them properly, so that their feet were supported and they felt more secure, and we took turns feeding them bits of lettuce and half grapes. Monkey and Rocket couldn't believe their luck at having someone to feed them endless treats, and soon got over their skittishness with Josh, climbing up on his lap while he sat cross-legged on the carpet to get closer to the food, and making him giggle with happiness. Dave and I kept catching each other's' eye, but we kept apart, and didn't touch at all, not wanting to confuse the situation for any of us.

Finally, Dave looked at his watch and said it was time to go home. Josh made an 'aaawwwww' noise and we reluctantly started putting our makeshift guinea pig city away.

'Can I come and see Monkey and Rocket again please Mrs Janet?' he asked sweetly.

'Of course you can, sweetheart.' I was pleased that I had met Josh, and touched that we had got on so well. He adored the guinea pigs, and I thought it was good for children to learn about animals.

'Janet's very busy, Josh.' Dave cut in. ' She was very kind to fix your knee but we need to go now.'

It was clear to me then that there would be no repeat visits from Josh. I did understand, really I did, we didn't want her getting suspicious if Josh kept on talking about his friend Janet and her guinea pigs, but at the same time I felt a pang of loss. I could easily have grown to love Josh as my own, and I found myself wanting to be involved in his life, and letting him do all the things that little boys loved to do, without treating everything like a photo opportunity. He was a just a kid, not an accessory to her fantasy life. If he was my child he'd be a whole lot better off.

CHAPTER TWELVE

Katie
September

My job hunt started to pay off as I was invited for interviews with several companies. I always booked the time off work, and never mentioned a word to anyone. That way, if I was unsuccessful, no one need ever know, and no one could say 'I told you so' when I was rejected yet again. There was one place in particular that I really wanted to work at, and I was due to see them later that day. They were a small, independent boutique recruitment agency who specialised in placing people working in unusual jobs or industries. The agency was looking for someone to cover reception and the switchboard, greet visitors and provide admin support to the recruitment team. It sounded varied and interesting, and I would get to meet a whole new range of people. My interview was at one o'clock, and I sat nervously at home that morning, mentally going through what I hoped were some intelligent sounding questions.

Good Luck XX Will be thinking of you. Love you.

Dave text me just before I was due to leave for the interview.

Thank you XX So nervous! Love you too.

He was meeting me for a late lunch afterwards and had promised wine so I could relax. I was stupidly early at the agency, and sat in the small reception area waiting to be called. It gave me time to study the layout, and to watch the current receptionist at her work. She seemed so confident and elegant, and I hoped my standard interview outfit of a black skirt suit with a plain top underneath would be formal enough. I eavesdropped on her phone calls and memorised the way she answered the phones and directed the queries. Moving into an office environment after working in a shop for so long was going to be something of a culture change, but I knew that if I got this job I would be on the path to a new, improved me. I really, really wanted it!

Finally, a door opened and a lovely, smiley lady walked out and held out her hand.

'Katie? She asked.

'Yes. Hello.' I stood up and met her handshake, hoping my palms weren't clammy with nerves.

'Lovely to meet you. I'm Debbie.' She beamed. I liked her on sight. 'Shall we go into the meeting room?' She led the way and indicated that I should sit down in the chair opposite her. A glass of water stood on the table and I nervously sipped at it, my throat suddenly dry.

'Now.' She had my application letter and CV in front of her. 'Let's start by you telling me why you have applied for this role.'

It went well, I thought, as I left forty-five minutes later. I had got through the nervous stage, Debbie had been great at putting me at ease, and I had hopefully given some good answers to her questions. The conversation flowed well and I managed to get in some questions of my own that weren't just about how much I would be paid and how many holidays I was entitled to every year. She promised me I would hear back from them with a decision in the next few days, so all I could do now was wait. I walked up the street to the centre of town, on time to meet Dave at the wine bar where we were due to have lunch. It had become a favourite haunt of ours, as it had a large rooftop seating area which looked down onto the busy street below. It meant we could get some sun, and watch the people on the ground rushing about their business, whilst hidden from view up in our lofty perch, so we had the privacy to pretend to be a normal couple. Dave was nowhere to be seen when I arrived so I walked upstairs, ordered a bottle of red wine and found the best table outside. He had been doing this to me a bit lately, being late for our dates, and sometimes we had barely half an hour together before I was due back to work. I was conscious that I had gained a reputation for bad timekeeping with my manager, and I was making a big effort to be on time every day. Dave annoyed me when he was late, it made me feel like he was taking me for granted and like his time was more precious than mine. Today, however, I was too keyed up to be irritated for long and five minutes after I arrived I saw him walking up the stairs.

'Hi, you OK? How'd it go?' He asked lazily. No apology for being late I noticed.

'Good, I think.' I poured us both a glass of wine. 'I'll know in the next few days anyway.'

At that moment my phone started ringing. The screen showed an unknown local number and I debated whether to let it ring out and go to voicemail. But, partly to punish Dave for being late to meet me again, and partly because it might have been someone about one of the jobs I had applied for, I picked up the call.

'Hello, Katie speaking.' I answered in an upbeat voice.

'Hello Katie, this is Debbie from Recruit Unique. Are you able to talk?' My stomach clenched, she was phoning me less than an hour after my interview – was that good or bad?

'Yes, Debbie. Hi.' I looked at Dave, mouthing 'It's them!', and I got up to walk to a quieter spot where I could hear better.

'Katie. Thank you for coming in today.' Debbie began. It was a 'No' then, I thought. Thanks, but no thanks. My heart sank.

'Katie.' She went on. 'We would very much like to offer you the position, on a starting salary of £25,000 per annum. Do you think that would be acceptable?'

'Oh My God, really??!' My voice went up several octaves. 'Yes, absolutely, yes! Thank you so much!'

'Wonderful!' Debbie sounded so warm and friendly, I could hardly wait to begin working for her. 'I'll get the paperwork out in the post to you today. Will you tell your current employers and be able to give me a start date?'

'I'll speak to them first thing tomorrow, when I'm back in.' I promised. I could hardly believe it. I had a brand new job! I had to give a month's notice but I had loads of holiday days left that I hadn't bothered to take, so I could, in all probability, start within a couple of weeks. The money was way more than what I was on now. I could put some aside each month, maybe find a cheap last minute deal and have a proper holiday for once, since my previous savings had been stolen by Adam to fund his luxury lifestyle in Thailand with his new girlfriend. Twat.

Hanging up, I rushed back to our table with a huge smile on my face. An evil idea popped into my head and I couldn't resist.

'That was my doctors' surgery.' I told Dave. 'I didn't tell you, because I didn't want you to worry, but I went to see them this morning before my interview. Darling...' I covered his hand in mine. 'such wonderful news.... I'm pregnant.'

He went white. Then slightly green.

'Wha...wha...what?' He stammered, looking for all the world like he was going to hurl. Damn, I couldn't keep a straight face, couldn't keep the charade going.

'JOKING!' I shouted. 'Ha, you should SEE your face!!!!' He groaned in relief and I laughed at his expression when it sank it that he wasn't about to be a father again anytime soon.

'But, seriously, there is wonderful news. I have a new job!' I couldn't help the smile on my face.

'Really? That's fantastic!' He whooped, standing up and running to my side of the table. He picked me up and whirled me around like we were in a cheesy movie. 'I'm sooooooo proud of you!' He bent his head to kiss me. 'You're amazing.'

'I couldn't have done it without you.' I laughed. 'You were the one who gave me the confidence to even try.'

'I love you!' He said. 'I LOVE YOU! What would you say if I went down on one knee, right now, in front of all these people, and asked you to marry me?' He looked at me, only half joking, the air between us suddenly charged.

'I'd say.....' I paused, considering. 'I'd say you had a lot of explaining to do to your wife if you came home with a new fiancée.' We both laughed, the awkward tension disappearing. Sometimes when he said such things to me, it was like he was prodding a bruise. He knew it was there and that poking at it would hurt, but he went ahead and did it anyway.

'Lets' get that wine down us!' I picked up my glass and waved it above my head. 'To new beginnings!' I cheered.

'To new beginnings!' He echoed. 'And to having the time of our lives!' He added.

Giving in my notice to my manager the next morning was one of the best moments of my life. To be fair, he took it well, and even congratulated me on my new career. Breaking the news to the rest of my team was bittersweet though. I called a quick staff meeting just before we opened as I thought it would be best to tell them all together, at the same time.

They were shocked, silent at first but then made a valiant effort to be pleased for me.

'Got your back, dawg!' Darren fist-bumped me as he walked out of the staffroom after the meeting.

'Got your back, dawg!' the others cried, each one filing past me and high-fiving or giving me a hug. Mel loitered at the back, waiting until all the others had left.

'Who are you?' She asked me bitterly, and fighting back tears. 'I just don't know you anymore. Taking up with that man has changed you, and not for the better either. I wish I could say I'm pleased for you and well done, but all I can say is good luck – you're going to need it.' She stormed past me before I could think of a reply, or tell her that I had recommended her as my replacement, complete with a place on the FastTrack Management Programme and everything.

I had agreed to work two weeks' notice and take the rest of my annual leave entitlement in lieu of the remainder of my notice period. I would be starting at Recruit Unique in just a few weeks' time. Having worn a uniform for so long, I panicked at my lack of suitable office attire, and dragged Dave around the charity shops at lunchtimes for days. I had no savings to buy a new wardrobe, so I slowly built up a capsule collection of mix and match skirts, blouses and jackets to get me through the five days per week looking like I was wearing something completely different and stylish every day. One day we were in Oxfam, flicking through the rails, when he said,

'Found something you might like'. I turned to him, and instead of a top or pretty scarf, he held an envelope in his hands. He handed it to me and simply said 'Open it.' It had my name written on it in his distinctive messy scrawl.

'What's this?' I was puzzled, it was the wrong shape to be a card and it was quite thick and bulky.

'You'll have to open it to find out.' He teased, looking like he was enjoying every moment.

'Now?.......Here?' I wondered why he had chosen the local Oxfam charity shop to give me a present.

'Now. Here.' He said firmly.

I eased open the envelope and drew out a sheaf of papers. They were print-outs of some sort. Opening them up, I saw they were booking confirmations for a flight to Rome, leaving this Friday and returning the following Monday. There was also a printed receipt for a hotel, for three nights. The bookings were all in my name. I stared at them, unable to understand.

'Surprise!'

'What the.......?' I was speechless.

'We're going to Rome!' He exclaimed. 'Next weekend. I've booked for me as well, but separately, and I put everything in your name and did it from my work email address so, you know, no one at home finds out.' No one at home meaning his wife.

'But.... How are you going to get away? What are you going to tell her?' I was still catching up with this turn of events, and couldn't think straight.

'She thinks I'm going to Manchester for the football. It'll be fine, she won't even notice I'm not in the country.' He was so excited I couldn't help but start to feel excited too. 'And if we're going to be in one of the most romantic places on earth.....' As if on cue, one of the elderly Oxfam volunteers appeared like a magician's assistant, holding out a dress in a theatrical manner.

'You'll need something to wear.' He finished. I took the dress, it was beautiful. A vintage dream in cream silk, it had a fitted bodice which clinched in at the waist, then flowed out to a swishy pleated skirt, a la Marilyn Monroe in that famous picture of her dress flying up in the breeze from the subway vent. 'Try it on.' He urged, when I stroked the smooth cream perfection of the fabric. I dived into the changing room, stripped off and stepped into the skirt, pulling the dress up and slipping my arms into the sleeves. It fitted like it had been made especially for me. I glanced at the label sewn into the seam, a long forgotten designer, the dress had probably been made in the fifties at the very height of debutante glamour. It spoke of cocktails at exclusive clubs, long white gloves and French cigarettes in ebony holders. The only problem was that I couldn't reach the zip at the back to do it up, or the hooks and eyes at the top of the neck. I poked my head out of the changing room curtail and motioned for Dave to come in.

'I need a little help.' I turned my back to him. He drew up the zipper and fumbled with the fastenings at the top. We stared at my reflection, at the way the dress skimmed over my body, draped in all the right places and made my waist look tiny and delicate.

'Perfect.' He stood behind me, his arms encircled me and he kissed my neck, the sensitive bit just below my ear. 'Just perfect. You'll be the most beautiful woman in Rome.' Rome! I could hardly believe it. It was somewhere I had always longed to go, and had never had the chance. Adam had preferred more tropical places, cheap and on the backpacker trail.

'Thank you. So much. You have no idea how much this means to me.' I could hardly get the words out. I could feel myself welling up with emotion and love. I leaned back against him and he tightened his embrace, burying his face in my hair and breathing in deeply.
Behind us, the curtain was suddenly pulled aside roughly and we sprang apart. The volunteer lady stood there.

'Let's have a look then, ducks.' She cackled, hacking out a 50-a-day smokers' cough. 'Oh I say, how lovely. Fit for a princess. You look like that Aubrey Hepburn lass from the pictures.' She tweaked the skirt here and there, adjusted the shoulders. 'Now, you just need some proper undies to go under it. We had some lovely ones donated in yesterday, nice and high in the waist with lots of room to cover all your bits!' She said happily. 'Good old flesh coloured cotton, they are, very practical, and I think I might be able to find you a sturdy bra to go with them.'

I didn't dare catch Dave's eye. The very thought of wearing some horrid old granny knickers under this heavenly dress – second-hand, horrid old granny knickers at that! It was enough to send us both into an unstoppable fit of giggles.

'Thank you, you're too kind.' I told her, trying to be polite while Dave sniggered into his hand behind me. 'But I have the perfect thing at home.' I resolved to dash into that posh sexy undies shop on the way home and pick up something that would give him a heart attack.

'No, it's no problem at all.' She went on as if I hadn't spoken. She was on a roll now, determined to see me kitted out in full. 'I'll just go and hunt them out, and then you can try them on.' She gave us a grotesque wink and bumbled off.

'Quick!' Hissed Dave, gasping for breath between giggles. 'We have to leg it before she comes back!'

He unzipped the dress and I threw on my clothes in record time. Paying at the counter (thirty quid – absolute bargain!) we ran out of the store and hid in the alleyway next door until we were certain the volunteer lady hadn't followed us out into the street, waving a pair of big elasticated bloomers.

'You do realise.' I panted. 'We can never, ever show our faces in there again!'

'Not unless we agree to buy their entire stock of stained Y-fronts and ropey old bras.' He agreed, mock seriously. 'Coast's clear - let's go, Aubrey Hepburn!'

CHAPTER THIRTEEN

Humming happily, I packed for our weekend in Rome, taking my best summer clothes. The hotel had a pool so a bikini was a must, cute summer dresses for the day and something smarter, including my new vintage silk beauty, now hanging up fresh from the drycleaners in its protective plastic sheath, for the nights. Jackie, my landlady, bless her heart, had offered to look after Monkey and Rocket at her place and I had paid her twelve-year-old nephew twenty quid to feed them and give them some cuddles whilst I was away. I downloaded a map of central Rome from our hotel website and literally Googled 'The Top Ten Things to Do in Rome', marking them all out, numbered one to ten on the map. I wanted to pack in as much as possible into the few days we were there, and I had carefully budgeted my spending money from the meagre amount of Euro's I had been able to afford to buy.

To get our flight, we had to get the train into London Victoria and then the Gatwick Express to Gatwick Airport. The flight to Rome wasn't until six in the evening but it would take us several hours to get to the airport so I arranged for the Friday afternoon, and the whole Monday off work, taking it as unpaid leave. Financially it would hit me hard at the end of the month, particularly as I had a bit of a gap between my last pay day at the book store and the next one at my new job at Recruit Unique, but I figured I would worry about that later – nothing was going to stop me from spending every moment of this weekend in a loved up state of utter bliss! Our first time away together, I thought, in a place where no one will know us and we can blend in with the crowds and be just another touristy couple in the eternal city of love. I imagined us strolling down pretty mosaic streets, holding hands and stopping to kiss in the cool shade of ancient buildings. We would marvel at the Trevi   Fountain,   run up the Spanish Steps, walk over the Bridge of Sighs – Whoops, that was Venice, not Rome – visit the Vatican and soak up the millennia of history and culture in one of the most beautiful cities in the world.   What an amazingly romantic man Dave was to think of organising this for me, he really did treat me like a princess. As if by thinking of him magically conjured him up, my phone buzzed with an incoming text.

I think we should get separate trains. X

What? Why would we need to get separate trains, part of the fun was the build-up and the excitement of travelling to the airport. I text back a simple

??

I knew he was planning on taking Friday afternoon off work as well, and we were cutting it quite fine to get to Gatwick in time for check-in as it was. Maybe he planned to go up to London earlier and meet me at Victoria for some reason.

It would just be safer. What if someone we know sees us on the train together? X

OK, point taken. We needed to hide, still. I checked the train timetables and the train we had planned to get was really the only viable option – everything else was either too early and would mean I had to take the whole day off, or too late, meaning we would miss the flight. We HAD to get the same train.

Just looked at train times, the 3.10 is the only one we can take.

He didn't reply for a while, but then he rang my mobile sometime later.

'I can't talk for long, I had to tell her I was getting something from the car.' He sounded stressed. 'If we get the same train, we'll have to pretend we don't know each other.'

'What? Do you mean ignore each other on the platform and sit in separate seats?' I asked, not believing what I was hearing. He had to be kidding.

'Separate carriages even.' Oh. He was serious. 'I can't take the risk of someone telling Vicki that they saw me on the train with another woman.'

'But.....surely we can sit next to each other?' I didn't see anything wrong with that, people had seen us walking around town together for weeks. What was so suspicious of sitting together on a train to London? 'She thinks you're going up to London anyway to catch the train to Manchester, and no one's going to notice us at Victoria. Chances of us running into someone we know on the Gatwick Express are slim to none.'

'Katie, please, be reasonable.' He sighed. I had thought I was, being very reasonable. 'We just can't take the chance.'

'And what about when we're at Gatwick?' I asked, sarcastically. 'Are we going to spend the whole time ignoring each other, just in case there might be someone there who knows you? What about on the plane to Rome? What about Rome itself?!' I was so angry at him now. It made me feel like he was ashamed of me, like I was a dirty habit he needed to hide.

'Don't be silly.' He snapped. 'I have to go. We'll talk about it tomorrow.' And he hung up without saying goodbye.

Furious tears stung my eyes. What was the point of even going if he was going to spend the whole time looking over his shoulder for fear of being caught out? All of a sudden I was sick and tired of the whole thing. What was I doing, putting up with being treated like this? There were plenty of men out there, available men, men with no baggage, men who were able to offer me a normal relationship. Why was I even with Dave? I asked myself. Even if he ever became free, if he left his wife or whatever, why would I want to be with someone who was happy, comfortable even, with lying and cheating on his partner? My phoned blipped again.

> **Sorry. But I just don't want to risk being found out. I will end up losing you and I can't do that. Love you XX**

My fingers hovered over the keypad, itching to reply with something angry and hurtful. Then I switched my phone off completely. We would see what Rome brought, but after that, when we returned home I would think long and hard about whether we had a future of any kind.

Vicki Campbell-Roberts@luckyladysoblessed
Letting him off the leash for the weekend! What will I do without my Love Bear for 3 whole days? #husbandgoals #hebetterbehave #football #missyou #emptybed #strongcouple #bestfriend #togetherforever #love #comehomesoon #absencemakestheheartgrowfonder #pamperweekend #beautytime #spaday #metime #hairtreatment #grindhardstayhumble #blessed

Katie
September
It was ridiculous, I huffed, as I walked to the train station dragging my wheelie case. Dave had gotten his own way, arguing patiently with me that a short train journey didn't make any difference to our weekend away, and that he's just not prepared to risk our whole relationship for the sake of a couple of hours on a train. Well, if he wanted me to ignore him, then he was in for some serious ignoring! At the very last minute I shoved a book into my bag. I hadn't planned on having any time to read in Rome but burrowing into a book on the journey would take my mind of it and save me from looking out for him, hoping to catch sight of him. Grabbing a takeaway coffee from Costa at the station, and struggling to wheel my case, carry my heavy handbag AND walk with a coffee in my hand, I stood on the platform, resolutely not looking at anybody on either side of me. When the train arrived I chose the carriage furthest from the front, and settled myself at a seat with a table. It was a thing for me – I had to sit facing the direction of travel or else I would get motion sickness. Instead of feeling excited about Rome, I felt lonely, like I was travelling on my own to a hospital appointment or a meeting with my divorce lawyer. I watched the bleak landscape roll past, lulled by the hypnotic sound of the train on the tracks. Every time the doors at the front of the carriage hissed open, my heart leaped, hoping it was Dave coming to find me, but it was only the snack trolley lady or the ticket inspector. I had thought we would at least make a game of it, this pretending to be strangers. Thought we would be sending sexy flirty texts to each other while we were sitting across the aisle, within touching distance but not allowed to touch, revelling in the delicious anticipation of being free to be openly affectionate in Rome.

The train rolled into London Victoria and it was a rush to find the right platform for the Gatwick Express. We had booked tickets but needed to print them out at one of the self-service ticket machines first. I queued up behind a snake of French teenagers, all shoving and shouting and getting on my nerves. When a machine became available I tapped the booking reference on the keypad as requested. 'Please swipe the Credit/Debit card that was used for payment at the time of booking' it flashed at me. Oh fuck, it wasn't my card that we had made the train bookings on – it was Dave's, and he was walking around the station somewhere with it in his wallet. Punching the screen hard to cancel the ticket transaction I bulldozed my way past the shouty French kids and anxiously scanned the concourse, in case he was on his way to the ticket machines. I tried calling his mobile, but it just rang out without him answering. Checking my watch, I saw that I had less than ten minutes to catch the train to the airport. My only option was to buy a completely new ticket on my own debit card, annoyingly it would cost me full price instead of the discounted advance rate we have got by booking online. Queueing up at the ticket machines again, the queue having grown by miles in the last five minutes, I prayed that I had enough money left in my account to cover the fare. Dave, you bastard, you owe me big time!

Running to the platform I was just in time to leap onto the train before the doors swished shut behind me. I scanned the passengers, hoping to see his dark hair and a free seat beside him. I couldn't see him but that didn't mean he wasn't on the same train but in another carriage. Lugging my case to the storage area I found half a spare seat next to some backpackers, who were taking up most of the room with their massive rucksacks propped up next to them, making it difficult for me to squeeze my legs into the space provided. They nattered away to each other in some

Scandinavian language while I perched miserably on the edge of the seat, sending him text after text and suggesting we meet up as soon as we got to Gatwick. He didn't reply and I sank further and further into a depressed gloom. This was hardly the best start to the romantic break I had envisaged.

Gatwick's South terminal was stupidly busy as always, and our flight was leaving from the North. I was running seriously late for check-in now and typically, the inter-terminal shuttle was running on one service and I had just missed one, meaning a seven-minute wait until the next. I tapped my foot anxiously on the floor as the waiting area for the shuttle started filling up with large groups of people. Families with overloaded luggage trollies and over-excited children pushed past me rudely, a group of young men probably on their way to a stag do swaggered up to me and said 'Awright darlin?' before belching beery breath into my face and laughing, sloping off to do the same to another single female traveller. I rolled my eyes, remembering that this was why I didn't like being in crowds of people, and prayed for the shuttle to hurry the fuck up. Finally, I was in the quieter North terminal and wheeling my case up to the check-in desk, which was thankfully still open with a small queue of people still waiting to be processed.

Ten minutes later I was through the departures door and in the long line of the security check, waiting not so patiently while the people in front of me expressed surprise and outrage at having to remove their shoes, or belts, or empty their pockets for the x-ray scanner, despite there being signs everywhere explaining what to do. One woman was arguing over the bottle of water she had just bought from one of the café's in the airport.

'But it's not even OPEN!' She shouted at the airport security guard. 'I just paid more than TWO POUNDS for it and you're telling me to THROW IT AWAY?!' The guard just looked like he'd heard it all before and trotted out the usual platitudes in a bored, robotic voice.

'Very sorry Madam, security policy Madam, huge signs explaining all this before you enter the security area Madam.' Another lady had silver bangles all the way up both her arms, and a gold chain attaching her earrings to her nose stud, and was slowly, painfully slowly, removing each item of jewellery individually with great care and placing it reverently in the plastic tray provided. Why, God, Why? I asked inwardly. Why do You let these people out into the world when I'm trying to get somewhere in a hurry? Why do You deliberately place these imbeciles in my way for me to trip over? Is it some kind of life lesson I'm supposed to learn, about tolerance and forgiveness and loving my fellow man? There was still no word on my phone from Dave when I shoved my bag and case onto the rollers and walked through the metal detector. It went off, of course it did. Motioning me to step onto the square marked out on the floor, the butch, bulldog-faced guard ran her hands all over my arms and legs and under my boobs. I'm sure she lingered especially long over my boobs. Deciding that I was no threat to national security she nodded me through, and I grabbed my belongings from the collection area and trudged through to the main departure lounge, loitering outside World of Whiskies to rearrange my bag and put my passport and boarding pass in a safe place.

'There you are!' Dave was standing in front of me, looking calm and unruffled.

'Where the hell were you? I couldn't find you!' I half wailed, feeling for all the world like I was going to cry. He wrapped me in a big bear hug and kissed my forehead.

'I will find you. Always.' He promised.

91

We were together now and that's all that mattered. We had a little time before we had to be at our gate for boarding so we stocked up on duty free spirits and lingered over a glass of overpriced vinegary wine at one of the lounge pub chains.

'I'm sorry I couldn't be there for you.' He picked up my hand and kissed my palm. 'I did look for you at Victoria station and I just didn't even think about the card thing.' I had vented the whole story about the train tickets, the miserable Gatwick Express journey and given him a detailed description of all the pain in the arse people I'd had to deal with, both on the way to and at the airport. 'Never mind' he soothed. 'Your holiday starts..........now!'

Our flight was called over the tannoy, inviting us to make our way to gate 104. As we had checked in at different times, our seats were miles apart. Dave went up to the service agent on the desk at the gate and had a quiet word. I could see the woman nodding and smiling, and sensed that Dave was using his easy charm to get her to move us to seats next to each other.

'Result!' he crowed. 'The flights not so busy so she's moved us so we've got a row to ourselves. Maybe we could join the mile-high club.....?' He raised his eyebrows suggestively.

I'd read enough tabloid newspaper stories about couples who were caught fumbling under blankets in full view of the other passengers, or falling out of the tiny aeroplane toilet door mid-flight in various stages of undress and in some cases, still physically joined together.

'Not happening.' I said flatly. 'You can wait until we're at the hotel.'

'Mmmmmm, I hear the pool's got some quiet hidden corners.' He leered. 'Perfect for getting up to no good. We could skinny dip under the stars tonight and I can ravish you in the water. Or you could ravish me.' After such a rocky start, he was doing a good job of lifting my spirits and the excitement I had felt in the build-up to this weekend now flared back to life.

'The room looks amazing!' I enthused. 'The bed is HUGE and there's plenty of room for two in the bathtub......'

'We won't need to leave, we'll just get room service every day and not set foot outside the hotel all weekend.' He was teasing me now.

'Oi, not a chance!' I laughed. He knew damn well I had a list of places I wanted to see over our couple of days.

'As long as it's not all fusty old museums and rip-off tourist traps.' He yawned and stretched his arms above his head. 'But I'd go anywhere with you, as long as we're there together it'll be heaven on Earth.'

The flight was smooth and uneventful – there were no under-blanket shenanigans and the toilets were at the front of the plane, which would have made sneaking into one together impossible without the rest of the passengers noticing. Disembarking at Rome's Fiumicino Airport, the heat haze from the tarmac hit us like a wall, even though it was past nine o'clock in the evening.

'Woo hoo! It's hot, hot, hot!' shouted Dave happily. The airport was a crazy maze of baggage halls and immigration queues but then we were out, and walking along the badly lit walkway towards the train station. The Leonardo Express took us directly into the centre of Rome and we decided that a taxi to the hotel would be the best bet, seeing as it was A) dark, B) we had no idea where the hotel was and C) we were knackered and looking forward to being in our hotel room together. I was in desperate need of a shower, needing to wash the breath and sweat of thousands of other people off me before I would feel clean again. Pulling up to the hotel in the taxi, we were amazed at how beautiful it was. It was lit up like a giant white wedding cake, set in lovely grounds where each tree had been transformed into works of art using different coloured spotlights, which lit them from trunk to top.

The room didn't disappoint either.

'It's fabulous!' I twirled around, trying to take it all in at once. It was on the very top floor of the hotel, and had quirky pointed ceilings which sloped down in places to meet the dormer windows. Dave had trouble standing upright in some areas, banging his head on the beams if he wasn't looking where he was going which made me laugh every time.

Double doors opened out onto a tiny balcony, lit with fairy lights and just wide enough for a small wrought iron table and two matching chairs. The view was stupendous, the centre of Rome showcased before us in an array of dazzling, sparkling lights.

Inside, the room was decorated in whites and pale greys, the king sized bed taking centre stage, draped in filmy organza curtains which could be drawn around the entire bed and made us feel we were sleeping safely within a celestial cloud. The bathroom was a clean, modern interior designers dream in marble, and was easily the same size as the entire bedroom.

Dave dumped our cases in the middle of the floor and in one smooth movement, picked me up and laid me not very gently on the bed, kissing me with the passion of someone who has been denied human comfort for a lifetime. He moved to start taking off my shoes, and I remembered I had been travelling for almost seven hours, and my feet, in fact all of me, probably didn't smell too fresh.

'Shower first' I insisted and sat up, trying to climb off the bed but getting trapped in its billowy white covers.

'Bed first.' Dave's voice was muffled by the feather duvet I had thrown over his head in my escape attempt.

'Shower!' He grabbed my leg and started pulling me back towards him on the bed.

'BED!'

'SHOWER! Trust me, you'll thank me later.'

'NOOOOOOO, BED BED BED!' He was still trying to pull me back.

'OK, compromise?' I tried.

'Compromise how? He said petulantly.

'Bath?' I suggested. 'Bath for two? With bubbles and candles and champagne? Well, bubbles and candles and duty frees....'

'Deal.' He grinned. 'But you're at the tap end!' He added, and leapt off the bed into the bathroom before I could get to my feet.

Giggling like children, we emptied every single miniature bottle of soap and shampoo into the tub, letting the geyser like taps whip up an impressively thick layer of bubbles. I found some tea lights scattered around the bedroom and balcony and took these all into the bathroom, lighting and placing them on every available surface. Dave opened the bottle of Courvoisier Brandy we had gone halves on at the Gatwick shopping lounge and found two sparkling crystal tumblers by the minibar fridge, pouring a generous measure into each glass.

Piling my hair up on top of my head and securing it with clips, I stripped off my crumpled travel-stained clothes. Feeling like the leading lady in a French erotica film, I climbed into the huge tub and lay back and closed my eyes, sighing in bliss, feeling the warm bubbles enveloping me and letting the stress of the day drain from my body. I heard Dave come into the bathroom and I opened my eyes as he handed me my glass. He stripped off his own clothes, giving me just enough time to admire the lean contours of his beautiful body, before climbing into the tub behind me, his legs on either side of mine and he drew me back to rest against him. Taking a sip of the brandy, I passed him my glass to put safely up high on the vanity unit, and turned over in the water so we were lying front to front, our bodies slippery with bubbles and heat.

'Let's make some waves.' I dared him.

Later, when we had moved from bath to bedroom floor, to actual bed, the brandy bottle half empty, we lay wrapped in each other's arms on top of the bedcovers. We hadn't drawn the thick blackout curtains and the lights of Rome played across our naked bodies. We were both exhausted, sore but sated for now and we murmured little secrets to one another in the half light.

'What would you have done if I had turned you down that day, the first time we went for coffee?' I was curious to know.

'Dunno' He said sleepily. 'Moved onto your friend Mel I suppose.' I slapped his bum and he laughed. 'I really hadn't thought about it, probably would have tried again the next day I think. Worn you down until you gave up and admitted you fancied me.' I slapped his bum again and he groaned and pushed against me, laughing 'Keep spanking me, I'm loving it.'
We were quiet for a minute, entwining our fingers together.

'Tell me about prison.' I ventured. 'What was it like in there for you?' I felt him tense, could feel his mind racing over what to say next.

'It wasn't all bad.' he started. 'But some things happened in there that I will never, ever tell anyone about.' I had an inkling as to what these things would have been, him being so young, and beautiful looking, he would have been a serious prize for some of the harder, long term prisoners he was locked in with. 'Being a first-timer on a relatively minor charge, and barely an adult, I was assigned an officer to look out for me, make sure I was making the most of the opportunities the prison service offered' He said this sardonically. 'Got me signed up for English classes so I could sit my exams in there and have some qualifications when I got out. He was a good bloke, had a son my own age so he did his best for me. There was an art teacher there too, who noticed that I wasn't bad at drawing and things, so he got me on a graphic design course as well through the Open University and made sure I had extra time in the computer labs so I could do my assignments. When I passed and got my certificate he brought me in a card, and a bar of chocolate to congratulate me, and then when I was released he pulled some strings, called in some favours, and got me a work experience placement at a design company he knew. All I had to do was sit out my two years of probation, keep my nose clean and work hard, and I would be free to move on to a paid job.'

I loved listening to him talk, loved feeling that he was sharing these memories with me, things that he probably hadn't told anyone else.

'I still have the box at home.' he went on, lost in remembering. 'It's the box they give you when you get released, the one with all your belongings in it. I keep it at the back of my wardrobe, with the original assignments and classwork from my graphic design course. I kept all the letters I got while I was in there, and the cards I got on my birthday, some of the other lads in my art class made me a card with a drawing of what was supposed to be Pamela Anderson on it, except it looks more like a pig with tits.'

I burst out laughing.

'Do you think it's weird?' he asked, turning to look at me. 'That I still keep the box of prison things?'

'No, of course it's not weird.' I looked back at him, and squeezed his hand. 'It was a big turning point in your life, and you can't change the fact that it happened, or what happened in there. It's a part of what makes you who you are today, it's only natural to keep some memories locked away and revisit them sometimes, good and bad.'

'Yes. 'That's exactly it, it made me who I am.' he sounded relieved, and like I'd just imparted some golden nugget of wisdom. 'She doesn't get it at all. She thinks I should throw the box away and can't understand why I would want to look through it now and again.'

I held my breath, it wasn't often that he opened up about her, his wife, so every little comment he did make I stored away for information purposes, to help exacerbate the ugly picture I already had of her in my head.

'She just doesn't get me like you do.' God, is he really going to trot out that old cliché - tell me his wife doesn't understand him?

'So why am I so different?' I knew I was skating on thin ice with this conversation but he had drunk enough brandy to be open and indiscreet, whereas usually he would button up and refuse to talk about her.

'You are a different creature altogether.' He touched my nose with his affectionately. 'You know how to show love, and you see the best in everything. Take this room for example. You were blown away by it, went mad for all the small things like candles, and the fairy lights and the mini box of welcome chocolates. She would have been complaining from the minute she set foot in here - the mirror would have been too small, or the light not flattering enough. She would have insisted that we get all dressed up and go out and be seen, so she could pose amongst the beautiful people in the fancy restaurant downstairs, and get that on her social media. She would have found fault with everything and I would have been the one to get the blame.'

'Is she really that much of a spoilt brat?' I asked, appalled. This man had organised, and paid for, the most perfect weekend away and there was no way I would have been anything but pathetically grateful. I certainly wouldn't have dreamed of complaining, even if the hotel had turned out to be a flea infested dump instead of the most luxurious place I had ever been in my life.

'Put it his way.' His voice became harder, sharper. 'A month after we got married she gave me back my engagement ring. It was too small, she said, and one diamond wasn't enough - she wanted three. And they had to be the best ones in the world, even gave me the name of the diamond dealers she wanted them from, along with the carat size of each one.'

'But the original one you chose for her.' I put in. 'surely she realised that you gave that to her as a symbol of your love?' Did she really just throw it back at him?

'I skinted myself for that ring as it was. Spent most of my savings on it, so the big bling ring she had in her mind was out of the question. I just couldn't afford it, even if I had been able to get credit or a bank loan I couldn't have done it. It was our first major argument.'
What. A. Bitch.
I lay there looking into his face.

'I will never ask you for anything you aren't able to give.' I said seriously. 'You already give me everything I want.'

We slept late the next morning. The dawn light was turning the sky silver when we had finally stopped talking and drifted off to sleep. I woke briefly to feel him spoon into me, moulding his body around mine in a perfect fit, before falling into the deepest sleep I had had for months. I woke to see him looking straight into my eyes.

'Morning beautiful' he yawned. 'Do you realise; this is the first time we've woken up together?'
We breakfasted by the pool, sipping proper Italian coffee from tiny cups, so strong that no amount of sugar could touch the burnt bitterness. I was itching to get going, couldn't wait to start exploring this iconic city.

'Where should we go first?' I took a huge bite of one of the warm flaky pastries from the basket on the table. 'Do you think we should just go for a walk, find our bearings?'

'Hmmmm?' Dave said distractedly. He was fiddling with his phone and not really listening to me.

'Shall we go in order of importance, visit the big sites first, so we don't run out of time and miss something?' I rabbited on.

'Damn Wi-Fi code's not working.' He muttered.

'Dave, hello, Earth to Dave...' I nudged his foot under the table. He looked up, as if startled to find me there, then remembered where he was.

'Sorry, sorry. Just got to get this working.' He rested a hand on my knee abstractedly. 'I need Google Maps so I can search for a sports bar showing the match today.'

'You what?' Did I hear that right? He was actually intending to watch football today, something he could have done on a normal boring weekend at home.

'But we're only here for such a short time, don't you want to make the most of it?' I wheedled.

'It's one of the most important games of the season.' He was trying not to show it but there was an edge to his voice. 'Besides, everyone thinks I'm at the game, how can I talk about it if I don't see it?' That was reasonable I suppose.

'So what am I supposed to do?'

'Go and look at some shops, that's what girls like to do on holiday isn't it? Look, I need to find a Wi-Fi hotspot, keep your phone on you and I'll text you and meet you somewhere after the game.'

Rome was an hour ahead of UK time so I guessed he wouldn't be finished until at least four o'clock that afternoon. He gave me a quick kiss on the cheek and was gone. I sat there, bloody well fuming.

I'd done a lot of travelling in my time so the thought of being alone in a strange city wasn't daunting. I was just acutely aware that, if I wanted to see the main attractions, I would have to do some of it by myself. There was no way we could squeeze Rome into one day so I would just have to get on with it – alone.

I ended up having a wonderful day anyway. I strolled through the Via del Corso, which dissected the historic centre of the old city, joined in a tour of the Vatican by tagging along with a group of fat, badly dressed Americans, who were on one of those different-port-every-day Mediterranean cruises. There were so many of them, shrieking at each other from under their sun visors and stretching fanny packs around their ample waists, that I reasoned one more quiet one wouldn't be noticed.

I found a vibrant street market in one of the squares and browsed the colourful stalls, selling everything from tacky souvenirs to scarves costing hundreds of Euro. Now and then I stopped for a coffee – everywhere sold coffee here, all the bars, little one person cafes, they all were happy to provide you with one of their tiny expresso's with a smile. They didn't make a big deal out of it, coffee, not like they do at home, with those hipster-bearded, top-knotted serious baristas at Starbucks who looked down their nose at you if you deigned to soil their masterpiece creations with milk or sugar. Here, it was served as it came, with a 'Ciao Bella' on the side, and you were left in peace to sit as long as you wanted, soaking up the culture and watching the beautiful people of Rome - the old men playing a convivial game of cards, the teenagers lounging on the street corners, eyeing each other up and looking impossibly lithe and sophisticated, and nothing like the dumpy chav's that littered our high street.

I sampled street food from the market, gobbled up one of the famous gelatos' then, as I couldn't decide on one flavour, I went back for another. One of the coffee bars served a tiny shot glass of Sambuca on the side, and I tossed the fiery spirit down my throat in one, much to the delight of the elderly gentleman who ran the place. He insisted on serving me another and sat down to join me, smashing our glasses together and shouting 'Saluta Roma!' I could live here, easily, I thought and imagined Dave and me in a tiny apartment off one of the town squares. We would be impossibly sophisticated and beautiful too, and live wild, fascinating lives which involved coffee and drinking and touring the country on a Lambretta scooter. Quite how we would fund this new life didn't enter my head, I was too busy fantasising about lounging half naked on our apartment balcony, shouting down greetings to the many interesting friends we would make here. My phone shouted at me, disrupting my daydream.

Where U? X

Bloody hell, it was gone half four already. I glanced around me, trying to find the name of the coffee bar, or a street sign, anything which would let me know where I was. I had just been wandering where my feet took me, neither wondering nor caring where I ended up. I went inside to the bar.

'Excuse me, can you give me the address of this place please? My friend's trying to find me and I don't know how to explain how to get here.' The old man held up his hand in the universal gesture for stop and I realised he didn't have a clue what I was saying. He reached under the bar and presented me with an IPad, already set to Google Translate and indicated I should enter my question, which the webpage would translate into Italian as I typed. That was bloody genius, I thought, all countries should do this. Once he had read the Italian translation he rapidly typed in a few lines and set the page to translate back to English, showing me the screen. I copied down the address exactly and text it back to Dave. I had no idea whereabouts in the city he was or how long it would take him to reach me. I spotted him walking towards me less than 5 minutes later, he was just around the corner the whole time, and luckily had been paying attention to the map and knew the way back to our hotel.

'Good day?' he asked cheerily.

'Wonderful. Shame you weren't here to be a part of it.' I couldn't resist getting in a little dig there, however it washed over him completely.

'I vote we go back to the room for a little.....riposo.' I doubt that what we would be doing in that room actually involved sleeping. 'And then get all dressed up ready for an evening out, make a night of it.' He was pleased with himself, his team must have won. We walked hand in hand back to the hotel, with the golden afternoon sun shining down on us.

Later, I was on my way to the shower to freshen up after a day of walking and an afternoon of hot, sweaty, messy sex. I heard Dave's phone ring just as I turned on the water and saw him reflected in the hallway mirror as he picked up his phone and left the room. I knew that he had to phone home sometimes while he was away, if only to talk to Josh once a day. He didn't keep it a secret from me, but he did make a point of walking out of my earshot when he called. A bit awkward talking to your wife in front of your mistress – apparently it was considered poor form according to 'The Married Man's Guide to Successfully Having an Affair and Not Getting Caught' handbook. I'm not sure if he thought he was protecting me, or avoiding me. I never mentioned these calls to him, by unspoken agreement we did not acknowledge that he had to check in with the wife and pretend he was on his own in a budget hotel in Manchester. I slithered into my wonderful, cream silk vintage gown. I had caught the sun and my shoulders were glowing prettily against the pale material, making me look healthy and radiant. I dried my hair with the incredibly slow hotel issue hairdryer. (Why these places don't invest in some super quick high speed ones, I don't know) I'd bought a small amount of make-up and dusted just enough on my face to compliment my already sun-kissed skin, and highlight my eyes which were sparkling with love and happiness. I fastened my silver fairy around my neck, it suited the style of the dress with its Art Deco lines. Dave jumped into the shower just after me, and was towelling off. He only had to rub his hair dry and jump into some fresh clothes and he was done.

'You look amazing.' He said sincerely, as I put on some high strappy sandals and picked up my evening bag. 'I've never seen you look so beautiful. I saw something today, and thought of you.' He pulled a small box from its hiding place under the cushions on the chair, and handed it to me. I sat on the edge of the bed.

'You really didn't need to…..' I started, but he dropped down onto his knees in front of me, laying his head in my lap.

'Open it. And you'll see why I did need to.'
Inside the box was a thin silver bangle. I took it out and saw the engraved words circling both the inner and outer surfaces.

Love is patient
Love is kind
Love is hope
Love believes all things
Love endures all things
Love is forever

'Oh, it's beautiful! I love it.' I tried it on and it rested perfectly, not too heavy on my arm.

'I love you.' He said simply. 'You are my world. And this love IS forever.'

CHAPTER FOURTEEN

It was a wonderful night – one I shall always look back on and remember every little detail forever. Well, almost every detail but more about that later. There was music and dancing, incredible food and drinking, so much drinking. We found a rustic little bar that looked as if it had been there since the days of Caesar. It was down some steps into a rough stone-cobbled yard. Lit only by candles it was dark and sinister looking, yet the sound of laughter and traditional Italian folk music coming from the back enticed us in, promising the warmest of welcomes. Ducking our heads in the low doorway we walked in to be greeted by a chorus of 'Amico! Amico! Amico!' meaning friend, and everybody's glasses raised in our direction.

'Is tradition.' The smiling bartender told us. 'All new peoples are helloed like this.'

The long counter was made from rough-hewn wood and we found two similar stools free at the door end of the bar. On shelves that reached up to the ceiling there was bottle after bottle of all kinds of weird and wonderful concoctions. We could see nothing that we recognised, nothing with Smirnoff or Gordons written on it. The bottles were beautifully decorated and warped with age, pictures of strange fruits or trees indicating that they held some kind of locally brewed liqueur.

'I have a brilliant idea.' Dave pointed to the far left bottle on the top row and indicated to the bartender to pour two shots. 'We each choose a bottle from the top and do a shot, then two from the shelf underneath, then three from the bottom shelf. Last man standing wins, loser pays.'

'A bit like an alcoholic version of Countdown then.' I was up for the challenge, despite not knowing what the hell we were about to drink. 'I hope you've brought your emergency credit card, because you are going DOWN!'

Tiny plates of snacks similar to tapas appeared next to us without asking. Shot glass after shot glass appeared in front of us, until we had no idea where we were even pointing anymore. Our drinking competition had roused the interest of our fellow customers and we soon had two teams on either side of us, clapping and cheering us on, and I swear I saw money change hands several times with people betting on the who would fall first. Both of us were too stubborn to give in, my head was spinning and my eyes stopped focusing. Dave looked like he was about to fall face down into his spicy meatball snack. The bartender opened the lift-up hatch and walked around to our side. He grabbed one of Dave's' hands and one of mine and raised them above our heads in a triumphant winner's pose.

'Un pareggio!' He shouted. 'A draw!'

The crowd roared their approval and the acoustic band started up again with a rousing Latin beat. The dancing began in earnest and both of us were dragged up onto the minuscule square of dance floor and thrown from person to person. We were offered coffee, and bottles of fizzy water with lemon, to help us cling on to some kind of sobriety, and within a short time we both felt absolutely fine again.

Moving onto a quieter restaurant, with hugs and kisses goodbye from our new friends, we dined on simple but delicious pasta with pecorino cheese and lashings of black pepper.

'Shall we get a bottle of wine?' Dave asked, running his eyes over the list. 'Italy's reds are some of the best in the world.'

'Do you think that's wise, given how much we've already had to drink tonight?' I laughed.

'Food this good was meant to be accompanied by wine, after all - when in Rome.....'

'OK, OK you win. Let's get wine.'

It turned out to be a really bad idea. I have a vague memory of walking back to the hotel and then nothing until I woke up the next day, naked, dizzy and unable to move. Apparently, according to Dave, we had made love twice and that it was fantastic - he was most put out that I couldn't remember a single thing about it.

Fighting back the hangovers the next morning we loaded up at the breakfast buffet on bacon, sausages and buttery toast. Neither of us could face the watery, lukewarm scrambled eggs, breeding salmonella in their silver dish. I really, really needed a proper cup of tea which, as everybody knows, is impossible to get abroad, so I alternated between mouthfuls of bitter expresso and sips of bottled water.

'I can't believe how much we drank last night.' I groaned. 'How are we not dead?'

Dave was sitting opposite me, grey-faced and concentrating on being very, very still, so as not to give in to the nausea that was threatening to put in a splashy appearance at the breakfast table.

'I think I am dead.' He replied. 'This is a special circle of hell where we spend the rest of eternity staring at fatty pork products and trying not to be sick.'

'Drink more water. As soon as you rehydrate you'll feel better.' It was our last full day in Rome, and my list was nowhere near done. Today I wanted to see the Coliseum, the Sistine Chapel and St Peters Basilica, which were all within walking distance of each other. It was a shame we didn't have the time to do some of the day trips that the local tour companies were offering. We could have gone to

Pompeii or taken a tour of the island of Capri, but the thought of sitting on a coach, or even worse, a boat, for hours was enough to make my already tender stomach somersault dangerously.

'Don't you even think of skipping out on me today' I said pointedly to Dave. I could read his mind and knew that all he wanted to do was to crawl back into bed. 'We have a full day of sight-seeing to do. I found this amazing gelato place yesterday that does fruit sorbets as well, a citrus one would probably cure your hangover completely so let's start there first.' I was already beginning to feel better at the thought of the sights we would see today. I wanted to get some photos so I could have one of us together, framed and by my bed, so I could relive the memories of this wonderful trip whenever I wanted to. With all the enthusiasm of a condemned man, Dave slowly got up from his chair and shakily followed me out of the dining room.

We did have a good day, in the end. I found it slightly surreal that I was standing in the Sistine Chapel, staring up at one of the world's greatest masterpieces known to man. Dave's mood had picked up considerably and he was as moved as I was by the sheer beauty and intricacy of the paintings.

'This was when people had real talent.' He whispered. 'Everything, their life's work, was dedicated to the glory of God, not taking selfies and sacrificing them to the false gods of Facebook.' He had a good point. The serenity and silence of the chapel soothed my soul, and I wondered if I was missing a trick here – maybe I should try going to church more often, if it helped me recapture some of the peace I felt here. I had no particular beliefs in God or otherwise. I had never been baptised into a church, my parents telling me that they wanted me to make my own choices about religion when I was old enough to understand.

Really, they were just being lazy and probably couldn't be arsed with organising a christening.

Dave couldn't take any photos as he was supposed to be in Manchester, so I snapped away and talked him into having one taken together, passing my phone to a nearby Japanese couple who were on their honeymoon.

'You look like you're in love too!' They squealed as they took several shots of us posed outside the chapel. I usually hated having my picture taken, but I was pleased with how these ones came out. We both looked happy and relaxed and, yes, in love – you would never know we weren't a proper couple.

That night we were too tired to go out drinking again so we settled on a takeaway pizza which, we reasoned, still counted as Italian food. We swam lazily in the floodlit pool, watching the last of the sun's rays fade behind the hotel's façade, and lounged on the pool chairs, munching on the cheesy dough and sticking to alcohol free Coke's.

'We should do this again.' Dave rolled onto his back and stared at the darkening sky, the first twinkling stars just visible.

'Do what? Eat pizza in a swimming pool?' I nudged him playfully.

'You know what I mean' He smiled and nudged me back. 'Do this. Go away together. Think of all the places we could see.'

It was a nice idea, but we both knew it was an impossible dream. Lack of money, lack of time, lack of feasible excuses for his weekend absences, all these meant that in reality, getting away together again would prove difficult, which only made this weekend all the more special.

In bed later our lovemaking was gentle and tinged with sadness.

'I feel so safe with you.' Dave nuzzled my skin, resting his head on my breasts. I stroked his face softly which I knew he loved. 'I can't imagine life without you now, you're the missing piece of the puzzle, you know?' I nodded, staring into the darkness, a single tear running down my cheek. I knew that tomorrow we would have to get up and go more or less straight to the airport to catch our return flight, and that this was the last time we would be like this, safely cocooned in our own little bubble. From now on we would be back to snatching a few stolen hours at my place, when he would get up in the middle of the night and shower me from him before going home, leaving me alone in my empty bed.

We slept embraced together all night, barely moving, waking occasionally to cuddle closer and share a soft kiss.

In the morning, we packed and walked to the train station to catch the train back to the airport. We were able to choose seats next to each other on the flight this time, and we spent our last few Euro on coffee and sweets for the plane. I waited for Dave to suggest we separate at Gatwick and make the journey back home apart, fearing being seen together back on home turf, but he said nothing; he just snoozed in his seat on the flight. Landing a couple of hours later he sorted out our Gatwick Express tickets with his card this time, giving me a rueful apologetic smile when he handed mine to me. We were silent on the train journey, feeling tired and down, and when we changed platforms at Victoria the silence had grown to feel awkward and heavy between us.

'This is where we should part.' Dave said, as our train rolled to a stop and the doors opened to let us on. 'I can't be sure she won't be at the station to meet me when we get in. I'll sit across from you though.'

It seemed such a seedy way to end the weekend and I was brought back to Earth with a bump. I was back on the bench, relegated to the 'other woman' status again, the dirty secret, the mistress, the ticking time bomb.

'Whatever.' I tried not to sound too bothered, but Dave caught my hand and gave it a squeeze.

'Meet at yours for a proper cup of tea later?'

On the train I toyed with my silver bangle, reading the engraved words over and over again. Dave had put his earphones in and looked like he was asleep, his hood up and his eyes closed. Bored, I rifled through my bag for some gum and found a cream envelope that I hadn't seen before. Inside was a postcard, one of the free postcards that had been in our room, with the name and picture of our hotel on the front. Flipping it over, I saw that Dave had scrawled a message.

To Remember Our Trip By XX

I wanted to give you a gift to say thank you for such a wonderful weekend away. I can't even believe it would have been as perfect as it was. Spending time with you is something I will always keep close to my heart. You are truly an incredible person, one that makes me so happy. Life is about living and feeling alive, and being with you is when I feel most alive. There is something about you that makes me feel so comfortable, it must be your beautiful eyes that I love staring into, losing myself in a wonderful world of us being together XXX. Hopefully we can do it again soon. XXXXXXXXXXX

He must have written this while I was in the bathroom, and hidden it in my bag, knowing I would find it later. Warmed right through, I read and re-read the card memorising the words then putting it safely back into the envelope. There was a hidden zip pocket inside my handbag and I would keep it safely in there, carrying it with me everywhere I went.

At the station he was up and off the train without so much as a goodbye, not even a look. I caught sight of him weaving his way through the after-work crowds, his holdall slung over his shoulder. There was no sign of his wife.

CHAPTER FIFTEEN

It was good to be home, in a way. I couldn't wait to have Monkey and Rocket back although I knew that had been taken good care of while I was away. Unpacking my case, I hung my vintage dress up in my wardrobe. Who knows when that'll get another outing I thought, it's not as if I had many opportunities to dress up and go out in my home town. I waited to hear from Dave, he had mentioned coming round to mine tonight but my phone stayed obstinately silent. Fixing myself a bowl of cereal in lieu of a proper dinner I powered up my laptop and went through my emails, expecting to see one from Debbie, my new boss, about starting next week. I only had a few more days at the bookshop to get through before I could embark on my new career as a Trainee Recruitment Consultant, well, Head of Reception and Administration at Recruit Unique – yes that sounded better. I wondered if I would get to have business cards. I pictured myself dressed in a power suit, having lunch meetings with important clients, shaking their hands and giving them one of my cards, being suitably busy and important. I know, I was just starting out on Reception but hey - no harm in a little bit of ambition!

I couldn't help it. I had saved Vicki's Instagram page in my Favourites and I clicked on it now, wondering if she had mentioned Dave being away for the weekend.

Vicki Campbell-Roberts@luckyladysoblessed
Because forever means eternity! A gift from the most incredible husband ever!
#surprise #eternityring #diamonds are forever #becausehemissedme #fairytale #feellikeaprincess #putaringonit #again #mrandmrs # couplegoals #weddingmemories #grindhardstayhumble #blessed

I couldn't breathe. After several banal posts about her make-up and announcing the new side parting in her hair, tonight she had posted a picture of a gold ring, tasteful and studded with diamonds the whole way around. An eternity ring? She got a diamond eternity ring while I got a cheap (twenty quid, I looked it up) silver bangle??!! He must have bought both things at the same time – unless he had chosen hers first, and then threw mine in as an afterthought. Way to make me feel special, Dave! My bracelet suddenly seemed like a tawdry fairground token, and I ripped it off my wrist and hurled it at the wall, denting it irreparably. I sent him a message.

Nice ring.

He didn't reply. Coward.

Katie
September

We didn't speak for a couple of days, not that he didn't try, I just ignored his calls and texts. I had two days left before I left my old job and I was busy tying up loose ends and making handover notes for the team so they could carry on in my absence. I deliberately made sure I was not anywhere near the shop floor during lunchtimes, so he couldn't stalk me and pounce, forcing me to talk to him, and I made sure I was too busy to take a break myself, fearing he would be hanging around outside waiting for me.

On my final day at the shop I had to suffer through the painful 'Leaving Ceremony' that the store managers insisted on. They had obviously had a whip round for a leaving present and presented me with a card and a gift bag containing a bottle of Prosecco, which they knew I didn't drink, and a voucher for afternoon tea at a posh country house hotel. It was a very thoughtful gift, and they'd even gone to the trouble of finding a 'Sorry You're Leaving' card with guinea pigs on it. The manager made a short speech about how I was bravely taking the next step in my life's journey (been reading through the self-help section again, Mr Jobsworth?) and wished me well. There was a half-hearted cheer from all the staff, and then we stood around awkwardly until Darren, bless him, said 'Got your back, dawg! Let's all go to the pub then!'

Away from the confines of the shop we relaxed, and I put the bottle of Prosecco on the table for the team, hoping they would see it as a gesture of generosity, and not that I just wanted rid of the vile stuff. Even Mel thawed out enough towards me to clink our glasses together. We got noisier and the laughter rang out around the table, and I looked around at these salt-of-the-earth people whose acceptance and friendship had got me through my divorce from Adam. Although I was happy, thrilled even, to have a better job and to be earning a lot more money, I would miss them, the sense of team and the almost unconditional friendship they offered.

When the evening was winding down and people were gathering up bags and coats, I took the chance to corner Mel.

'Mel, I think you were right. About Dave and all that.' She held my gaze steadily, not giving anything away. 'We had an amazing weekend away, and then just like that, he made me feel cheap, and second best. I think I'm going to end things with him, make a fresh start.' I hadn't really intended to say this, but as the words left my mouth I knew it was right. Mel softened.

116

'Maybe it was a case of you having to find this out for yourself, love.' She looked at me so kindly I nearly lost it, and I gulped back the tears that threatened to spill. 'I could tell you were infatuated with him though, and no amount of advice from me would make a difference. So I had to take a step back and just let you get on with it.' She rubbed my arm affectionately. 'Maybe some good's come out of it anyway, eh? You got a great new job out of it, much better than dying of boredom with us lot anyway. You just take this chance and make the most of it. Things will come right, you'll see, it'll all come right in the end.'

'I'm sorry I didn't listen to you' I said mournfully. 'I know you were only looking out for me.'

'Ah no bother, luvvy.' She gave me a bony hug. 'Just be glad you saw sense before any damage was done.'

Walking home later, I felt more at peace with the world than I had done in a long time. I would call it a day with Dave, but nicely, with no hard feelings on either side. I wanted him to be happy and there was to be no happy ending in our story. I would set him free and he could decide what he wanted to do – whether he wanted to continue in his miserable marriage for Josh's sake, or to try and build a life on his own as a single Dad, amicably sharing custody with his wife. Either way, I didn't want to be a factor in his decision. My brief yearning to be a proper mother to Josh still caused a pain in my heart but it was not my place to interfere. I was not going to be his stepmum, and he would never be my son.

I was walking down the alleyway to my gate when a hooded figure appeared in the darkness and ran towards me. I stifled a scream and turned to run back to the safety of the main street with its orange lamps, and the chance that there were other people who would save me. He caught my arm and this time I did scream.

'Katie, ssshhh, it's only me.' Dave let go of me, and pushed his hood back so I could see his face.

'What are you doing?' I hissed like a pissed off cat. 'You scared the shit out of me! What are you even doing here?'

'You won't answer your phone, you don't reply to my texts, you hide whenever I come in the shop, what am I supposed to do? He folded his arms across his chest and glared at me. 'I intended to leave you a letter, that's why I came round, but then I decided I'd stay and wait for you. That was two hours ago.'

'I didn't ask you to come round. You shouldn't have waited.' I ducked around him and opened the gate.

'Wait.' He started to follow me. 'Can't I at least come inside so we can talk?'
The childish me wanted to slam the gate in his face in retaliation for giving me such a fright. I hoped he didn't think he was coming in to have sex with me.

'I hope you don't think you're coming in to have sex with me.' I said shrilly, sounding like I was about fifteen.
He grinned wickedly.

'Never crossed my mind.'

Inside, I put the kettle on to boil. I wasn't about to offer him a drink but I was gagging for a cup of tea. Dave leaned up against the kitchen counter watching me, but making no attempt to touch me.

'You're mad at me.' It was a statement rather than a question.

'I'm not mad at you.' I said dully, clearly meaning the opposite. 'I just didn't like the way you made me feel when you left me on the train.'

118

'So this isn't about the ring?' He had to go and poke that bruise, didn't he. 'I'm sorry you saw that post...' There was a 'but' on its way.

'But.' See, there it was. 'If you insist on snooping at Vicki's Instagram then you're going to see things you don't like.' He had rehearsed this speech, probably while he was sitting outside in the gutter tonight, waiting for me to get home.

'Dave, you dumped me as soon as we got on the train at Victoria. We had the most amazing weekend, you said I made you feel safe. You swore to love me forever, or didn't you read the words on the bangle?' Sarcasm was my shield.

'Love forgives all things, love endures all things.' He quoted the verse back at me.

'And then I find out that you gave HER an eternity ring! I went on. 'Do you really not see the problem I have with that?'

'So it is about the ring?'

'Of course it's about the fucking ring!' I shouted. 'And all that shit she put up about weddings and couples and you missing her...' I trailed off, unable to keep back the tears.

'Shhhh, don't cry.' He was at my side in an instant, pulling me to him and rocking me in his arms. 'It's what she expects. You have no idea the promises I had to make to get her to agree to me going away for the whole weekend. Buying her jewellery buys me my freedom. And you should know by now that the bullshit she spouts on social media is her way of setting herself above everyone else. She'd be over the moon if she knew she'd made you so jealous. She has no idea who you are, or what you mean to me, but inspiring envy in other women is her ultimate goal, it means she's won.'

'I'm not jealous.' I sobbed into his chest. 'I just hate that you can love me one minute and walk away from me the next, like I mean nothing, like I am nothing.'

'I'm sorry. ' He whispered, smoothing back my hair and wiping my eyes. 'I never meant for you to get hurt in all this. I wouldn't want to cause you a second's pain, and to see you like this kills me.' He sat down on the couch and pulled me onto his knee, cradling me like a child.

'I think I need more.' It was painful to admit. 'I know I promised not to ask you for more than you could give. But I don't think you can give me what I want.'
He winced and closed his eyes.

'I only ever wanted to make you happy.'

He had to go, was expected at home.

'I promised Josh we'd make a start on his new Lego set tonight. It's a Star Wars one, with storm trooper Lego men and all.'
It went unsaid, but we'd both agreed to take a step back and see what happened. The few days in Rome had been so intense, an overload of all our senses, that we weren't thinking straight, and maybe a few days apart would do us good.

CHAPTER SIXTEEN

I had my new job to concentrate on and I didn't want the distraction of having to think about meeting Dave at lunchtimes, especially as I wasn't sure what the correct office etiquette was when it came to lunchbreaks. As the new girl would I get choose what time I went, or would I get the worst time slot of twelve to one by default? I was used to eating late in the day so an early break would make the afternoon seem endlessly long.

Early on Monday morning I was standing in front of my bedroom mirror, criticising my third outfit of the day. I didn't have to wear a uniform anymore, and I had forgotten the anxiety that came with making a decision about what to wear every day. I wanted to make the best first impression I could. Was my skirt too short, my jacket too boxy? Would my new workmates be able to tell that everything I had on came from a charity shop? I discarded the jacket for committing the crime of being too eighties, the shoulder pads sticking up so high they made me look like I had no neck. Christ, all I needed was some big hair, some bright pink blusher and gigantic dangly earrings and I could give Joan Collins a run for her money! Sticking with the biscuit coloured pencil skirt, I teamed it up with a plain oyster silky blouse, and added a soft scarf printed with colourful sausage dogs, to add a bit of fun and make me seem more likeable.

If it was going to take this long to get dressed every day, I'd have to set my alarm for an hour earlier. I resolved to put together some more outfit choices tonight, enough to get me through the week. Finally satisfied with my appearance, I grabbed keys, phone and bag, told Monkey and Rocket to be good today, and walked the new route to my new job.

Good luck today. You'll be great! Let me know how you get on.

Dave had stopped putting kisses and 'love yous' on his texts, but it was nice of him to send me such a sweet message. I was feeling better about things after the weekend, mostly due to seeing a cryptic post on her Instagram.

Vicki Campbell-Roberts@luckyladysoblessed
Sometimes strong women need to be show men how strong they can be. #badday #strong #win #itgetsbetter #boxitout #gymrage #standyourground #inspirational #women #notequals #betterthanthat #sisters #grindhardstayhumble #blessed

She had added a photo of herself, of course. An extreme close up of her at the gym, her face tomato red and sweaty, her eyes squinting madly – oooohhhhhh angry squashed squirrel is not happy! It seemed all was not well in Vickiland. Did they have a fight? I wondered. It was rare for her not to bang on about her hair or her clothes, or gush about love and couples and goals. She still had the ever-present, idiotic 'grind hard stay humble' hashtag and always, always ended with 'blessed'.
Hashtag annoying, hashtag stopit, hashtag sithefuckdownbitch!
It cheered me up no end though. Things must be bad for her to share with her legions (324) of fans that she had had a bad day. What did a bad day constitute on Planet Vicki? Split ends? A spot? Husband in love with someone else? Ha! - My turn to be smug.

At Recruit Unique Debbie was waiting for me in reception. She held up two mugs of coffee and waved them in the direction of the bright 'Welcome!' banner that was pinned up behind the desk - my desk.

'Happy first day!' she cheered. 'Pop your bag and stuff under your desk and I'll give you the grand tour.'

Walking with our coffees, she led me around the building. The offices were small and all on the one level, with interview rooms, a meeting room and a tiny kitchenette and bathroom at the very end of the main corridor. It would be part of my job to make sure these spaces were tidy, and set up for client meetings. I would also be responsible for the presentation of the reception area, and would be expected to offer water or tea and coffee to all of our visitors. It all seemed fairly straightforward – tea, tidying and answering the phone, I could do all of those things. The door opened and the glamorously shiny girl I had seen on the front desk on the day of my interview walked in.

'Katie, this is Adele. Adele is moving up into a consultancy position, hence the need for a new receptionist.' Debbie introduced us.

'Hi. Cute scarf!' Adele shook my hand. Yes! I knew the sausage dog scarf was a winner. 'I'll be showing you the basics with the booking system and getting you started.'

The rest of the day passed in a blur and it seemed no time at all when Adele asked what time I wanted to take lunch.

'I don't have any plans. Whatever fits in with you.' I was shamelessly sucking up but I wanted this impossibly beautiful and confident creature to like me. We agreed on one o'clock and I skipped out into the sunshine, relieved at how well things were going on my first day. Wandering around the shopping centre aimlessly I soon got bored. I was so used to spending every lunchtime with Dave I didn't know what to do with myself now that I was on my own. I sent him a quick text.

Going really well. Just on lunch now.

He replied straight away.

Want some company?

We weren't supposed to be seeing each other. It couldn't hurt though. I justified it to myself - I was itching to tell someone all about my first day.

Hanging around outside Starbucks. If you can make it here in five minutes I'll buy you a coffee ☺

He must have already left his office, knowing I would say yes to meeting him, as he rocked up three minutes later. I got us both takeaway drinks and we walked outside to the square, finding an empty bench to sit on. We chatted easily about my morning and he was genuinely pleased for me when I told him how much I was enjoying it.

'Do you know if you're allowed your mobile on you when you're working? He asked. I wasn't sure yet, I know some places can be funny about using your phone at work and I wasn't about to knowingly put a foot wrong so soon.

'I'd better not, for now.' I stalled. 'They've not said I can't but…….'

'I can text you at lunchtime though?'

'I have my own company email address now, I'm sure they're not monitoring those, although there's probably some kind of swear word filter, you could email me instead?' I gave him the address on a scrap of paper. No one had mentioned business cards to me yet – maybe I should bring that up at the first staff meeting.

'Cool. I'll send you some funnies.' He put the scrap of paper safely in his wallet.

It was time I was heading back so I gulped down the rest of my too hot coffee and binned the cup.

124

'Well. Nice to see you.' I said, excruciatingly politely as I stood up to go. He made a noise in his throat, halfway between a laugh and a groan.

'Yeah. You too.' He said flatly. 'Take care.'

Honestly, what did he expect? Hugs and kisses? We had agreed to cool things off for a while. I had other things on my mind today and no time to worry about how he was feeling. Returning to the office, Adele started showing me the administration side of things. I was to screen all new applications from people looking for work placements and divide them up between the recruitment consultants, depending on their area of expertise. I would then arrange consultation appointments for them, if we thought we could successfully find them work. It felt good to think we were helping people find their dream jobs, and that I was now an integral part in that process. Apart from jazzing up a few CV's and answering the phones, there wasn't much else to the job really, and I felt sure it wouldn't take me very long to pick things up.

Debbie was pleased with me at the end of the day.

'It's like you've been here for ages.' She beamed. 'You already feel like part of the family!'

I beamed back. There was a lot of beaming in this place. If they wanted me to beam, I would beam. Beaming at people was now part of me new professional, capable me – I had successfully reinvented myself.

I had no need or desire to spy on some silly bitch's made up life as told through her Instagram profile. I was above all that now. Wasn't I?

Vicki Campbell-Roberts@Luckyladysoblessed
Life can be short, full of ups and downs and the thoroughly unexpected; so celebrate the good moments, tell the people you love that you love them, drink the French champagne, take the leap of faith because it just might pay off, and don't wait around for life to happen! Live every day 😲❤ xx #morningthoughts #instadaily #quotes #insight #wisewords #liveyourlife #loveyourlife #celebration #family #couplegoals #belikeus #champagne #veuvecliquot #treatmelikeaqueen #forever #mymanlovesme #dressup #karenmillen #grindhardstayhumble #blessed

Grrrrrrr. She still had the power to make me grind my teeth in anger. Wittering on like she was the world authority on happiness, making out she's some kind of celebrity life coach. The photo this time was an artsy black and white shot of her and Dave at a black-tie event, posing together like they were a red carpet couple. Her new eternity ring sparkled on her finger as she lovingly placed a hand on his chest and gurned toothily for the camera. I knew I should have let it go and let karma sort that shit out but the gall of the woman was incredible. My mum used to tell me that pride came before a fall, and my God - did I want to see her fall! Off a very high building. On to a very hard surface. Splat.

CHAPTER SEVENTEEN

Katie
October

The weeks flew past, and the nights drew in, heralding the arrival of autumn. The mornings were darker, making it harder to get out of bed when the alarm went off. With the help of my first new and improved pay packet I had added to my working wardrobe, and had even bought several brand new items from the high street shops. I still loved browsing the charity shops though, and I got into a new Dave-less routine of spending my lunchbreaks rummaging through the bargains and the sale rails several times a week.

It was coming up to my birthday and, as usual, I was avoiding thinking about it. I would get the usual cards from my sisters, probably flowers delivered by Interflora from my mum and dad. They always went for flowers every year, except one year they FORGOT! They had upped and moved to New Zealand when I was in my last year of school, and they weren't that fussed when I said I didn't want to go with them. I was in love with Adam at the time, and wild horses wouldn't have parted us, so I arranged to go and board with his aunty until I finished school and found a job. We got married soon after, when I was nineteen. Stupid, now I think back on it, and people tried to tell me, but you think you know it all when you're nineteen when really, you know nothing. Mum and Dad did not come back for the wedding and we were on distant but polite terms now, strangers really. They still had no idea that Adam had left me and we were now divorced.

Other than that, my birthday would go unmarked. I hadn't mentioned it to my new workmates but was planning to buy some cream cakes for everyone. I was still well and truly in the new-girl-sucking-up stage.

I was in our local branch of the British Red Cross shop as they were known to have better quality women's clothing, relatively new with good labels, and I could usually depend on spotting an absolute find, when I saw Dave flicking through the men's shirts on the rail at the back of the shop. Shit – do I say hi or do I avoid him; could I leave the shop before he saw me? Too late. He must have had a sixth sense when it came to me because he turned and we locked eyes.

'Oh, hi.' I said weakly, totally faking being pleased to see him.

'Hey you.' he walked over and kissed my cheek. 'Long time no see, how's it going?'

'Good, yeah. You?'

'Fine.'

Is this how it was going to be? A whole stilted conversation based on one syllable words?

'Still not daring to show your face in Oxfam yet?' His eyes twinkled naughtily, remembering the day we bought my vintage dress, and had had to run away from the bossy volunteer lady. I laughed.

'Our photos are probably on their wall – Oxfam's Most Wanted!' I joked.

'God, I miss you.' He sounded so sad. 'No one can make me laugh like you do. No one can even make me smile anymore.'

Cue awkward silence.

'It's your birthday soon, isn't it?' He changed the subject, thankfully. 'What are you doing for it?'

'Not much.' I grimaced. 'I don't really make a big deal of it.'

'We could go out for dinner. If you want to, that is. Just as friends.' He was quick to add.

128

I searched for a suitable excuse. Damn, I'd just told him I hadn't made any plans. The British politeness in me mutinied and overthrew my brain, and I found the words 'That would be great' coming out of my mouth, even as my brain was desperately shouting at me to shut the fuck up. He looked surprised, then pleased.

'Good. That's settled then. What do you prefer? Thai, Indian…..'

Don't say Italian.

'Italian?' The word was loaded with meaning.

'You choose, I don't mind. I need to get back to the office, text me about it later OK?' I knew I was being brusque but what was he playing at? Dropping our memories in my lap like they were precious gems. I didn't want to think about what we used to have together, I've moved on - wish you all the best, let's stay friends, no hard feelings kind of moved on. I was so over him.

At home later that evening he sent me a text.

I've booked Thai Palace for your birthday. Let me know if that's ok. X

Kisses had made a reappearance on his messages. I sighed. It was so obvious he wanted to rekindle things between us and, while it was true that I did miss him, I couldn't forgive the duplicity he had shown. He seemed to have no problem jumping from me to her and back again, splitting his life down the middle, playing us both.   I imagined fast forwarding years from now, picturing his funeral with her dressed in a black designer dress with a fashionable veil, grieving prettily in the front row of the church, whilst me and our ten kids stood ragged and barefoot outside in the snow. His other secret family. Ok so I was being a bit Dickensian and dramatic, and there was no way we were going to have ten kids, but point made.

Sounds good. See you then.

No kiss. He had to learn.

Katie
October
The day of my birthday dawned bright but cold, the wind whipping the leaves off the trees in the park as I walked to work. Flowers from my parents had arrived the day before, and Jackie had left a gift wrapped bottle of wine on my doorstep this morning, so I already felt like it was a special day.

When I got to the office everyone was really sweet and wished me a happy birthday. The cream cakes I had bought in the bakery on the way in went down a storm. For skinny women who are always on diets, they can certainly cram the cakes down them. I had settled into my role nicely and had lost that uncertainness and lack of confidence that comes with learning something new. I was fairly sure I could handle most things they asked me to do now and they were pleased with my work, so I was sure I would pass my probation which was due just before Christmas.

I had agreed to meet Dave before dinner tonight. He was treating me to a birthday cocktail at the wine bar first, the same wine bar where we used to meet, before we moved on to our eight course tasting menu at the Thai Palace. I loved tasting menus – you got to try a little bit of everything and had a different wine with each course. Because he had made such an effort I dressed up a little bit, wearing a bronze and black mini-dress, with proper hold-up stockings underneath and my highest heeled knee high boots. The dress was quite short and I flashed the lacy top of my stockings every time I crossed my legs, but I was in the mood for teasing him, punishing him by showing him what he could no longer have. The look of naked admiration on his face when I took off my coat at the bar was worth it.

'You look incredible.' He pulled out my chair for me to sit down and I saw him clocking the peep of lace at the top of my leg.

'This is nice.' I said brightly, sipping my Mojito through the straw. It was sweet and packed a kick and was utterly delicious. Dave had ordered a Caipirinha and offered me a taste, it was also good so we decided on another round and swapped drinks. Someone should have warned me of the way cocktails do that thing of pretending not to be full of alcohol. I was already starting to lose control and we had eight different wines to get through yet. Walking arm in arm (I was a bit wobbly on my heels) to the restaurant we were seated at the best table in the window.

'This is a bit, er, public for you, isn't it?' I couldn't resist a dig at his paranoia of being seen together.

'She's away. Taken Josh to her parents for a couple of days, so we won't be caught.' He knew exactly where I was going with this. 'From outside it looks like we're sitting with loads of other people anyway, so no need for anyone to know it's just you and me.'

The waiters started bringing us dishes of sumptuous food and we relaxed, the world shrinking until there was just the two of us in it. Dave dared me to eat a prawn, offered to pay me if I did so I took a tiny bite out of the ugly pink body. There was enough chilli and garlic on it to disguise the taste but to me it was like chewing on the end of a rubber-tipped pencil.

'Pay up!' I crowed, and he threw ten pence over the table at me.

'It was worth that just to see the disgust on your face.' He laughed. He topped up our wine glasses again.

'I've missed this.' He held my gaze. Finally, I looked away and he cleared his throat.

'Anyway, it's someone's birthday.' he sang, and pulled several brightly wrapped boxes from underneath his chair. At this, the waiting staff formed a line by our table and sang 'happy birthday to you' with more enthusiasm than skill. Another member of staff came through the door leading to the kitchen, holding a mini cake with a single lit candle in the middle, and presented it to me with a flourish, the words 'Happy Birthday Cattie' in sloppy white icing were sliding down the sides.

'Did you organise this?' I asked, lost for words. I remembered his love of grand gestures -the unicorn balloon, the surprise trip to Rome.

He was pleased with himself, openly enjoying the look of surprise on my face.

'Presents!' He said. 'Can't have a birthday without presents. We have cake, we have wine and now we have presents!'

He pushed the small tower of gifts across the table to me. Diners at the other tables clapped and cheered, and shouted 'Happy Birthday!' I had never had such a fuss made of me - I'm not quite sure I liked it.

'This one first.' Dave picked the largest box up and passed it to me. 'It's the most special.' The waiters craned their necks to watch as I unpeeled the paper. The box was large and rectangular and I had absolutely no idea what it could be. Pulling the last of the paper away I turned the box over.

Dave pissed himself laughing. The waiters exchanged horrified glances and scuttled away, unable to look me in the eye. The rest of the restaurant froze, waiting to see my reaction.

With it's clear plastic window showcasing the contents, I was looking at a very black, eye-wateringly large, thickly veined dildo. Dave was now slumped halfway off his chair, unable to breathe for laughing so hard.

'Awww, you got me a replacement for you!' I exclaimed loudly, so everyone could hear. 'I'm going to call him..... "Bigger Dave".' The restaurant exploded into laughter, and several women at one table drunkenly offered to buy it off me.

Still gasping for breath, Dave wiped his eyes and said 'Fair play! I deserved that one.'

'Are the rest like that?' I pointed to the remaining boxes. 'A bottle of lube, a butt plug?' This set Dave off again and he literally fell on the floor, clutching his stomach from the stitch in his side.

'No, the rest are real presents, I promise.' he said when he had recovered enough to sit up.

And they were. He had given me a smart black leather Radley purse, with loads of clever compartments and spaces for cards.

'To replace that one that's falling to bits.' He said of my old pound shop special. 'You can put all your business cards in this one.'

In the next box was a pretty silver watch, with a mother of pearl face and a ring of diamantes circling the outside. It was just to my taste, not being too showy, and I would be able to wear it every day. I had moaned to him ages ago that my beaten up old Quiksilver watch, an eighteenth birthday present from Adam, was looking too scruffy now that I had to dress up a bit for work.

'So you do listen to me sometimes.' I couldn't help but be impressed. He had chosen perfect presents for me, practical but classy, well - apart from the dildo, which I vowed would never leave its boxy home.

'There's still one left.' He nudged the last, smallest box closer to me. It was jewellery, of that I had no doubt. It looked suspiciously like a ring box too.

'It's not silver.' he said nervously, when I stared at the contents without speaking. 'It's white gold, and they're real diamonds.'

It was a perfect replica of the eternity ring he had given his wife. Burnished, matt gold - white gold, as he said, with tiny diamond chips studded evenly around the outside. It was nowhere near as expensive as hers, but I guessed he'd had to hunt far and wide to find something that was so similar, in the colour I preferred. It was meant to be worn on my ring finger, too nestle in close in partnership with my fictional wedding and engagement rings, but this was taking the pretence too far and I jammed it onto my index finger instead and held it up to the light.

'It doesn't matter if it was made of tin and glass beads' I reassured him. 'I know what you were thinking when you bought this for me. I know what it means and I know what you're trying to say.'

'It means, my night time Goddess, that you are my moon and stars.' As opposed to the sun, which her gold version represents, I thought meanly.

'It means that you are staying at my place tonight.' I signalled the waiter for the bill, and started gathering up my belongings. 'Coming?'

'Do we get to christen 'Big Dave' tonight?' Full marks for optimism, Dave. He couldn't pay the bill fast enough.

'Only if we try it out on you first.' I said sweetly, and the wince on his face said it all.

CHAPTER EIGHTEEN

Katie
November

We were lying in bed early one Saturday afternoon, listening to the rain and hail batter the windows. We had slipped into our old ways almost too easily. Meeting every lunchtime, seeing each other a couple of nights a week, but this was a new thing. Dave had started coming round to my flat after dropping Josh off at Soccer Stars on Saturday mornings, staying a few hours until it was time to pick him up again. I wasn't usually out of bed so early so I gave him the spare key, and he let himself into my house, slipping in naked next to me in my bed and warming his frozen skin on my warm one.

'We need to go away together again.' Dave said sleepily, playing with a strand of my hair as I lay with my head on his chest.

'Go where?' I wasn't really listening, just concentrating on the feel and smell of him, knowing he would have to shower and leave soon.

'I don't know, somewhere, France maybe? He shifted under me and moved to sit up. 'Just a weekend. I'll have a look at the football fixtures and see which weekends I could pretend to go up to Manchester again'

'I don't think that's a good idea.' I said, reaching out to caress his back. 'It's just too risky, and I don't fancy being dumped at the train station again.'

'I didn't dump you, I was protecting you.' It was the same tired, old argument that we resurrected now and then. He walked naked to the kitchen and flicked the kettle on, reaching into the cupboard for mugs and teabags.

'Alright if I make some toast?' He put two slices of bread in the toaster.

'Why don't we find somewhere closer to home, instead of travelling all that way just for one weekend? Cornwall, or Brighton maybe. Places like that will be cheap at this time of year, we can find a really nice hotel.' I was warming up to the idea now. 'A spa hotel, with a heated indoor pool, and couple massages.' I added with glee.

Dave padded back to the bed and handed me a cup of tea.

'Yeah, that would work.' He stepped into his boxers and pulled them up. Buttering his toast and taking it to the couch, he picked up the remote and switched on the football, flopping down onto the cushions. 'Have a look, see what you can find and we'll book something soon, beat the Christmas rush.'

With Christmas being only weeks away, I started to think of presents. Specifically, what to get Dave. He was so generous when it came to giving, he was always finding little somethings which he thought I'd like, and giving them to me for no other reason than "just because". Buying him stuff was harder though. I couldn't see what excuses he could come up with to explain away any mystery gifts that appeared at home, so I had to think carefully and strategically. I had managed to start putting aside a little bit of money each month and, although small, having some savings stashed away was a comfort. Blimey! I thought. I'll be in a pension scheme next; and I own my own hoover and iron – does that make me a proper grown up at last? But I was still far from being able to afford to pay for a weekend away for us both, however much I wanted to, and which would have made a perfect Christmas present.

Spending most of my free time with Dave made it hard to go present shopping but I managed to sneak a couple of lunchtimes to myself, inventing a doctors or dentists' appointment as reasons why I couldn't meet him. I knew he had a thing for Paul Smith stuff but as I browsed the concession in a department store my heart sank. I couldn't afford any of this. Three hundred quid for a shirt! And buying clothing for someone else was so personal, it was hard to choose the right thing. Slinking out of the shop before one of the snooty assistants decided to "help" me, I spied something on the mannequin nearest the door. Draped around its neck, in classic Paul Smith colours, was a woollen scarf. Perfect! Dave did wear scarves a lot but his were tatty old ones he'd got for a pound at a charity shop. He would love this one. Paying before I could change my mind – fifty flippin' quid for a flippin' scarf! – I found a smart gift box to put it in at the party shop next door and went back to the office, pleased with my efforts. I would get a couple of joke things from the seedy sex shop, maybe a bottle of his favourite wine, and Whoop! Present shopping done!

We had been a bit short staffed in the office due to seasonal colds laying a couple of our recruitment consultants low. As a result, and as they were so pleased with my progress so far, Debbie asked if I would like to take over some of the feedback duties. This was when new applicants sent us in their CV's, and asked for our advice on wording, layout and how to whittle down the information so it was relevant to the position they were applying for, but not swamping the employer with pages and pages of detail. I was flattered that Debbie thought I was capable enough to advise other people on their job prospects, it was the first step to becoming a consultant like Adele.

I was at my desk with a stack of application forms from new people interested in finding employment through Recruit Unique. Feeling important I shuffled through them, making notes on each one, and marking the good ones, indicating that they were worth bringing in for an interview with us.

Halfway down the pile, I found an application form from a Mrs Victoria Campbell-Roberts.

No way! Insta-squirrel had only gone and applied for one of our advertised jobs! Scrolling down the application form I saw she was after one of the supervisor roles at a new nursery which was about to open, as part of the local primary school, and under the authority of the local education services. There were several jobs on offer, and would attract a lot of applicants as they were offering "Mums" hours, working around school hours and would be term time only, the staff not being required to work through the school holidays. The layout of her attached CV was similar to mine so I guess Dave had worked his graphic design magic on hers as well. Reading quickly through, it was a pity, I thought, she was actually very well qualified for one of the vacant positions and I would have no good reason not to put her forward for consideration. She had included a photo of herself, grinning confidently at the camera. Putting a photo on your CV was considered a no-no these days, in the wake of a tidal wave of new discrimination and data protection laws, but she would have been unable to resist, vain little piece that she was. It wasn't even just a professional head shot, which would have been borderline acceptable, it was a full-on full body, hand on hip, tits out pose, more suited to a porn mag than a job application. She was wearing a hideous neon yellow asymmetrical sundress, frilly on one shoulder, the other shoulder bare, and there was no way a prospective employer would think her suitable for working with babies and toddlers. I looked back at her application form and saw she had ticked the box to indicate she would like us to contact her with feedback on her application. Brilliant. I could go back to her with detailed reasons as to why she wasn't going to make the shortlist. In some cases, we were encouraged to use social media sites like Facebook and

Instagram to help us build up a bigger picture of a particular applicant, especially if there was something potentially damaging or incriminating in their profiles. Employers were relying more and more on using these sites to get a better understanding of the image someone publically projected. It helped filter out the morons, the party animals who would phone in sick every Monday, the wannabe terrorists who would blow themselves up on the way to work, the all night gamers, the political activists, the Nazi sympathisers and, the image obsessed. That was her category. Too self-absorbed to pay attention to anybody else's needs, she could not be relied upon to have the attention to detail, and the ability to multi-task, that was crucial when working with children. I could not, in all good conscience, recommend her for the position. And I just didn't want her to get the job. It wouldn't hurt for her to fail at something once in her privileged life.

I opened my Outlook and began to compose an email to her.

Dear Mrs Campbell-Roberts, I typed.

Thank you for your application for the position of Nursery Supervisor at Bouncy Beans Nursery, advertised through us at Recruit Unique.

On your application form, you have indicated that you would like us to give you some feedback on the quality of your application and CV, and we are pleased to provide the following observations.

Whilst your CV is of a good standard, and you are suitably qualified for this position, we have taken the liberty of investigating your various social media profiles, as this helps us to better understand the personality of our applicants.

I am sorry to say that both your Facebook and Instagram profiles do not project you in a favourable light. You come across as being vain, self-obsessed, and boastful, with an over-inflated sense of your own importance. Your images indicate that you are more interested in social climbing and giving nonsensical and fabricated lifestyle advice for your own personal advancement rather than giving serious consideration to your career as a professional childminder. I would suggest that you think about posting less pictures of yourself, your hair, your fashion choices and your obvious smugness. Please also be advised that the face you pull in these selfies makes you look ridiculous. The current colour of your hair is of no importance to the world and what you are wearing, even less so.

Therefore, Mrs Campbell-Roberts, I am sorry to advise you that Recruit Unique will not be progressing your application any further.

Kind regards

Katie Fernley
Recruitment Consultant.

There! That should do it. I wasn't quite a Recruitment Consultant but she wasn't to know that. I hit send and then quickly deleted the email from my sent folder. I would shred her application and deny all knowledge of it if necessary. Before I did though, I took a photocopy of her CV, which had all her personal contact details on it – her email address and mobile number. It wouldn't hurt to keep a copy for myself. You never knew when such information would come in handy.

Katie
December

There was no comeback from the email I sent. No reply from her and she didn't post anything about it on her pages. Dave didn't mention it so I guess she was too embarrassed to share it with him. I hoped it had knocked her right off her ivory tower. Grind hard and stay humble about that, bitch!
We were still looking for the chance to get away together and I was avidly searching the last minute deals websites for, well, a last minute deal. It had turned bitterly cold and snow was forecast for the weeks ahead. The bookies had slashed the odds of a white Christmas and it seemed we were in for a magical festive season that usually only existed in cheesy Disney movies. I had passed my probation at work with flying colours and was welcomed onto the team as a permanent member of staff. No one had rumbled me over the email, and no one had even noticed her application was missing from the pile.
Dave had had a bout of man-flu, and had been moaning and groaning about his sore throat for days. We both had our respective work Christmas parties coming up and had arranged to meet at my place after his, to swap presents and celebrate our own little Christmas together. He would be in Scotland at her parents for the whole holidays, only returning to be back at work for the first week in January, so I had volunteered to work between Christmas and New Year. It scored me a whole bunch of brownie points with the other staff who had kids, as it enabled them to take the time off to spend the festive season with their families, while I only had myself to worry about. And Monkey and Rocket of course. I didn't mind spending Christmas on my own. I would do a mini-roast, and stock up on wine and special nibbly treats for me and the guinea pigs. I had loads of DVD's that I was dying

to watch and anticipated spending the whole long weekend in my fleecy pyjama's, not bothering to get dressed. Dave being away was an added bonus actually, I didn't need to bother washing my hair or shaving my legs, in preparation for one of his surprise night time visits.

On the night of his Christmas works do, he sent me a text me at eleven o'clock.

Can you pick me up? I'll walk to the car park. X

Picking him up meant getting dressed. I was lounging on the couch, dressed only in a scanty pair of lace knickers and one of Dave's t-shirts. Grumbling, I threw on my biggest, warmest coat and a pair of trainers and went out to my car in the sleet that was driving sideways and stinging my bare legs. I'd had a glass of wine while I was waiting for Dave so I hoped I wouldn't get pulled over in a road check, but the multi-story car park where I was picking him up wasn't far. I waited in one of the empty disabled bays on the ground floor and sent him a text.

Here waiting. On ground floor. Come now. X

I shivered, and kept the engine running so the heater would stay on. Come on Dave, I did not fancy waiting around in a deserted car park while you had one last drink with your boss. Twenty minutes and four increasingly shitty texts from me later he finally appeared, weaving around the bollards at the entrance to the car park. He had on a huge, green and red stripy elf hat, with a bell tinkling merrily at the top. It was about three-foot-high and he had accessorised it with a shockingly bad Xmas jumper, featuring prancing reindeer and scary gingerbread men with smiles like serial killers. He had a bulky plastic carrier bag with him which swung dangerously close to the concrete barriers as he tried to keep his balance, drunkenly over-compensating by flinging out his arms whenever his feet failed to walk in a straight line. I started the car and reversed out, picking him up at the car park exit a few feet away. He opened the car door and tried to get in still wearing the tall elf hat, and nearly decapitating himself in the process. He fell into the passenger seat beside me.

'D'ya like my hat?' he yelled in my ear, misjudging the distance between us and slobbering over my cheek. 'S'great eh? I made Alan wear one as well.'

Alan was Dave's boss, a serious, somewhat dour, older man with no sense of humour that I could see. How on Earth Dave had persuaded Alan into a silly hat was beyond me.

If we were to have any chance of the romantic, quiet special pre-Christmas present giving ceremony that I had envisaged tonight, I needed Dave to sober up a little bit. A bit drunk was fine, but any more alcohol tonight would turn him into a messy wreck, which I knew from experience would make him fall asleep, snoring and drooling, and I would be unable to rouse him.

'Tea!' I said brightly. 'I think. When we get home.'

'Home.' He slurred. 'Home is where you are.' He slid his cold hand up my bare leg onto my thigh, reaching the lace of my tiny panties. 'Home is here.' God, his fingers were bloody cold!

Thankfully, a cup of tea and no more alcohol did the trick and Dave sobered up enough to be good company. I had lit several scented candles and we lay on the rug in front of the couch in the flickering light. The flat was warm and cosy and we had made a nest of blankets and pillows to cuddle up in. We had diverged ourselves of most of our clothing as soon as we had walked in the door and were now mostly naked, drowsy in the warmth and semi-darkness.

'OK.' Dave sat up. 'I have some presents for you but you have to agree to something first.'

'The last time you asked me to agree to something first I ended up naked, except for your England football shirt, and doing the reverse cowgirl.' He grinned delightedly at that memory.

'Oh yeah......' he drawled. 'Definitely have to do that one again. Anyway, as I was saying, I have something you can wear but you need to put it on straight away, so I can see it on you.'

'Sounds intriguing. I have something you can wear too so you also need to put it on straight away, so I can see YOU in it.'

'OK' Lets swap and I'll go into the bathroom and you stay out here, and when we're both ready we'll go for the big reveal!' His mood was infectious and this sounded like it would be a right laugh anyway.

'Deal!'

We threw our bundles of presents at each other and Dave disappeared into my bathroom and locked the door.

The first gift I unwrapped was some thick knitted socks, made to look like cute polar bears, and trying them on they came up over my knees. The second was a shiny gift box, containing an exquisite set of very, very expensive underwear. I could see now why he wanted to see me in them as soon as possible. There was a tiny scrap of black lace, masquerading as a G-string, and a gorgeous black and red embroidered satin basque, which fastened up the front with dozens of tiny hooks. Trying it on, it squeezed me in, in all the right places, but left my boobs to spill out lushly over the top. Completing the ensemble, there were delicate, sheer proper stockings, with elastic loops which secured to buttons on the bottom of the basque. The last parcel contained a set of twinkly star fairy lights, powered by a small battery pack so there was no need for them to be plugged into a power supply. When I had figured out how all the underwear went on, I unpacked the string of tiny silver star lights and draped them round and round my body, and tucked the battery pack down the back of my G-string. The lights twinkled and flashed and lit me up like a Christmas tree. Those, the sexy undies and the over the knee woolly socks made a very fetching festive sight.

'I'm ready.' I sang through the still closed bathroom door.

'Nearly there.' came the muffled, laughing reply. 'I can't believe you did this to me. You're an evil bitch, you know that?'

The door opened and I took in the once-in-a-lifetime sight of Dave, still wearing his elf hat, crammed into a red Lycra Santa mankini complete with white cotton wool where his pubic hair should be. Several sizes too small, it left nothing to the imagination and his testicles bulged grotesquely out from the where the mankini stretched painfully up into his bum crack. He minced into the room gingerly. I clapped my hands over my mouth to stop me from combusting with laughter.

'Awesome scarf though!' The Paul Smith scarf was wound gently round his neck and he picked up the end and nuzzled his face into it. 'So soft. I love it! It's the best present I ever got.'

We took in each other's outfits and burst out laughing.

'You look incredible' he fingered the top of the basque, running a finger over the swell of my breast, thrust into unbelievable proportions by the tight satin. 'Those lights definitely add something! Not so sure about the socks though.' He looked at my feet, encased in thick wool, with the little polar bear noses bobbing on my toes.

'Oh, I don't know.' I snapped the tight Lycra on the back of his mankini, making him jump. 'I think they're the perfect match.'

I kissed him hard, and then said 'Smile!' before snapping a picture of us both on my phone. This would be one Christmas party photo that I would never let him forget.

CHAPTER NINETEEN

The real Christmas Day came and went exactly as I planned, in my jammie's with Monkey and Rocket on my knee, all three of us wrapped up snuggly in a blanket on the couch and watching telly. Guinea pigs love soft textiles, and will happily spend hours snoozing under a fleecy cover. As an added bonus they were brilliant little hot water bottles for my legs.

On Boxing Day, I got a call from Mel, inviting me to join her and her dog Maxie on a windy day walk.

'To blow away the cobwebs.' She insisted. Maxie was a sweet whippet/lurcher cross with an unfortunate incontinence problem, and the need to stop every few steps, making our progress very slow. We walked along the sea front, watching the heavy white breakers crash upon the pebbled shore, and getting whipped by the salty spray.

'You still seeing him then?' Mel said shortly, although resigned now to the fact that Dave and I were, to all intent and purposes, a couple.

'When I can.' I replied. 'When his other life doesn't get in the way. I'm way down on his list of things to do, after job, wife, son, and football.'

'There's something I never told you.' Mel said in a strained voice as she tugged on Maxie's lead when she stopped to sniff a car tyre. 'When I was much younger, I was involved with a married man too.'

I stared at her open mouthed. Oh it all comes out now!

'I expect you think I'm being hypocritical, judging you, but having done the exact same thing myself.' She took the words right out of my mouth. 'It's because of that I don't like seeing you do what I did. I don't want you to end up like me. OH IT'S ONLY A BIT OF WEE!' Mel yelled at a passing couple who were looking at Maxie in disgust as the dog crouched and squatted on the footpath to relieve herself. 'I wasted the best years of my life on that man. Spent years waiting for him to leave his wife like he promised me. Only he never did. Always had some excuse, the kids were too young, her mother had died, she wasn't well herself. Excuse after excuse after excuse.'

'It's not the same for us, Mel. I don't want Dave to leave his wife. He's already told me that's not on the cards, ever, so I'm not waiting for anything.' I wasn't holding out any secret hope that something would happen to make Dave change his mind.

'All the same.' Mel continued. 'There's no future for the two of you. Do you still think you'll be his secret lover twenty years from now, that's if you don't get caught first?'

'It is what it is Mel.' I said philosophically. 'And it'll do for now. It stops me being lonely, and we do have a lot of fun together.' I shrugged. 'It won't last forever, we both know that, but for the time being there's no reason to stop.' Mel huffed but wisely kept her counsel.

'Come on, let's have a cuppa at mine. Best get Maxie home before she collapses with dehydration from too much pissing.'

Vicki Campbell-Roberts@luckyladysoblessed
Happy New Year from our house to yours. Thanks to all for making it another magnificent year. Raising a glass to all of you this fine (hail stoning) December evening ♥ xxx
#nye #Hogmanay #langmayyerlumreek #bestwishes #lovingthoughts #mothersandsons #daddyslittleman #family #mumanddad #bestparenstever #checkoutmybag #mulberry #bestpresentever #bestfriend #dearhusband #selfie #letsgetdrunk #screwthediet #thinkiwannamarryyou #again #love #soulmate #grindhardstayhumble #blessed

Katie
January
I hadn't heard from Dave over the whole Christmas period. Not a single text. Back at work after the holidays the January blues settled heavily on my heart. The agency was quiet for now as there was usually a lull at this time of year, before employers shook off the Christmas glitter and tinsel and decided they had better pull finger and get those jobs filled. I had brought my star lights to work and wrapped them around the peace lily that was on my desk, adding a cheery bit of much needed sparkle to the office.

Trawling through the spam emails that had crowded up my inbox over the last week, a new message popped up on my screen.

From: Dave@Eye4Design.co.uk
To: Katie.Fernley@RecruitUnique.org
Subject: Meet for lunch today? XXX

He had added a hilarious picture of two guinea pigs in Santa hats, fighting over a piece of carrot. I replied that I would see him at one o'clock and don't be late!

'So how was your Christmas?' I asked as soon as we sat down on our favourite couch in the fuggy café.

'It was the worst Christmas I've ever had.' he announced dramatically. 'I spent the whole time in bed with tonsillitis.'

'Boo, rubbish present Santa!'

'I know!' He fiddled with the spoon in his latte. 'All my presents were rubbish – apart from my Paul Smith scarf.' He was wearing it today, and stroked the pile with reverence. 'The in-laws gave us all books. My wife gave me books. And poor Josh got loads of clothes that were far too babyish for him.'

I scooped the froth from the top of my drink and slurped it up messily.

'Pig.' he said affectionately, throwing a cushion at me. I grinned a mouthful of foam back at him.

'What did you get your wife?' He sighed and put another cushion over his face, muffling his reply.

'I got her what she asked me for. A Mulberry handbag, in blue, that cost me four hundred and fifty quid. Only it was the wrong one. I got the smaller one and she wanted the bigger version – the one that cost over a thousand pounds! A thousand pounds for a handbag! She sulked all through Christmas dinner. I had to take it back on Boxing Day and buy her the better one.'

'Nice.' I put my glass down. So that's the best present ever she was bleating on about in her New Year's Eve post. 'I don't know why you put up with her tantrums.'

He didn't answer, just sprawled over the couch with the cushion still on his head. I leaned against him and lifted up the cushion. Holding up my phone, I showed Dave the photo

I had taken of us dressed in our Christmas gifts. I did this every time I wanted to make him laugh. And every time I wanted him to remember how much more fun I was than her.

CHAPTER TWENTY
Katie
January

'Mrs Janet! Mrs Janet!'

It was freezing cold blustery Saturday morning. Planning on making a huge batch of my Granny's winter vegetable soup to ward off the chills, I was trudging to the morning market to stock up on everything I would need.

'MRS JANET!' A small hand tugged insistently on mine and I turned to see Josh, grinning up at me in delight.

'Mrs Janet, I called and called and you didn't stop!' He admonished, throwing his arms wide in an exaggerated gesture of annoyance at me.

'Josh! I'm so sorry, I didn't hear you - I must have been in my own little world.' Either that or I wasn't used to answering to the name Janet. I crouched down so we were eye to eye.' Are you alright? Where are you off to? It's cold out today'

'Mummy's getting me some new shoes for school. I growed out of mine already.' He lifted his foot to show me and his shoes did indeed look too small, his little toes were poking out through a hole in the top. Taking a proper look at him, he had no socks on, no hat or gloves or scarf and his coat was far too light for such a cold day.

'Josh, aren't you cold? Why haven't you got a hat on at least?' He shrugged and carried on grinning at me.

'I looked for you at the library but I didn't see you. I wanted to know if I could play with Monkey and Rocket again because it was so much fun, and I think they really like me.'

'I, er, don't work there every day, so you must have been there when it was my day off.' I improvised. 'Monkey and Rocket did like you, I could tell. They're always asking me when their friend Josh is coming to play again.' He giggled at the thought of my talking guinea pigs, knowing I

152

was joking but thrilled that they liked him. I was dimly aware of another person walking up to where we were crouched on the street.

Well, well, the squashed squirrel herself, in the actual flesh. She was standing looking at her phone, glued to whatever was on the screen. She looked up and gave us a cursory glance, barely flicking an eye over me before dismissing me as of no interest whatsoever, and going back to her phone. I looked at her out of the corner of my eye, watching as she tapped the screen furiously. She was even shorter than I'd thought. I took in her skinny jeans, her designer spike heeled boots and her fake fur jacket. She was wearing huge mirror lensed sunglasses, even though it was a dreary overcast day, and she had her thousand-pound Mulberry bag slung over one arm looking for all the world like a short Victoria Beckham being papped by Heat magazine. Her hair was loose, and fell in the type of loose waves that can only be achieved by hot brushes and hours of patience.

'C'mon Josh. We're going now.' She turned away from us and started walking away, her attention still firmly on her phone. Her voice was flat, uninterested and I doubt she would have noticed if I had picked Josh up and carried him off home, which I certainly felt like doing. He was woefully underdressed for the winter and looked like he could do with a hot drink and a bit of fussing.

'Josh.' She called again, sounding impatient. 'Now'.

'I gotta go now.' Josh shifted from foot to foot. His hands were starting to look blue with cold and he shivered in the biting wind.

'You take care Josh.' I stared at him, taking in the dark eyes and hair that were so like his dads. He made me think of Dave when he was a little boy, living in squalor and near poverty, and I wanted to hug him to me so badly 'Tell your Mum you need more clothes if you're cold.' I added, glancing down the street to where she had strutted away, not bothering to wait for her small son. She was still messing about on her phone, not paying any attention to other people who were trying to walk past, and were having to veer madly around her as she barged straight at them. I watched as Josh ran to catch up with her, then kept watching in horror as I saw her grab Josh's small hand roughly and drag him into the road after her, straight into the path of an oncoming car, which screeched to a halt inches from them both. She had walked straight out without looking, her nose almost touching the screen of her phone as she blithely carried on across the road, ignoring the shouts of the furious driver.

That poor boy. She was totally irresponsible, not even teaching him where it was safe to cross the road, and to look both ways. She did not deserve to have that child, I thought and briefly considered calling Social Services to tell them what I had just seen. It would reflect badly on Dave if they got involved though, so I would take it up with him when I next saw him, and tell him in no uncertain terms that his wife's behaviour was unacceptable, putting their son's life in danger like that. And her a bloody nanny and all! I hoped that she took better care of the children she was being paid to look after. I wondered if it was worth me finding out who she worked for, and sending them an anonymous letter warning them of her callous attitude, and that their children might not be safe with her. It was something to consider, anyway.

'Just leave it' There was a world of warning in his voice. 'I'll deal with it.'

'But she put him in danger! He was almost hit by that car and I doubt he would have survived if it had hit him, he's so small.' I had relayed the disturbing events of Saturday morning to him, pointing out the lack of warm clothes and the slapdash attitude of his wife.

'I said, leave it.' He gritted his teeth. 'Whatever else Vicki is, she's a responsible mother. Josh is one of those kids who runs hot all the time anyway. It's hard to get him to wear things like scarves and gloves.'

'Dave, he looked freezing. And unhappy.' I couldn't let it drop, not if Josh wasn't being looked after properly. 'Your wife is permanently on Planet Selfie; she was superglued to her bloody phone.'

'Are you still stalking her on Instagram?' Dave was belligerent now. 'You're the one who's obsessed. You need to get a life of your own and stop gate-crashing mine!' He had tipped over into dangerously angry now and bellowed out the last few words at me.

'It's not stalking. I'm not even following. She puts that shit up for one reason only – so other people can see it. Anyone in the world can look at her if they want to. You want to be careful what secrets she's sharing, who knows what weirdos are watching her.'
Making a visible effort to calm down Dave rubbed a hand over his face and let out a long sigh.

'It's not healthy, this habit you've got. Just leave it alone. Please.'
But I couldn't promise him I would. I had to keep up with her posts. It helped reassure me that she was still as vain and awful as ever, and it made me feel like the better person. It was also how I found out what Dave got up to when he wasn't with me. Seeing posts of the nights out, the family days, the three of them on a cosy evening at home, it all helped me add to the bigger picture. Whenever he left out details of what he had got up to at the weekend, or where he went when they had a night out, I got the truth from her pictures. He had lied to me several times, and the posts she

155

put up later told a completely different story from the watered down version he had given me. It was hard to know which one of them was the worst liar, they were both so comfortable with twisting the truth.

Katie
February

'Southend!' Dave cried triumphantly.

'What about it?' I asked, puzzled. He had just slid onto the stool opposite me at our table in the pub. We were right next to the roaring log fire and our skins were being sizzled from the welcome heat.

'We're going to Southend-on-Sea!'

'Why ever would we want to do that?' Southend had never been high on my 'must visit' list. It had one of those long, long piers that was full of noisy fair rides and slot machine arcades, a bit like Blackpool, and the town was tatty and tacky. It was one of those places where high unemployment, a high percentage in teenage mothers, and even higher percentage in people who were drug and alcohol dependant made the resident population seem chavvy, criminal and common. I know, I'm being a snob, I am my mother's daughter after all, and yes, I know Jamie Oliver has a restaurant there but that doesn't change the fact that everyone in that town smells of chip fat.

Dave leant forward, his excitement was undimmed in spite of my unenthusiastic response.

'You know Danny?'

'Yes, I know Danny.' Danny was a mate of Dave's from his football team. Danny was loud and coarse. Danny took far too many drugs. Danny still thought farts were funny.

'He's getting married, to Liz. About time, seeing as they've already got three kids with another one on the way, but Liz put her foot down and threatened to leave him unless he agreed to get married.'

'Good for Liz.' I thought privately that Liz should probably cut her losses and run, instead of saddling herself to Danny in permanent wedlock.

'So, Danny want's his stag do to be in Poland. He's got some idea that you get a better class of prostitute over there, better value for money, plus the booze is cheap so he's organised for a few of us to go over for a week. EasyJet fly there for peanuts, but the catch is that they fly out of Gatwick but back into Southend airport, so I'll be in Southend on the way back. You could meet me up there and we can spend the night together.' He sat back, thrilled with his grand plan.

'So let me get this straight.' My mind was spinning and had got stuck somewhere around the time I heard the word "prostitute". 'You're going to Poland for a week on a stag do. You're planning on visiting some brothels while you're there. And then you're expecting me to meet you in Southend afterwards, welcoming you with open legs?' My voice was getting higher and louder and just as I said 'open legs' there was a lull in the noise in the pub, so the words carried over to the rest of the bar, prompting some quizzical looks from the other patrons.

'Shh. Not so loud' Dave laughed. 'Yes to the stag do, no to the brothels, yes to meeting you afterwards. Danny's the one who wants the shag some Polish prozzies before he gets hitched, the rest of us will probably just go to a strip club.'

'Oh that's alright then.' I was still disgusted at him. 'I'm not sleeping with you until you get tested for disease though.'

'It's not like that. It's just a club like any other except some ropey old birds with floppy tits get up and dance for money.'

'Yeah. You're not selling this to me.' I accepted that a strip club was par for the course on a stag do, but the way Dave had been so blasé about going to a brothel make me feel horribly seedy and used.

'Plus,' Dave went on. 'Danny knows this bloke there who can get us some cheap gear, so we can probably get away with bringing some back and making a bit of money on it. Dave always sounded like he was in one of those 'Mad fer it' Manchester indie bands from the nineties', whenever he started talking about drugs. I knew that him and his mates did a fair bit when they were out on the town, and he smoked a bit of weed most nights, but his increasing intake of cocaine was becoming a bit of a problem with me. I didn't do anything like that myself, didn't even smoke despite that fact that both of my parents were die-hard pack a day cigarette fiends. Some nights when Dave came round to see me, he would text that he was on his way at nine o'clock, then not show up until gone midnight, buzzing with unnatural energy and almost chewing his own face off.

'You're also going to smuggle A class substances back into the country? This was getting better and better. 'I hope you don't expect me to meet you at the airport? I'm not your mule.' I grumbled.

'All you need to do is find us somewhere nice to stay, a B&B will do. I'll get the train from the airport and you can meet me at the station in town.'
He made it sound so easy, and we hadn't managed to get another weekend away together since Rome, even though I looked for last minute deals every day.

Back at work that afternoon, the warmth from the pub fading, I went online and started researching places to stay in Southend, and worked out the trains I would need to get there. It wasn't as simple as I thought. I would have to get one train up to London, change at Fenchurch Street station, and catch another train to Southend, almost doubling back on myself. I had more luck with B&B's though, finding a lovely one that was right on the seafront, and boasted of being the winner of Channel 4's Four in a Bed programme. Being February it was ridiculously cheap to stay for one night, and we would treat it as a belated Valentines celebration. The real Valentine's Day had been and gone with muted cheer. We had exchanged funny cards and he had given me yet another silver bracelet, this one a chain of Celtic love knots, linking together to form a circle. I needed more arms. I still wore my silver fairy every day which drew many admiring comments, my Love bangle from Italy and my white gold ring. Any more jewellery and I would feel like a pearly queen. She had posted a picture of two valentine cards, one addressed 'To my Beautiful Wife.

Vicki Campbell-Roberts@luckyladysoblessed
Celebrating another year together and still so very much in love. #valentine #husbandandwife #cards # steakdinner # Malbec #cuddlesonthecouch #celebration #love #always #hubby #wifey #best guy #luckygirl #ladyhaveitall #grindhardstayhumble #blessed

God. When would she ever get over herself?

CHAPTER TWENTY-ONE
Katie
February

It wasn't as bad as I'd imagined. Southend-on-Sea had easy transport links, most of the big high street chains, and several interesting looking places where I thought we could have dinner later that night. I had enjoyed the train journey, the broad expanse of flat salt marshes dotted here and there with ancient country inns, and the view of the wide channel reflected silver from the cold sky. I got in with several hours to kill before Dave's flight landed at the airport. It would take another hour or so for him to get through the airport, provided he didn't get arrested first, and into the town by train. I had found where the station was - there were two in Southend, who knew? - and his was the other one from the one I had arrived into. I had checked into our B&B, a large Georgian house which was so quiet, I felt sure we were the only ones staying tonight. Having a mooch around the town, getting my bearings and browsing through Primark, I stocked up on foodie treats from Marks & Spencer, in case we didn't want to leave the room in search of food later. Grabbing a couple of bottles of wine, I went back to the B&B and made it all cosy and welcoming for Dave. I had brought the special underwear he had got me for Christmas, it was the perfect opportunity to wear it again, and once I'd squeezed into it I covered up with a soft grey jersey dress which would be easy to throw off in a second. Dave was going to text me when he landed so I knew what time to leave for the station. It was only a fifteen-minute walk, and I got bored waiting for him so I opened one of the bottles of wine and helped myself to a glass. At least I would be in a cheerful mood when I met him off the train, and he was probably still drunk from his week in Poland.

I was ticking quite nicely when I arrived at the train station. Figuring I had about ten minutes to wait I sat on a cold metal bench, which had a good view of the tracks stretching out into the distance so I would be able to see his train coming in. I waited, and waited. Several trains came and went. There were only two platforms so I knew I wouldn't miss his. Getting too cold and feeling faintly silly in my tight basque and stockings, I wandered the station, leafing through the magazines in the tiny shop until the man behind the counter 'ahem'ed loudly at me, ruffling the pages of the magazine he was reading. It was OK for him, he seemed to say, his beady eyes behind his glasses taking in my slightly inebriated state, but customers were not allowed to read the merchandise if they had no intention of buying. Reminded of my own shop days I put the book down with an apologetic smile. He harrumphed again and went back to reading his Woman's Own. There was still no sign of Dave, nor had there been any message for me on my phone, so I went over to the tiny ticket office and enquired when the next airport train was due.

'They come in every forty minutes or so.' the officer told me. 'One's just arrived ten minutes ago so's you got a half hour wait for the next'

It was getting colder now, and dark, and I debated going back to the warm room at the B&B, leaving Dave to find his own way. He might have missed the flight for all I knew. Or maybe he HAD been arrested, and wasn't able to phone me and let me know. I walked up and down the waiting area to ward off the cold, watching as other people were reunited with their loved ones. Small children running up to their dads and lifting up their arms, demanding to be swung up in a big daddy cuddle. I would wait for the next train only, I decided. Dave had the details of the hotel so if he was delayed for any reason he could get a message to me there.

At last there was a light in the distance and a train chugged softly into the station, hissing to a stop just the other side of the barriers. A few people got off, none of them Dave though, and then I saw him, at the far end of the train, walking slowly and carrying his heavy holdall on his shoulder like it weighed a tonne. Even at this distance I could see there was something wrong. He stooped, like a man with the weight of the world on his shoulders, and walked tiredly up to me and passed through the ticket gate.

'Hello, handsome stranger.' I leaned into him, expecting him to grab me in a clinch and plant a big kiss on my mouth. Instead, he awkwardly hugged me with his one free arm and pecked me chastely on the cheek.

'Alright?' he was quiet, and looked like he hadn't slept in days.

'You OK?' I asked. I knew he'd probably be rotten with a hangover from the stag do but this was something else, something had happened. 'Did you make it past the border then?' I thought maybe he'd had a run in with her majesty's custom and excise officers at the airport, that they'd confiscated his duty frees or something.

'Yeah.' Was all he said. 'Let's go.' We made small talk on the short walk to the B&B, it was hard to get anything out of him, and he only spoke briefly about his week whereas usually he would be brimming with excitement and telling me hair raising stories in great detail.

'I got wine.' I said when we were on our way up to the room. 'And snacks, if you're hungry now. I've found a couple of places that look like they could be fun to eat at later. There's a cellar bar called the Charles Dickens which serves Victorian style food, sawdust on the floor, barrels of brandy as tables, that kind of thing.' He just listened morosely.

'Maybe later.' he shrugged.

162

Once in our room, I stripped off my jersey dress in one fluid movement and turned to him, basque, G-string and stockings all on show.

'Don't I get a proper kiss then?' I demanded cheekily, running my hand down his cheek. He caught my hand in his, stopping it dead and looked past me.

'What's wrong?' I whispered, scared now. He was so cold towards me, so distant.

'She knows.' He said flatly.

'Who? Knows what?' I asked stupidly, my brain refusing to catch up with the words he had uttered.

'Vicki. My wife. She knows about us.' He sank onto the bed and put his head in his hands.

'How?' There was no way she could know. He was on his way back from Poland, would be home tomorrow. How on Earth had she known we were here in Southend together?

He groaned and lay back, blinking rapidly.

'I sent you an email, yesterday, to your work email address. Only I tried to do it from memory and it must have been wrong, because it pinged back to my email account as undeliverable, and she read it.' The words were delivered in a monotone, as if relaying something that had happened to someone else.

'What did you say, in this email I never got?' How could he have been so stupid? And why does she read his personal emails anyway?

'Something like, I love you and can't wait to be with you tonight. I think it said that you are the love of my life and I'm only happy when I'm with you. I dunno. I was drunk when I tried to send it.' He looked at me at last. 'All true. I did, I do, mean that.'

'Only now she knows it too.' I said. She knows my name. Would she put two and two together and realise it was me who sent her the shitty email from Recruit Unique? I could be in a whole bunch of trouble if she did.

'What did she say?' I could only imagine.

He let out a deep breath.

'I'm denying it all. Said it was a practical joke that one of the other lads had done, sent the email from my phone knowing she'd see it. It's weak, but I've got tonight to work on my story.' He heaved himself up into a sitting position. 'I need a shower. We'll go out after if you want.'

He was trying to be normal, like this bombshell hadn't just detonated between us, showering us both in sharp shrapnel. He went into the ensuite and shut the door firmly. Any other time and he would have bundled me into the shower with him but tonight, it seemed, he had failed to be struck by my charms.

I sat on the edge of the bed, trying to digest what had happened. She knew. She fucking well knew! I heard the shower start up and at the same time his phone started ringing. Picking it up from where he'd left it on the side table, it said 'Incoming call. Vicki Roberts'. I KNEW her name wasn't Campbell bloody hyphen bloody Roberts! I wondered what would happen if I answered it. Would she realise who I was or would I get away with saying I was the B&B owner, and I had found Dave's phone on the floor outside his room? I let it ring. He would have a hard time persuading her of his cock and bull story of his mate's prank, without me adding to the drama.

His phone blipped with a message. It was still in my hand and I read 'Just tell me the truth.' The shower hissed off so I put the phone back where he had put it. Honestly, if I hadn't had a few glasses of wine, and if I wasn't wearing this ridiculous tacky red satin outfit, I would have been out that door and on the first train back to London. I seriously wondered if there were any more trains tonight, and whether I would be able to get back home or would I be stuck at Fenchurch Street until morning. Dave opened the door of the bathroom, fully dressed in clean clothes. He went straight to his phone and picked it up, checking the screen.

'I'm going outside for a smoke.' He put his phone in his pocket and walked out, leaving me sat on the bed, staring after him. He was gone for almost an hour. I had snuck downstairs to the front door and looked up and down the street, wondering if he had left. But his holdall was still in our room so he couldn't have done. I heard him shout and in the darkness I could just about make him out. He was across the road, near one of the fair rides, now boarded up for the winter. He was pacing up and down, shouting into the phone and waving his arms around angrily.

'Will you just listen?!' I heard him yell. It didn't look like he was having any luck convincing her of his story. I left him to it, went back up into our room and closed the door. Coming back in later, his face red with either cold or anger, or both, he gathered up his wallet.

'Coming?' He said sharply. I had taken off the underwear, he had not even noticed I had been wearing it, and changed into comfy jeans and a plain black jumper, ready to leave at a moment's notice if I had to.

'Where are we going?' I wasn't sure I wanted to be anywhere near him when he was in this mood.

'Gotta eat something.' He muttered. 'I've just spend a week living on cabbage and soup. It was only the Vodka that stopped me from dying.' There was a flash of the old Dave in there, cracking jokes, so I reluctantly let him lead us into the main shopping precinct in search of somewhere that would serve us at this late hour. We settled on the Dickensian bar I had found earlier and sat through a silent dinner of chicken and mashed potatoes. I was throwing back the wine as fast as I could, determined to drink away the feeling of being cast off that had been hanging over me since Dave had first broken the news.

We both avoided talking about Vicki, and the email that went wrong. I could see Dave's mind ticking over with various excuses, weighing one against the other in the search for the one that would get him off the hook.

'I think, tomorrow, we should go to the station separately.'

I stopped chewing my lukewarm chicken and gave him a level look over my glass of wine.

'If you think so.' I wasn't going to argue with him about this again. We would travel as we did on our way to Rome, apart, pretending not to know each other. It didn't bother me as much now as it did then.

'And we should get separate trains home too.'

'Fine.' I had no wish to be with him when he was like this anyway. 'If I could have, I would have gone home tonight.' I told him frankly.

'That might have been best.' He was equally frank. For the rest of the dinner neither of us spoke a word.

We shared the bed that night out of necessity, although I told him he should make up a bed on the floor if he couldn't bear being next to me. We both went to sleep quickly, me from the large amount of wine I had consumed probably. He reached for me in the night and we had perfunctory, unsatisfactory sex; and the thought occurred to me that this might be our last time.

In the morning I woke early. The room was light with the morning sun and Dave was still fast asleep next to me. I watched him for a while until he stirred and then opened his eyes and looked at me. In the next few seconds I saw

166

everything I needed to know in the three emotions that passed over his face. He had just woken up and had not yet had the chance to put the mask on and hide his true self from me. First, I saw confusion. He didn't know where he was or why I was here. Secondly, disappointment. It was the wrong person in bed next to him. I was not the woman he wanted to see when he woke up this morning, and finally, fear. Pure naked fear when the penny dropped that he had been found out and it was highly unlikely he would be able to talk himself out of it this time.

In those few moments, I knew. When it came to it, and he was forced into making a choice, he was not going to choose me.

'I'm sorry.' he whispered softly. 'I love her.'

I had lost. She had won.

PART TWO

CHAPTER TWENTY-TWO
Dave
February

Why did I start the affair with Katie? Yeah. I don't know why I did it really. A combination of boredom, feeling neglected and just to prove I could I suppose. And, I must admit, I got a real kick out of shagging Katie at her place then going home and having sex with Vicki that same night. What man doesn't dream of having two different women in one night?

I never meant for it to go this far. Katie knew the score, she told me she didn't care that I was married so I thought 'why not?' She was available, made it clear she fancied me. And she was funny, I mean really funny. We had so many laughs and the sex was great. I wasn't lying when I said it was the best sex I'd had in years. Vicki was a virgin when we got together so she had no idea really, and when Josh was born it was months before she let me touch her again.

The image she projects is no real comparison to the real thing. She goes on about date nights and cuddles on the couch when really, she's got her head up her arse and her hands on her phone, and I'm there wishing I could sneak out and see Katie.

To be fair, I was feeling wretched when I got in from Poland. We'd been on the lash for days and there was mountains of coke available everywhere we went. The story I'd told Katie about sticking to the strip clubs wasn't strictly true either. The girls in the brothels were more than happy to see a group of fit young men, with plenty of money and willing to pay whatever they asked to do whatever we wanted. Some of those girls knew a thing or two, I tell you! It's a shame I wouldn't have the chance to teach Katie some of their tricks now.

When I got the first call from Vicki I was balls deep in one girl who said she was eighteen but was fourteen if she was a day.

A bit young for me, I don't go in for all that normally, but it was either have her, or wait around for one of the other lads to finish with their girl and put up with his sloppy seconds. Anyway, my phone kept ringing and ringing and when I finally got around to answering it I had twenty-seven missed calls from Vick, and over forty text messages each calling me something worse than the last. Speaking to her, it finally dawned on me just how much of fuck up I had made but I was frozen, not thinking clearly and on a massive come down from the night before.

She was screaming her head off at me, demanding to know who Katie was and why I was sending her emails telling her I loved her. Because she doesn't hit me up for thousand pound handbags I wanted to snap. Because she gives me the attention and affection that you don't. I played dumb though, made out like I had no idea what she was talking about, and I rang off before she could shriek any further.

When I saw Katie waiting for me at the train station I'm ashamed to say I took my bad mood out on her. It wasn't her fault any of this had happened but just her being there was a nuisance. I could have done with just having a night to myself to be honest, so I kind of resented her for hanging around. She was good as gold though and didn't pester me too much with any silly, girly 'what happens now?' questions and when I woke up in the night, hard from a dream about the young hooker, she was there, warm and willing and she let me use her as I wanted. She's got no respect for herself has Katie.

The other thing I wasn't so honest about was that it wasn't Danny's stag do in Poland, it was mine. So now I've got my work cut out for me, getting Vick to believe my story about the lads sending the email as a joke, a wind-up before our second wedding goes ahead in a few weeks. I'll get Danny onside, get him to 'own up' to it. There'll be nothing she can say after that. But it's curtains for Katie I'm afraid. I hold my hands up. I played with fire, got my fingers burned and now I need to throw that book of matches away. It'll be hard, saying goodbye to her but it's time things came to an end anyway. We couldn't go on forever. She knows that. She needs to go quietly though, leave me and Vicki alone to work things out. I can't have her moping about, calling me and begging me to take her back. We're over now. I love my wife.

Katie
March

When I got out of the shower Dave had already gone. The coward had packed his things and left the B&B without a word, leaving me to travel back on my own. I had a raging hangover from all the wine I had drunk the night before and I couldn't face the kind landlady's offer of breakfast, not even when she offered to make me a banana smoothie to take with me.

Dave would have gone straight up to London on the train by now and I wouldn't have run into him but even so, I hung around Southend for a while, mooching around the shops. I stopped at a greasy spoon café for tea, then found that I was ravenous so I ordered the full English breakfast and scoffed it all down, even wiping my plate clean with the limp white bread toast. Feeling much better with a full stomach I walked up to the train station and waited for the next train to Fenchurch Street station. With a bit of luck, I could get a connecting train more or less straight away and I could be back at home in a couple of hours.

I had no desire to see or even speak to Dave. The way he had treated me last night was appalling, like it was my fault his wife had found out about us. If he hadn't tried to send that email, relying on his alcohol-sodden brain instead of checking he had the right address, she would have been none the wiser.

You know what? I thought. It was his problem, not mine. If he wanted to save his marriage and stay with her then he deserved everything he was going to get. There was no way I was going to take any of the responsibility for this one. He knew the risks when we started going out and he went ahead and did it anyway so he can bloody well sort out his own mess.

Back in my flat later that day I realised just how much I valued my own space. I was back on my feet again for the first time and I was making a success of my life now. I didn't need a man to take care of me, I had been doing just fine on my own for years now. I had just never realised it. I wondered how Dave was faring, whether he'd been able to weasel his way out of this one. She would have to be pretty stupid if she believed that 'my mates did it as a joke' rubbish. As if he was still able to read my mind a text appeared on my phone.

> **She won't believe me when I said Danny sent the email for a laugh. I'm going to have to say we only just met and it was your idea to meet in Southend. You're going to have to take the blame. I think it would be best if we didn't see each other for a while.**

No shit, Dave. We wouldn't be seeing each other for a very long, long time.

> **I am not taking the blame for your fuck up! If you won't tell her the truth, the REAL truth, then I will.**

172

Man up, you spineless idiot! Own up to your infidelity and take your punishment like a man. The trouble with Dave is that he's spent so long lying to everyone around him, he couldn't tell the truth now if he wanted to.

You don't need to tell her anything. I will deal with this my way.

I threw my phone down onto the bed without replying. He would lie and lie and lie, painting a completely different picture to what had really happened. No doubt I would be the one who would end up looking like the home-wrecking, man-stealing tramp while he would make himself out to be the wronged party, guilty of a moment of weakness only. How could he have said no when I'd come onto him so strongly? Boys will be boys when it's offered up on a plate.
If there's one thing I hate most in life, it's injustice of any kind. Unfairness. Someone getting the blame for something they didn't do. Well I was not that useless trodden-down doormat of a woman any longer and I'll be damned if I was going to meekly accept being the only one at fault here.

CHAPTER TWENTY-THREE

After a restless night's sleep I carried my rage and bitterness with me when I went into work the next day.

'Did you have a nice weekend away?' Debbie asked me innocently. I wondered what she'd say if I turned around and said 'No, actually, my married lover's wife found out about our affair and now he wants me to take the blame to get him off the hook.' No doubt Debbie would find something positive to say, she was that sort of person. Instead I just smiled weakly and murmured something noncommittal.

I spent most of the morning Googling stories about men who'd had affairs and got their comeuppance in various painful ways, just to make me feel better. I also looked at 'Best Ever Petty Revenge Stories' for some ideas on how to get back at Dave for making me feel so used. There were some brilliant examples – mostly about how people had taken a wee into their enemies' fruit juice or cut up all their clothes or secreted rotten prawns in their cars. I thought briefly about hacking into his email account and sending a confession letter to all of his contacts. I would make it look like he was owning up to being unfaithful to Vicki and begging for forgiveness, and I would send it to everyone – his in-laws, his work clients, Josh's school, Vicki's friends - everyone. I might even put something in there apologising to me for being such an arsehole and absolving me of any of the blame. But I couldn't figure out a way to do it, I supposed I would need access to his PC at work and I couldn't see a way of finding out his passwords anyway.

There was a hilarious revenge story online about a woman who had swapped her lover's shampoo for super strength hair remover and laughed when all of his hair had fallen out or was so badly damaged he had to shave his head completely. Again, although I would have loved to try this one – Dave was particularly sensitive about losing his hair and was forever asking me if I thought his hairline was receding – there was no way of pulling it off. I would have to break into their house or stalk him in the chemists hoping he would put a bottle of shampoo in his basket, and then swap it for one I had prepared earlier, full of Veet. The idea was great but the execution of it was impossible.

I hated the thought of both of them laughing at me, Dave describing me to his wife as a pathetic, sex-starved loser, desperate for any attention. Although I accepted, welcomed even, that our affair was over, it was far too galling to allow him to carry on as if nothing had ever happened between us, as if he had never said he loved me or begged me not to leave him. I wanted her to understand just how serious we had been, and how he had showered me with affection, love and presents. I wanted her to realise just how much I knew about her true personality and how I could see right through the thin veneer of fake perfection she plastered over every area of her life. She needed to know that someone out there had enough information on what she was really like, that a few select examples of just how selfish and mercenary she was, would topple her off the golden throne she had set herself upon and bring her false kingdom to come crashing down around her ears.

I didn't just have to exact revenge on Dave alone. What I had planned would be revenge enough to take them both out. Target one and you hit the other as well.

What a marvellous thing the internet was! That night, fortified by a family bag of Galaxy Minstrels and a bottle of Merlot, I learned all about creating a social media profile that could not be traced back to me. I created a new Google Mail account, using a fake name and address and choosing a random set of numbers and letters as my account name.

Using this fake email address, I signed up to Facebook as a new user, finding a photo for the home page by doing a simple search for images of a neutrally pretty blonde woman. She looked sporty and sensible without being too attractive, the kind of person you might instantly like and trust. I called my new identity Pippa Adams; and Pippa Adams soon had a complete history. Where she worked, what clubs and groups she belonged to, what music and books she liked, it was all there for people to see. I had added the name of a prestigious girl's school not far from our town as where Pippa had graduated, thinking that that was where some of Vicki's online friends may have gone. They were all called things like Pippa, Isobel and Chloe anyway, so one more Pippa would sneak in unnoticed. They would assume she had a married name by now so if they didn't remember going to school with her it wouldn't matter.

Calling up the Facebook page of Vicki Roberts, sorry – Vicki Campbell-Roberts – I scrolled down the list of her friends and casually invited them to be my friend as well. Avoiding Dave's own Facebook account, I sent friend requests to her family members, to the mums of other kids in Josh's class, to her hairstylist and contacts in the fashion industry. Lastly, I sent a friend request to Vicki herself.

'Hi Vick!' I gushed in my message. 'Just moved back to the area after living abroad. Been following your Instagram for ages, so thrilled for you! You look like you live the perfect life! XX.' She would be so smug, getting a message like that. She would presume Pippa was an old friend from way back and Vicki was the kind of person who only cared about the numbers of followers she had and the number of likes she got, she wouldn't care where they came from or if she actually knew this person.

Satisfied I had done a good night's work, I shut down the page and switched off my laptop. I would wait until tomorrow night to see how many people had responded to my friend requests. Once I had a decent audience I would start putting things up on my Facebook wall for them all to see. I hugged myself with glee. This was going to be fun.

Vicki Campbell-Roberts@luckyladysoblessed
Tuesday date night with the love of my life - you can never have too much vegan Thai food XX #foodporn #goodcompany #sauvignonblanc #vegan #vegetablesonly #thaifood #vegancurry #eatcleantraindirty #veganlifestlye #nomeatinthishouse #couplegoals #husband goals #fashion #ralphlauren #raybans #storyofmylife #ladyhaveitall #grindhardstayhumble #blessed

OK. Now I wanted to throw acid in her face.

So she was a vegan now? What a stupid idiot - she was only claiming to be vegan because it was so on trend at the moment. Ariana Grande and Beyoncé had both recently been spouting on about the benefits of going vegan so it wasn't surprising that she was jumping on that bandwagon too. Probably not the best idea to post a pro vegan message whilst wearing a leather jacket though. Or leather boots. Really, did she even have a brain in that ego stretched head of hers? Duh - hashtag dumb bitch. And where was the news about her lying, cheating husband? She had just found out he was seeing another woman, had planned a weekend away with this other woman, and she was still bleating on about date night with the love of her life.

In the photo she was wearing a lacy scarlet slip type thing with a shapeless leather coat of some kind over it, like a biker jacket but without the zips. She had the biggest smirk on her face and those stupid mirror sunglasses on. Did she sleep in those or what?

Logging on to my new Facebook account as Pippa Adams I was ecstatic when I saw that more than forty people had accepted my friend requests, most of them were linked to her as well, as my mutual friends' counter told me. Some had sent me puzzled messages asking if we had gone to school together and there were a few messages from people inviting me to join various online groups or forums. Best news of all though, Vicki had accepted me as a friend, no questions asked and I now had access to even more information about her made-up life. It was like she had never grown out of the childhood game of 'Let's Pretend' where she was always the princess and everyone else had to be her minions. Looking at her Facebook page gave me the chance to have a nosy at Dave's page as well. I looked down the names of his friends, recognising a few and sending them the invite to be my friend too. Interestingly it looked like he was Facebook friends with his mother, the woman who had abandoned him and his brothers when they were just children. It surprised me, he had always vehemently denied having anything to do with her these days, and he only accepted contact from her when it had some benefit for Josh, his birthday or Christmas. Curious I sent her a friend request as well. That could be very useful indeed.

The plan was developing perfectly. It was time to put the next stage into action. The one where people would find out how much Pippa Adams knew about a certain well-known mutual friend of theirs. Using a computer program called Snipping Tool I carefully lifted that latest Instagram post from Vicki and copied it into my Facebook page. I loved Snipping Tool. It allowed me to clip a small piece of any internet page I wanted and paste it into a blank document.

It was a bit like a screen shot but I could be much more specific on what I wanted to show. Placing the snippet onto my page I left the following comment underneath:

Can you really claim to be a vegan while you're wearing leather? I thought veganism was about eschewing all animal unfriendly products? Does anyone else agree?

Almost immediately I started getting likes. Some people left their own comments underneath mine.

- **This is really wrong! I'm a vegan because I don't like animals being farmed for human consumption. This is actually quite insulting to true vegans.**
- **I know this woman and she's not a vegan. I had a bacon butty with her at the weekend!**
- **Why is she wearing those sunglasses? It's dark.**

Clapping my hands, I let out a laugh made of pure evil glee. This was great! She was getting slated by the very people she claimed were her friends. I knew I would only have a very small window of time to put up some more snips before people cottoned on that I was actually trolling Vicki and they would start to block me from their accounts. Working late into the night I pasted copies of all of her most braggerty posts onto my wall. Underneath the one she had posted on New Year's Day, the one with her modelling her new Mulberry handbag, I added:

I heard she ruined Christmas for everyone because her husband got her the wrong bag. She threw a tantrum and sulked until he went and swapped it for the one she wanted which cost more than twice as much.

179

There was the post she put up just before the weekend Dave and I went to Rome, the one where she called him her Love Bear. To this I added:

You do realise that he was sleeping with someone else all weekend? I heard her husband has been having an affair for months.

I added the picture she had entitled Post Photo Shoot Nap and outed her publicly:

She's not a model. She had a money-off voucher for a family photo with a cut-price photographer.

Similarly, with the fake business woman post I wrote:

She's not a business woman flying business class. She was on her way to Lanzarote with EasyJet.

On and on I went, finally finishing with the picture of her, Dave and Josh on their couch at home. Dave had lied straight to my face when he told me it was an old photo from ages ago. I knew better than to believe anything he said now.

They look like a very happy family, don't they? Only he's been having an affair for the last eight months and she is the type of woman who puts her tiny son in mortal danger. I witnessed her dragging him in front of a moving car without looking. She is not fit to call herself a mother.

By now the comments were flooding into Pippa's Facebook page thick and fast.
- **Who are you?**
- **How do you know these things?**

- **Does Vicki know you're saying these horrible lies?**
- **I don't think you're being very nice.**
- **You shouldn't be using Facebook for slagging someone else off.**
- **Wow. She seems like a right bitch.**
-

That last one warmed my heart.

Logging out I closed the laptop lid with a satisfied sigh. I had achieved what I set out to do. There would probably be complaints to the company behind Facebook, and no doubt people would be un-friending Pippa in droves, but it didn't matter.   Pippa Adams would not be logging into her Facebook account ever again.   I only hope that the comments I posted were shared and shared again. She would see them eventually. Even now there could be one of her so called friends texting her.

> **Think you should check your Facebook. Someone has been leaving the most awful things about you. Just thought you should know.**

There would be pretend horror and sympathy but really, they were probably secretly thrilled that someone had finally called Vicki on her bullshit.

Vicki Campbell-Roberts was a complete sham.   And the whole world knew it.

CHAPTER TWENTY-FOUR

I know it was you Katie. Or should I say Pippa?

Ho hum. Really Dave. Is that the best you can do? You'd have to be thick as a plank not to have worked that one out.

We could press charges against you if we wanted to.

No you couldn't.

What for? Telling the truth? Last time I checked that wasn't a crime.

He didn't reply.

Feeling triumphant I breezed into work the morning after shutting Pippa's account down. Getting those pathetic texts from Dave during the day had only served to make me feel even more victorious. If he had seen Pippa's comments, then I could guarantee she had too. It was a sweet, sweet moment and I savoured every second of it. Who said revenge was a dish best served cold? Revenge was swift, brutal and satisfying. I made a good woman scorned I thought, hell could take lessons from me when it came to fury.

The feeling lasted all week. Dave had scuttled back under his rock and had not sent me any more mildly threatening texts. It was only when I got back to my flat on Friday afternoon that I found a letter from my doctor's surgery waiting for me on the mat. Puzzled, I opened it thinking it was a reminder for a smear test or something routine but the words it contained made my scalp prickle with embarrassment and fear.

Dear Ms Fernley, it read.

It has come to our attention that you have been named as the sexual partner of several of our male patients.

These men have come forward to be tested for sexually transmitted diseases after experiencing some worrying symptoms and unfortunately they have all tested positive for both gonorrhoea and chlamydia. The men have expressed their concern that you are most likely the source of their infection and claim that you continue to be sexually active with multiple partners whilst knowing you have these diseases, causing the infections to be spread further.

It is in your best interests to be tested for both gonorrhoea and chlamydia as soon as possible so we can tailor a course of treatment for you. I would advise that you cease all sexual activity immediately until you are clear of any infectious diseases. For your information I have enclosed a leaflet on the symptoms, treatment and effects of both of these conditions along with details of our free sexual health clinics which you may benefit from attending.

I look forward to hearing from you soon.

Yours sincerely

Doctor Martin Davis

Devondale Clinic

It wasn't true. I didn't have any diseases. I couldn't believe my doctor would actually write a letter like this to me. As for multiple sexual partners, I had only ever slept with two men in my entire life so I could hardly be classed as promiscuous. Who were these men that claimed they had had sex with me? It was disgusting. Who would want people to think that I slept around........? Dave. Of course it was. He was behind this, it had his name written all over it. The other men who had tested positive for sexually transmitted diseases were no doubt Danny and the rest of the blokes who went to

Poland on that stag week. They had probably caught all sorts from going with prostitutes and were now trying to blame me as the source of the infection. They had seriously crossed the line this time. I would march down to the surgery directly, first thing tomorrow morning and, for want of a better way of putting it, get this all cleared up!

I alternated between seething rage and debilitating embarrassment all night. Fear made me paranoid and I began to question whether I had noticed any unusual symptoms 'down there' recently. Apart from a nasty bout of cystitis after we got back from Rome I had been in perfect health but this didn't stop me from checking my underwear for signs of an unwanted discharge.

Devondale Clinic was all the way across town and I knew they had a drop-in style surgery on Saturday mornings where you didn't have to make an appointment in advance. These drop in days were always heaving with sick humanity and I took my place in the queue at the reception desk behind an old man who coughed phlegm over every surface, and a whiny child loudly complaining about not being able to have Cocoa Pops for breakfast that morning. When it was finally my turn I waved the letter at the elderly receptionist.

'I received this in the post yesterday. Could I please speak to Dr Davis about it?' I spoke quietly, not wanting to be overheard by anyone in the crowded waiting area.

'Speak up.' The receptionist bellowed. 'I can't hear you if you whisper.' She snatched the letter out of my hand and scanned the contents. 'Oh. I see.' Her lip curled up as she looked at me with pure disgust on her face. 'I think you want the Sexual Health Clinic. We don't hold them on Saturday mornings, the next one will be on Wednesday evening. Do you want me to book you an appointment? I think you need one urgently, all things considered.' Her voice carried across the entire room like she was a trained actress projecting to the very back of a theatre.

'No. You don't understand.' I said firmly and holding out my hand for the letter back. 'I received this in error. There has been a mistake.'

'Our doctors don't make mistakes.' Her mouth was pursed into a tight line. 'Looks like you've been no better than you ought to be and now it's all caught up with you.' She tapped a few keys on the computer. 'I've booked you in to be tested for both Gonorrhoea and Chlamydia next Wednesday at six fifteen. Perhaps I should make it an extra-long appointment, there may be other diseases we need to check for.' She said this as loudly as she could, the mouldy old bitch. I was almost crying now in frustration and anger.

'No. I don't need to be tested for any of these.' I protested but she turned away from me and shouted 'Next!' Our conversation was over. I was dismissed.

Fighting my way against the tide of genuinely sick people waiting to be seen I had just reached the clinic doors when a light hand touched my shoulder. Looking round I saw a pair of concerned, but friendly, dark brown eyes gazing into mine.

'Are you OK?' She was wearing the clinic's uniform of a pale blue smock over skinny jeans. There was a badge with the words 'Julia. Practice Nurse' pinned to her chest. 'Come on. I can see you're upset about something. I have a private room where we can go and have a chat. I'll just get you some water first.' She steered me gently but firmly to the corridor at the end of the waiting room, never letting go of my arm. I found I didn't mind. She radiated warmth and kindness, and she was so calm I had no reason not to think that everything would work out OK.

Opening up one of the side doors, she guided me into a small, scrupulously tidy office. It had all the paraphernalia of the other doctor's offices I had been in but seemed more welcoming somehow. There was a playpen in the corner with lots of soft toys waiting to be played with by chubby, baby hands. She had a big box of tissues placed right in the centre of her desk. I guess she sees a lot of crying. Patting my hand, she waited until I was sitting down and had recovered myself a fraction.

'I'm sorry about Hazel on reception. I overheard some of your conversation I'm afraid. Couldn't help it really, the woman's deaf as a post and shouts everybody's business out loud all the time.' Her voice had a lovely melodic lilt, with just a hint of a Caribbean accent. 'From what I could gather you are having some problems with your sexual health?'

'No' I cried, sniffing back the tears again. 'I'm not. Not at all.'

'It's nothing to get embarrassed about.' She soothed. 'Anyone can get an STI. Anyone at all. We're not here to judge.'

'Tell that to the dragon on reception.' I muttered.

'I saw how she treated you. You have grounds to put in a formal complaint over her behaviour. She shared your extremely personal details with a number of other people and that is reason for dismissal.' She leaned in and whispered conspiratorially. 'Go on. You'd be doing me a big favour. I've been trying to get rid of that cantankerous old bitch for years.'

A laugh escaped me and Julia grinned widely.

'That's better! Now, what can I do to help you today?' Wordlessly I passed her the letter. She skimmed it, her smile dimming slowly until she was out and out frowning.

'This doesn't make any sense.' She exclaimed. She clicked on the mouse next to her computer and looked up my file. 'Just as I thought.' She said a few minutes later. 'There is no record of us having sent you a letter in the last

186

few months. Reading this, it is highly unlikely that we would have written to you on the basis on another patient's diagnosis anyway. I can safely say that this was not written by a doctor, at least, not any doctor worth the name.' She ripped the letter in two and threw it into the circular bin by her desk.

'Katie, it seems you have been the victim of a very cruel practical joke, my dear.'

CHAPTER TWENTY-FIVE
Dave

The letter was a stroke of genius. There are some advantages to being a graphic designer. Namely, it's easy to create all kinds of fake documents and make them look like they're the real thing. Faking a letter from her doctor's surgery was one of the easiest things I'd done. I lifted the surgery logo of their website, looked up a few of the doctor's names and – done! The leaflet about the sexual health clinic was a nice touch though I thought. I got the idea off Danny. He had been scratching like a baboon for days and been diagnosed with a dose of crabs, most likely picked up from one of the dirty bitches in Poland. He was sitting morosely in the pub with us one night sharing his experience.

'The doc gave me this.' He handed round the leaflet. It was full of extremely graphic close-up photos of all sorts of infected willies and gashes. Honestly, it turned our stomachs looking at the pictures of genital warts and deformed knobs. 'He said I was lucky I didn't get anything worse. Apparently girls can have Chlamydia for years without even knowing about it, and they can pass it on to you even if you only have sex once. Crabs is easy to get rid of, just got a special wash to use. I'm supposed to tell Liz so we can boil wash all the bedding and towels and stuff. I'm not going to though – she'll chop my dick off.'

We all agreed that is was probably best not to tell Liz. If I was in Danny's shoes I wouldn't want to tell Vicki either, and Liz was ten times scarier than Vick.

After that stunt Katie had pulled with the fake Facebook page I'd had no end of hysteric tears from Vicki. She needed constant reassurance all of the time - she was livid that several of her followers had dropped out, disappeared when Katie's comments had gone online.

'I was well on my way to getting over five hundred followers. If you get so many you get noticed by the big advertisers and approached to promote their clothes and make-up. I could have had Gucci and Prada begging me to model their stuff if I gave them a mention. And now I've gone back down to below four hundred and they won't give me the time of day.' Vicki wailed on my shoulder and I patted her awkwardly. Female emotions still had the power to scare the shit out of me.

'Just ignore it, Vick.' I told her. 'Just keep on doing what you do and in a few days' time no one will even remember Pippa Adams ever existed.' I knew Pippa Adams didn't exist anyway but Vicki was convinced she had been to school with her.

'She was always jealous of me.' Vicki moaned. 'She was never in the popular set I was. She isn't even pretty. But what I can't figure out.' she went on 'is how she knew so much about me. I mean, no one knows about my Mulberry bag except you and me.'

I gulped. Vicki was genuinely puzzled now but she'd work it out eventually, bless her low IQ. I did not need to own up to telling tales on her just yet.

Vicki Campbell-Roberts@luckyladysoblessed
The family are off to snowy Scotland again tomorrow! Two weeks of skiing, snowball fights and après ski hot whiskey toddies! Stay tuned for a big announcement soon!!! XXX
#snowtime   #skigirl   #snowboarding   boy   #marriage #weddingbells   #familygoals   #strongcouple #togetherforever   #loveinyoureyes   #fairytale #dreamscometrue   #thanksdaddy   #rayban   #skiwear #canadagoose   #brunette   #greeneyes   #sizesix #ladyhaveitall #grindhardstayhumble #blessed

Katie

Thank you squirrel-face. You've just helpfully told me your house is going to be empty for the next two weeks.

Julia's kindness over the bogus letter had given me the strength to face the remaining people in the waiting room who had heard the bitchy receptionist redirect me to the sexual health clinic. Julia had seen me out of the clinic doors, loudly exclaiming as we walked through the hushed whispers.

'That's right. There nothing the matter with you. Your notes must have got mixed up with someone else's. You're in perfect health, every inch of you.' She glared at the old woman behind the reception desk who seemed to shrink down into herself like the wicked green witch in the Wizard of Oz. 'Let me know if you decide you want to make a formal complaint.' Julia added, not releasing the receptionist from her laser like stare for a second.

I couldn't thank her enough. She had saved me from disappearing into a deep pit of despair. Had I not gone to the doctors today I would have spent the whole weekend convincing myself that I had somehow infected most of the men in this town with something icky, and Julia's calm, no nonsense approach had given me the reassurance I needed. I was not going mad after all. Not going mad, but I was mad. Mad as fuck.

Seeing Vicki's post about going to Scotland, accompanied by a cute photo of Josh dressed in skiwear and sitting cross-legged inside a large suitcase, (a Louis Vuitton suitcase no less, bet she picked up a cheap knock-off at a market somewhere) meant two things. One – I would not have to run into Dave unexpectedly as he would be out of town for a couple of weeks. I doubt I would have been able to face him, not without blushing bright red as I remembered the accusations of the fake doctor's letter. He would have been full of himself as well, unable to resist having a good old gloat so I'm glad I would be free of him for a little while. The second thing was that their house and car would be left unsupervised. They always flew when they went to Scotland, Dave had told me months ago. Poor Josh gets dreadfully car sick on the long journey and her parents are always happy to pay for the return flights. I'd had enough of dreaming up clever schemes for revenge. I was going to get him back in a good old fashioned time-honoured classic.

I waited a couple of days after they had gone before driving over to their street one night. He would know it was me behind it though so I needed an alibi for the time their car was vandalised. It was quite a clever plan, I thought. I drove to the train station and parked in the car park on the other side of the road, the one that didn't have security cameras, before buying a one-way ticket to London, leaving at seven o'clock that evening. All I had to do then was get on the train, making sure I was easily recognisable on the CCTV cameras, and get off at the next station, jumping on a return train twenty minutes later. I changed my coat for one with a big furry hood for the return journey so my face could not be seen, and paid cash for both tickets so they could not be traced. Then I simply got into my car and drove over to Dave and Vicki's house.

I had been there once before, when Dave had forgotten his wallet one day and we had driven over there in my car one afternoon so he could pick it up. No one else had been at home. Josh was at school and Vicki was at work so Dave invited me in while he searched for his wallet. I remember being quite shocked at the state of the place. The entrance hall smelt badly of damp and sweaty trainers. There was mess everywhere, piles of clothing and scattered make-up and hair products scattered all over the lounge suite. The kitchen was an absolute pigging bombsite and Dave surprised me by saying 'Oh, looks like someone's had a tidy up.' He wasn't joking either. Apparently that was what passed for clean and tidy in their place. Luckily Dave was only two minutes and I could escape back out to my car. It had rattled me, seeing the marital home. If I had been on my own I would have had a good snoop, particularly at their bedroom, opening cupboards and poking in drawers looking for any secrets.

That night, however, I wasn't interested in what was behind closed doors. Their silver Audi Estate was parked on their driveway, right up close to the high neighbouring wall and shrouded in the darkness. There was no light from the street shining on it and the entire neighbourhood was silent and deserted. I parked at the end of their road, well away from their house but close enough to be back at my car within a minute if I needed to get away quickly. Their car had one of those sickly-sweet window stickers on the rear window. Three stick figures, two large and one a lot smaller, with the words 'Our Family. Mummy, Daddy and Me' printed underneath. Sliding around to the side of the car that was closest to the wall I pulled out the collection of sharp knives and kitchen utensils I had put in my coat pocket specifically for this reason. Not being too sure at what would work best, I'd never done this before, I had a small paring knife, a vegetable peeler, a three pronged roasting fork and a small grater. I think the grater was for nutmeg or something. I found it at the back of the kitchen drawer and it had been there long before I moved in. I figured it could do some serious damage though. It wasn't enough to just scratch the car up a bit. I wanted to do some real damage, something that would require every panel to be replaced and cost them a fortune.

Using the knife for starters, I crossed my fingers the car wasn't alarmed. Scraping the tip of the knife along the doors as hard as I could I was satisfied to see great big scratches appear in the paintwork. For maximum effect I went over the same scratches again and again, gouging out huge chunks of paint. The vegetable peeler was good for denting and scratching; the fork was next to useless but I got a few hard dings in with it. The best result was from the little grater, it scuffed the paint up so badly the damage went through to the metal underneath. Sweating by now, it was hard work, I moved to the front of the car and scratched the fuck out of the windscreen. I bent back the wiper blades so they were twisted pieces of uselessness and had a go at slashing the tyres but I just couldn't punch the knife in hard enough. Satisfied I had done as good a job as possible, I pocketed the weapons and crept to the end of the wall. Apart from one light on upstairs in the neighbouring house all was quiet. Not a single car had passed while I was busy working, and there was not a soul to be seen. Strutting like a peacock, and resisting the urge to whistle, I walked casually back to my car.

CHAPTER TWENTY-SIX
Katie

I probably would have left it at that if I hadn't seen the post she put up. I was still looking at her Instagram page every day, still inwardly seething at the sheer narcissism and blatant ego of the bitch. It isn't stalking if you're looking at the stuff she wants people to see, is it? She's putting her personal details up on a public platform, the whole world can see it if they want, so she can't complain about being judged on it.

This one had a whole slideshow of photos attached to it. It showed her and Dave, somewhere snowy so I'm guessing Scotland, on a mountainside. She had on a full, white lacy dress, he was in a white tux.

Vicki Campbell-Roberts@luckyladysoblessed
Love is your eyes, family is your smile and home is in your arms. Still can't believe I married my best friend - twice! #brideandgroom #wedding #winterwonderland #weddingdress #pronovias #whitetieandtails #couplegoals #support #trust #compassion #recipeforlove #buildtogether #workforeachother #kingandqueen #empire #always #forgiven #weddingofthecentury #blessed

Feeling sick, I clicked through the photos attached to the post. There was no mistaking it, they had got married again, renewed their vows to one another. This must have been the big announcement she had been referring to last time. Bear in mind, this was only a couple of weeks after the disastrous night in Southend, so for them to have a big, white wedding in the Scottish Highlands so soon they must have organised

194

it ages ago, well before she found out about us. Dave had never said a word. Don't get me wrong, I was hardly sitting around crying my eyes out and playing sad love songs over and over on a loop. In fact, I hadn't shed a single tear over the end of our affair. It was if we had never met.

I wasn't upset at all, but I was numb. The thing that bothered me, really hurt me, was that Dave had walked out on our friendship without so much as a backwards glance. He'd walked away like it meant nothing, like I was nothing. So seeing these photos of their second, expensive looking wedding made me so angry that for a second I wanted to kill them both. Really kill them. At that moment I completely understood what people meant when they said they saw red, and why some of them went mental with machine guns in shopping centres, but I would describe it as more of a white rage. A cold rage. Looking at them simpering sickeningly at each other I promised myself that I would get even with them both. He didn't get to be happy, not after treating me the way he had, they didn't have the right to be happy when I was the one who ended up on my own. They would not get to have their happy ever after - not after I'd finished with them.

I kept sticking a finger in that open wound and swirling it around to cause the most pain possible. I went through those wedding photos frame by frame with a magnifying glass. The dress she bragged about as being from a top London bridal store hung on her like a shapeless rag on a washing line. It was backless, very lacy and had a long train which dragged in the dirty snow at their feet. She had no proper boobs to hold it up so it gaped at the neck, giving the effect of a little girl playing dress-ups. Her hair was a tangled mess and it looked like it had gotten wet, and she'd left it to dry in rats tails down her back. There were shots of their parents, crikey! - her Mum was a bit fat - easy to see what Vicki would look like in thirty years' time, and there was Josh in a miniature tux, looking heartbreakingly small and fit to burst with pride. She had rustled up some girlfriends from somewhere, maybe they were hired for the day, and draped them in red crushed velvet dresses. Skin-tight and plunging, they were deeply unflattering and looked cheap and nasty. Looking closer the whole wedding looked vulgar and tacky, a tasteless display of wealth without class.

Some of Dave's friends had made it into the photos, so there's no way they could have pulled this shindig together in such a short time. It would have taken months to organise. Dave was planning to vow his love and fidelity to his wife, before all of his friends and family, and under the eye of the God he believes in, when the whole time he was sleeping with me. I looked at his face in the photos. There was no trace of shame, or guilt. And why hadn't I noticed how weird his hair parting was, or how oddly shaped his face was, making him like a badly boiled potato. He'd obviously indulged in a bit of snow himself before the ceremony because his eyes had that manic gleam I'd come to recognise so well. I wondered if she knew about his nasty, expensive little habit. He had moaned about spending so much on her Mulberry handbag but he was spending just as much on the shit he shovelled up his nose.

Dave
March

The whole second wedding/second honeymoon thing was all Vicki's idea, naturally. We hadn't had a proper wedding the first time around, she argued, her dress had been all wrong and we had just gone to the registry office, so there were no decent photos. Being such a Daddy's girl, she had sweet-talked her father into giving us the money for this wedding and the honeymoon to Florida, but he had insisted that the ceremony take place in Scotland, near her parent's place, so he could control all of the details. I wasn't bothered either way, it was all for show, didn't mean anything. I got a free holiday out of it and my mates got to have a blast at the after party so it was worth gritting my teeth and putting on that stupid white tux for a day. There were some advantages in marrying into money after all.

Katie sent me a shitty text a few days later so she must have been snooping at Vick's social media again. It read –

> **Just seen your wedding photos, looks like you renewed your vows. A bit hypocritical don't you think? Guess I never meant the world to you after all. Don't ever contact me again.**

I didn't bother replying; she was just a jealous spiteful cow. I'd dumped her and she couldn't let it go so she thought a few pointed messages would rattle me. As if.

I wish she would stop looking at Vick's profile though, she'll only see things that will upset her and the thought that she's spying on us makes me a little bit uneasy.

Katie
March

I lay in bed that night, my mind swirling with ideas for payback, coming up with more and more elaborate schemes in which I would see them both publicly shamed and humiliated, and Dave would be begging me to forgive him. I see now that it was all lies - the presents, the compliments, the 'I love you's' were all about keeping me sweet and compliant. The fact that I had my own flat so close to town must have been an added bonus for him, somewhere to spend a couple of hours with a willing available woman before he went back to his real life.

I was disgusted with myself as well, the way I had let myself be so easily led, and so easily fooled. Just a few well-chosen words and I believed him wholly, he must have thought I was so stupid he probably couldn't believe his luck. Eventually, I got up and took one of the sleeping tablets my doctor had prescribed for me in the weeks after Adam had left. I wasn't keen on taking them, they were far too strong and made me fit for nothing the next day. The last time I had taken one I sat in my bed crying my eyes out as I hallucinated my paintings in their frames, melting down the walls; and the cushions on the couch were jumping about like little horses. Hilarious when you think some people pay good money for drugs that have that exact same effect, and my doctor gave them to me for free, literally forcing them into my hands.

Crashing out twenty minutes later, my last waking thoughts were of the plan I had half formed in my head. It would be fun, I thought, it was genius, simple to execute and with maximum effect. I would enjoy every second. I fell asleep, smiling.

The next morning, fighting off the chemical hangover left by the sleeping pill, I struggled into work bleary eyed, carrying a large empty box and a bin bag full of stuff. Despite the tablet I had been up early, putting the beginnings of my plan into action and gathering up every single thing that Dave had left at my place. If the girls at work had noticed that I no longer went out at lunchtimes, and had been a bit quiet lately, they hadn't said anything, knowing I preferred keeping to myself.

Mid-morning, when all the consultants were in meetings or interview and I was sure I was on my own in the office, I quickly printed out an address label on my printer, addressed to Mrs V Campbell-Roberts and stuck to the cardboard box I had lugged in with me this morning. Sneaking down the corridor, on high alert for anyone who might see me, I made copy after copy on the office photocopier and tiptoed back to my desk, ready to start working on the 'wedding present' I was about to send to Vicki.

First into the box went his clothes. There was the England football shirt he had left behind one night, a scarf, not his favourite Paul Smith one unfortunately, a jumper that was easily recognisable as his as he was hardly ever seen out of it and his special beloved Man City t-shirt, the one he liked to lounge about in at my place, usually while watching a film before he initiated sex on the couch. Next, in went the big black dildo, the one he had bought me as a joke present for my birthday last year. It was still in its box, unused, but I took it out and laid it amongst the clothing, hoping she would think it had seen a fair amount of action. The packaging for it was a problem, I would have to hide it in a carrier bag and run out later to throw it into a bin somewhere. I couldn't chuck it into the office bin for anyone to find.

In went the photocopies. I had diligently copied every single thing he had ever sent me. Every card, every letter, every email, and the postcard he had given me after our trip to

Rome, the note he had sent with the unicorn balloon, it all went into the rapidly filling box.

I sat at my desk for hours that day, painstakingly transcribing and typing up onto sheets of A4 paper every incriminating text he'd ever sent me. I kept them all you see, couldn't bear to delete even one, not the ones where he said he loved me and not the ones which proved the time we spent together. There were a fair few explicit ones as well, he had liked to spell out his fantasies and tell me exactly what he wanted me to do to him when we met up later that night. It took ages to type up, and it ran to almost ten pages of notes but the end results were worth it. I had added in the dates of when the messages had been sent so she could chart the progress of our relationship, right up to the one where he begged me to meet him in Southend, even though their second wedding preparations were probably well under way by then. In went a copy of the few photos I had of us together, the one taken outside the Sistine Chapel, both of us looking loved up, and the one I had taken at Christmas - me in my red silk basque and stockings, Dave in his Santa mankini and elf hat, his cock clearly sticking through the side of the red Lycra.

Folded up neatly under the photos was the basque outfit, with Dave's little stretchy mankini draped across it. I did not include my vintage dress. That was worth money so I would sell it on EBay; I wasn't stupid.

It was almost as if I was preparing a time capsule, a box shaped cross section of our whole affair. I was enjoying myself. I took photos of every single item of jewellery Dave had ever bought me and emailed them to myself, printing out the images on our colour printer and including them in the package, along with notes on exactly when and where he had given them to me. I wasn't going to return any of it. I planned to sell each item either on our local classifieds website or to a silver dealer for scrap, but I had a special plan for the silver bangle, with its verse about loved engraved on each side, the one he had given me on that amazing night in Rome. I would advertise it for sale online, through our local paper's buy and sell website, with the following description

– "For Sale, one sterling silver bangle, engraved with the words 'Love is patient, Love is kind, Love is hope, love endures all things, love forgives all things, love is forever'. Unwanted gift from DAVE ROBERTS, of Brooke Street, who didn't understand the concept of 'forever'. Best offer secures."

That should get his attention. Loads of people in our town used that website so it was bound to be seen by several people who knew him, and who would ask some difficult questions. Maybe I would find out the address of Vicki's parents and send them a copy. The box was full now and almost ready to go, there was just one final thing I needed to add. Starting a new blank document on my computer, I constructed a covering letter. It would be the first thing she would find when she opened the box.

Vicki, (I debated putting 'Dear Vicki' but it seemed a little too friendly)
Please find enclosed everything your husband left at my place during our eight-month affair. I don't know what he has told you, but knowing Dave as well as I do, I can guarantee it was only half the truth, and presented so it would show him in the most favourable light possible. No doubt he has concocted a fabricated story of how I came on to him, and how he resisted as best he could before succumbing to my temptress's wiles. I beg to differ.

However, I will let the contents of this box tell their own story. Instagram THAT, bitch.

Short but succinct I thought, before sealing up the box with parcel tape. I would take it to the post office this afternoon, and she would in all probability get it tomorrow. Perfect. Tomorrow was Wednesday and Dave always went straight from work to football practice on Wednesdays so there was no chance he would get home before her and find the gift I had so lovingly prepared before she did.

He would have no chance to hide it from her, and he wouldn't know what hit him when he got home that night.

CHAPTER TWENTY-SEVEN

Katie
April

How I would have loved to have seen her face when she opened the box. She probably thought it was a belated wedding present, which in a way it was. I thought I would be able to hear her shrieking in anger from my house. There was no way Dave could charm his way out of that one.

It looked like I had got away with the vandalism of their car too. Neighbours reported the damage to the police the day after I had done it. They must have contacted Dave as the registered owner, interrupting his wedding celebrations, because I had two police officers turn up at my place on Wednesday late afternoon.

'Are you Katie Fernley?' The older one of the two stood in my doorway, notepad in hand.

'Yes. Why? What's happened?' I hoped I managed to look suitably surprised and shocked, those being the only acceptable emotions to show when the police arrive unexpectedly on your doorstep.

'Mrs Fernley...'

'Ms.' I insisted.

'Ms Fernley, we are investigating an incident of deliberate vandalism on a parked vehicle in Brooke Street two nights ago.'

'It wasn't my car. What's it got to do with me?' Pretending to look baffled, and not guilty as hell was hard.

'The owner has insinuated that you may know something about it. He claims you and he were in a relationship recently but, when he decided to end it you, ah, didn't take the news too well.' Older cop was being very professional. Younger spotty cop behind him was smirking into his chest. 'He thinks you may have damaged his car as a way of getting back at him.'

'Pffft.' I huffed. 'I presume you're talking about Dave Roberts?'

Older cop didn't even need to look at his notes.

'That's correct. Yes.'

'Do you know Dave Roberts?' I raised one eyebrow as I asked him.

'Not personally, madam, no.' Older cop admitted.

'Well I do, and he's a liar. And a dick. Just when was I supposed to have committed this act of deliberate vandalism?' I added heavy emphasis on the last two words.

'Monday night. A neighbour of Mr and Mrs Roberts noticed the car had been scratched the next morning and called us.' I glanced at younger spotty cop. He looked thrilled at the prospect of actually arresting me. Sorry buddy but I'm about to rain on your parade.

'Well, then it can't have been me. I was in London that night. I caught the train up at seven o'clock.' Triumphant, I crossed my arms and leaned against the wall.

'Do you have any proof of this?' Older cop raised his eyebrows.

'Er, yes, I think so anyway.' Pretending to be flustered, I looked like I was thinking hard. 'I have the ticket somewhere. Come in for a minute. It's probably in one of my coat pockets.'

I knew exactly where it was, I had anticipated this visit and planned ahead. Older cop followed me into my lounge while I pretended to search through various coats and turn out my handbag. Younger spotty cop could stay outside.

'Cute.' His voice was a smile as he caught sight of Monkey and Rocket. 'My granddaughter has some. She loves them to bits.'

'Yeah, they're great.' Pleased to have this common ground I continued. 'What does she call hers?'

'Custard and Coco.' he proclaimed. 'Lovely little things they are. Big personalities for such small creatures.'

'I totally agree.' I put my hand on my used ticket. 'Ah, found it. Here it is.' Waving it with a flourish I passed it to him. He checked the date and time and made some notes in his notepad.

'Well. There doesn't seem to be any reason to keep you any longer. It's quite clear you weren't in town when the crime was committed.' Older cop winked at me. 'Mr Roberts must have some other people who don't like him very much.'

'That's more than possible.' I agreed. Putting his cap back on his head he shook my hand.

'That will be the end of it. Look after those little monkeys won't you.' Younger spotty cop looked like he was going to cry with disappointment and I couldn't resist poking my tongue out at him when they turned to leave. He scowled and looked like he was about to say something but older cop stopped him.

'Off we go, Webb. No need to bother the young lady anymore.'

Laughing softly, I shut the door in his face.

I kept a close eye on her social media posts, looking for something which would give me a clue that she had finally realised what a loser she had married, twice, but there was just the usual blonde hair vs brunette hair, look what I'm wearing today, selfie in the mirror posts she always put up. Until one day, two weeks after I had sent her the special box of home truths.

My addiction was getting worse, I checked her Instagram at least three times a day. It was on my favourites tab on both my work and home computers so I could click straight onto it when I got in in the mornings, or immediately when I got home at night. Some of the others at work had noticed how much time I was spending on her pages and came over for a closer look.

'I don't know who she is' I lied. 'Someone just put me on to her Instagram because she's just so awful. It's becoming an internet sensation - just how vain she is.' The others looked and laughed, agreeing that - yes, it was funny, wasn't it, this ordinary looking woman bigging herself up like she was an A list persona. No one seemed to recognise her name, maybe because of the fake double barrelled surname she used, but at least no one said 'Oh it's her, she's one of our clients!' From then on it became the office game, on our morning tea break we would look at her most recent post and howl with laughter, pouring scorn on her latest look - see how much weight she's put on? Check out that hideous dress she's wearing. Why does she wear big diamante sunglasses that make her look like Elton John in drag? It was good to have some playmates joining me in my little habit.

So anyway, back to the day she posted about her honeymoon. Yes, that's right folks, they were off on a second honeymoon. And you'd think, that with her expensive tastes and penchant for the high life, they would have gone somewhere exclusive, somewhere that was beyond most of the rest of the population financially. The Seychelles, or the Maldives maybe, both of those destinations would have provided a spectacular backdrop to the endless bikini shots she was so fond of sharing. Both would have been eminently suitable for an Instagram princess.

They went to Florida. They went to bloody Harry Potter World in Florida. Not joking. I thought they must have taken Josh with them, which would have made sense, going to Harry Potter World when you had a five-year-old in tow but, no; it was just the two of them. I cringed in embarrassment - for fucks sake, what kind of grown up couple would choose the film set of a kiddie's movie as a honeymoon destination? For the next three weeks there was post after post after post - Harry Potter this, Disney World that, selfie of her in the mirror bragging about how thin her legs were getting after doing so much walking, selfie of her in the mirror having gone from brown to blonde again, selfie of her in the mirror gushing about her Bardot top, her green eyes, her own natural beauty.

It was also Dave's birthday while they were away and there was a cheesy, staged photo of the two of them at the breakfast table, with pancakes and fruit, coffee and a copy of the Wall Street Journal laid carefully over his plate. I rolled my eyes - as if Dave had the intelligence to read the flipping Wall Street Journal. I had to hand it to her though, to the unsuspecting passer-by they would look every inch the famous Hollywood couple having some down time between shooting scenes. She had half a grapefruit on her plate, he had a cigar in his hand - who the fuck did they think they were? John and Jackie fucking Kennedy? I couldn't resist, OK the bottle of wine I had drunk while I was looking at their photos couldn't resist, texting Dave.

Happy birthday, I hope you both liked my present. If you thought I would just go away quietly - you were wrong!

I didn't get a reply. I wasn't expecting to. I wasn't sure if he was picking up his texts while he was in Florida, but just the act of sending it made me feel like I was back in control again.

Dave

Florida was great. Made all the more sweeter by not having to fork out for a single thing. The whole trip had been paid for by Vicki's dad, including a generous wodge of spending money. Josh was staying with them, the grandparents, while we were away and I think this was the reason why her dad had been so keen to get rid of us for a few weeks. They adored having the little guy to stay, and Josh would get three weeks of too much food and too much fussing and would be a whiny brat when he was returned to us.

Yeah, it was nice and all that. A bit heavy on the theme parks for my liking but that was Vicks' taste not mine. It got a bit boring, surrounded by cartoon animals and weirdo boy wizards all of the time, and I got fed up with being with Vicki all day, every day. Still, I made the effort. I had to be on my best behaviour, I wasn't completely out of the doghouse yet. When I got the call about my car being scratched to fuck I knew it could have only been Katie. It had been attacked with some considerable force, the sergeant had told me, and there was a fair amount of rage behind it. It was personal, not opportunistic, done by someone with a grudge not one of the bored kids who ran about on our estate thinking they were in gangs.

I happily gave them Katie's address. The car being damaged didn't really bother me too much. Insurance would cover most of the cost but it was a bit inconvenient, I suppose. I couldn't believe Katie had done something so stupid and obvious. It surprised me, actually, that she wasn't boxing a bit cleverer.

I never heard any more from the cops. When I phoned for an update after we got back home and saw the damage for ourselves, I was told that the investigations were still ongoing, and no charges had been brought against anyone yet. It puzzled me, how had she got away with it?

We settled back into normal family life. Everything was planned around Josh's sports club or school activities, or Vicki's hair appointments and beauty treatments, so I just did what I was told, and went where I was sent. It was one Saturday a few weeks later when Vicki and I were walking into town. She had her eye on some shoes, or something, and they were a bit out of her price range so she wanted me to put them on our credit card. She suggested we make a day of it, while Josh was playing football. We could have lunch somewhere nice. Somewhere nice meant somewhere expensive, somewhere where she could be seen. My card was going to take a pounding today.

Walking around a corner past the pet shop a slight figure burst out of the doors and literally slammed into me.

'Gosh! Whoops! Sorry!' My hair was in my eyes and I couldn't see where I was.........' I stopped short as I recognised that breathy, laughing voice. Katie stopped laughing when she saw who she had bumped into. We stared at each other for a long moment. Vicki stood next to me, looking from me to Katie and then back to me again. It took a while before the penny dropped.

'OMG! Is this HER?' Vicki shrieked.

Katie went to barge her way past us but she was laden down with parcels and shopping bags, and Vicki casually stepped in her path, forcing Katie to stop again. Vicki looked Katie up and down slowly and I recognised the gleam of pure malice that distorted her features.

'So this is the shameless slut who tried to break up our marriage.' Vicki was still addressing me but her eyes never left Katie's face. 'Really, Dave, you never told me she was so......fat!' she finished spitefully. Katie looked incredulous and opened her mouth to retort but Vicki was quicker. 'All I can think is that you must have been curious.

209

Wondered if the rumours about fat girls being desperate and willing to do anything were true.' Vicki ground her heel and spun around, eyes glittering with victory. 'Thank God you came to your senses and realised what you had at home.' She pulled on my arm. 'Come on. Let's leave this cheap white trash whore on the street corner, where she belongs.' We had taken just a few steps when Katie called my name.

'Dave.' She said softly, dangerously softly. 'Lost for words?'

'I have nothing to say.' I replied stiffly. Fuck, this was awkward.

'That's funny. You always had plenty to say when you were in my bed. You weren't so quiet when you were begging me to stick my finger up your....'

'STOP!' I shouted. Was it hot today or was it just me? 'There's no need for bitterness Katie. It's all water under the bridge now. You should move on.'

'Oh I have moved on, believe me, and he's a hell of a lot better than you.' Katie turned to Vicki with a look of fake concern. 'I feel sorry for you. Being shackled to a man like this. I mean, being such a terrible lover and all. All the right equipment with no idea how to use it.' Vicki's eyes almost popped out of her head with rage. She looked like a mean pug who'd been kicked in the balls. But Katie wasn't done yet. 'But I guess you wouldn't know any better, Dave always told me how bad you were in bed, how boring, how vannnnilllla.' She stretched the out word vanilla slowly and provocatively, before turning on her heel and walking away. I could feel Vicki's rage building and building, she was going to implode any second.

When the hell had Katie got so.....ballsy? She always seemed so meek, it was part of the reason I had been attracted to her; she would do what she was told and never challenged, never complained. I grabbed hold of Vicki and led her away.

She was stiff with outrage, and fuming that she had not had the last word. I would pay for this later, in more ways than just money.

Katie

It was a good feeling. Skipping as best I could with bags of hay and straw for the guinea pigs, I couldn't keep the smile off my face. She had thought she had got the better of me, calling me names in the street like any common fishwife. I couldn't believe my ears when she called me fat though. I'm a ten on a good day, a twelve when I'm due my period and bloated out with gas and water. There's no way that could be called fat. It was on the tip of my tongue to say that with her height, she wouldn't ever look anything but dumpy, and some of the things she wore made her look like a pig in a dress.

Dave had stood by, getting redder and redder in the face, and looking at anything and anywhere but the two of us wishing the ground would open up and swallow him whole. When Vicki had finished her vitriolic spat by calling me a cheap white trash whore I nearly laughed. I had grown up with two older sisters, both who delighted in seeing who could come up with the most original insults and names for me. I was well practiced in the art of the ultimate comeback. If Vicki wanted a slanging match she picked the wrong person. Her insults fell well short of their mark.

Throwing scorn on Dave's performance in bed was a cheap and dirty way to cut them both. He would forever ponder if what I said was true, that he was rubbish in the bedroom department, and she would feel the words 'boring and vanilla' like a brand. It wasn't true that I had another boyfriend but they weren't to know that. I hoped I had ruined their day, both of them.

CHAPTER TWENTY-EIGHT
Katie
April

The days ticked slowly by. Spring was making an entrance at last and the watery warmth of the sun on my face as I walked to work was a welcome sensation. I had heard nothing from Dave since that unfortunate run-in in town, not that I thought I would. I had taken my silver fairy necklace to an antiques dealer specialising in antique jewellery – he had offered me eight quid for it. Turns out it was pretty but almost worthless. Ironic actually, that was the perfect way to describe the man who had given it to me – pretty but worthless.

I was feeling better, generally, and had a new optimistic view on life. I was over Dave; that was certain, I don't think I was ever really that into him, I think I was just taken in by the flowery words and extravagant gestures. It was certainly a relief not to get any texts from him in the middle of the night, begging to come round for sex.

Walking into my reception area at work that day there was a distinct air of foreboding, like a black shadow had been cast over our offices. Puzzled, but shrugging it off as nothing to do with me, I took off my coat and settled myself at my desk like I do every day, opening my Outlook and starting to go through the emails which had come in overnight. There was an unnatural hush. Instead of the usual busy bustling morning noises of phones ringing, people talking and laughing, there was silence, but it was a loaded silence, like a gun about to go off. I got the impression that something had happened, and that everyone knew about it except me. I caught Adele giving me sympathetic glances now and again but before I could ask her what was going on, my desk phone rang.

'Ah, Katie. You're in, good.' Debbie was not her usual warm and bubbly self. 'I will need to see you as soon as possible. I've booked meeting room four, and Adele will cover the phones and reception, so as soon as you can please.' She put the phone down before I could utter a word. Silently I logged off my computer and walked to the meeting room, filled with trepidation and the certain knowledge that I was in deep, deep shit. Debbie was seated at the table, some papers in front of her and a sealed A4 envelope was placed on my side of the laminated surface. There was another woman in the room, someone I didn't know, who had a notepad and was busy making notes, deliberately not making eye contact with me.

'Take a seat.' Debbie's voice was steady, but distinctly unfriendly. 'This is Lorna, a representative from our human resources business partners at Baines & Winter Law. She will be taking the minutes of this meeting today. Now, Katie, I have to ask you first – do you know why you've been called in to see us today?'

'No.' The word stuck in my throat, and I coughed. Reaching for the glass of water that had been set before me I took a sip, mind racing. 'No Debbie. I've no idea.' I said, stronger this time.

Debbie studied me for a moment.

'Katie, I'm afraid we have had a complaint regarding your conduct. Do you recognise this email?' She pushed one of the sheets of paper across to me. 'Dear Mrs Campbell-Roberts.' I read. 'Thank you for your application for the position of Nursery Supervisor at Bouncy Beans Nursery, advertised through us at Recruit Unique.....' I didn't need to read anymore. How the hell had they got a copy of this? I was so sure I deleted it off the system the second I sent it. The IT geeks must have found a way to retrieve it.

'This email was forwarded to us a few days ago, along with a formal complaint to the directors of the company.' Debbie went on. 'Would you care to explain to us, why you would send such a derogatory and personal attack to one of our potential clients?'

So she had sent it in after all, she must have been biding her time, just waiting for the right moment to strike, like the venomous snake she is.

'I can explain.' I took a deep breath. 'It was when you asked me to take on some of the feedback work, back when there were so many staff away sick and you were short-staffed. You always encouraged us to look people up on social media, try and gauge what type of personality they were, and if there was anything on there that rang alarm bells, so once I looked at her Instagram profile, I felt, in all good conscience, that she would not be suitable to put forward for the role. I admit I may have gone a little overboard in my email, but it was only that I felt so strongly she was not a good role model for the children.' I paused, letting that sink in. Debbie and the other one, Lorna or whatever, glanced at each other. 'I still feel that my instincts were right and I stand by what I have done.' I lifted my chin up, I would not back down and they couldn't make me apologise to anyone.

'Please, open the envelope in front of you.' Debbie nodded to it. 'Take a moment to read the document inside and tell us your thoughts.'

Sliding out the sheaf of papers, I could see it was some kind of legally binding agreement, between myself and Recruit Unique. Skimming the legalese, the summary of the document seemed to be saying that my employment had come to an end. I went cold all over.

'What is this?' I whispered.

'It's a legal agreement between us at Recruit Unique, and yourself.' said Debbie briskly. 'The basic terms are that we will give you three months' notice, effective immediately, even though we are only legally required to serve you with one month only. You will not be required to work your notice period, therefore, your three month's salary will be paid to you in one lump sum on the usual pay date of this month. In return for this you will leave today. We are prepared to provide you with the standard reference stating dates of employment only, but you must understand, we will not be able to provide a personal character reference for you in the future.' She paused, giving me time to take this all in.

'You're sacking me?' I asked in disbelief.

'Given the circumstances, we're really being very generous. The damage you have caused to the reputation, not only of this poor woman, but the reputational damage to the company, well, we could have called it gross misconduct and you would have been dismissed immediately without any notice or pay.'

Anger flared in me.

'OK, there's something you need to know about this woman. She is the most irresponsible, uncaring, egotistical ......' Debbie cut in, talking firmly over me.

'My understanding is that you've never even met this person, so I'm at a loss as to how you could form such a strong opinion of her.'

'I saw her,' I was spitting out my words now. 'I saw her drag her own son out into the road in front of a speeding car because she was too busy fucking about on her phone to take any notice of where she was going! And I have met her – she called me fat! Look, if she's going to make a complaint about me then I reserve the right to put forward my side of the argument.' Debbie looked at me pityingly.

'Katie, you misunderstand.' She said gently. 'The complaint wasn't from Mrs Campbell-Roberts at all. The complaint was made by her husband.'

I walked out of the office for the last time ten minutes later. I had one week to seek independent legal advice, like I could afford that, and sign the paperwork accepting their offer or take the agency to an employment tribunal and argue the toss. Either way, I was out of a job. The three months' salary would see me through for a little while, I had to grudgingly admit that it was pretty generous of them, but I was effectively unemployed, with no means of supporting myself.

Debbie had shaken her head in disappointment when we had wrapped up the meeting today.

'I had such high hopes for you.' She sighed. 'Why did you have to go and throw everything away for the sake of your petty jealousy?'

I couldn't believe Dave had done this, it was beyond spiteful. He had been the one to forward my email directly to the directors, copying in the local school board as well. I could see why the agency had had to take it so seriously. The mayor was probably calling for my head on a plate. Dave must have known I would end up losing my job over this.

Glumly, I trudged back home. It was barely eleven o'clock and my normal daily routine had been knocked on its arse. I crawled fully clothed under my duvet and shivered pathetically for a couple of hours, feeling very sorry for myself. My optimism of that morning had taken a nosedive and I wondered how I would find another job if it got around that I had been sacked from Recruit Unique. Eventually though, I got up and made a comforting mug of hot cocoa. There was no point putting off what needed to be done, I chided myself, as I fired up my laptop ready to take on the search for a new job yet again. I had no one but myself to fall back on, I could only rely on me. Look at where placing your trust in someone else had got me – first Adam, now Dave. What is it about me that make men think they can walk all over me like I'm some kind of doormat?

Her Instagram page was now my home page and the internet browser automatically opened it up whenever I switched on my laptop.

Vicki Campbell-Roberts@luckyladysoblessed
I love this man more than I love pink champagne and Minnie ears…. #pinkchampagne #honeymoon #husbandgoals #Disney #memories #takemeback #seeyounextyear #couplegoals #abercrombieandfitch #summervibes #Orlando #minniemouse #waltdisney #magic #dreamscometrue #bestmarriage #darkhair #greeneyes #nyxhighlighter #thewayhelooksatme #somuchlove #thelifeyouwant #grindhardstayhumble #blessed

You wouldn't think, to look at Dave in that photo, that he'd just spent the best part of an entire year fucking someone else.

But you would think, to look at Dave in that photo, that he was absolutely off his tits on cocaine. Which gave me an idea, my best yet.

Remember how when he went to Poland, him and his mates were planning on smuggling back some illegal substances to sell on? I know he did, because I saw the packages in his case when we were at the B&B in Southend. I wasn't snooping, they just weren't hidden very well. God knows how he got through border control with that lot but I guess they aren't too bothered at little airports like that. If the rest of them managed to smuggle to same amount in my guess was that they had a whole heap of it stashed somewhere ready to sell, and knowing Dave's Obsessive Compulsive Disorder-type need to organise things, I figured that the stash was under his control, and in his house somewhere.

We had one of those local Crimestoppers numbers, where you could phone the police and grass somebody up, with total anonymity, and a guarantee that your call would not be traced back to you. All it took was one sweet, sweet phone call. I gave them Dave's name and address and said I knew for a fact that there was a large amount of Class A drugs hidden on the premises, that he was planning to sell for a huge profit. They happily took down all of the details about what flight he had been on and where it had come from, and never once asked me how I had come by this information. Promising they would look into it, I hung up, feeling on top of the bloody world once more.

Don't mess with me Dave, you will not win.

CHAPTER TWENTY-NINE
Katie
May

Once again I didn't hear anything more about it for a while. I had signed the paperwork for the agreement the agency had offered me and the lump sum, which seemed a huge amount to me, sat in my bank account. Aware that I would possibly have to eke out this amount for as long as it took me to get another job, I started using the huge amounts of free time I now had to cook large cheap meals from scratch, and freeze them into single sized portions for future consumption. I was in the middle of stirring up a huge batch of spaghetti bolognaise and singing along to the local radio station, the one with the playlist firmly stuck in the 80's, when my ears pricked up at the mention of a familiar name.

"Local police have arrested a man who was badly injured in a dawn raid on a house in Brooke Street this morning. Officers uncovered a large amount of what appears to be an illegal substance at the premises and were in the process of arresting the man, thought to be in his thirties, when the suspect made an attempt to jump out of a first floor window, severely injuring his ankle in the event. After taking him to hospital in handcuffs his ankle was confirmed as broken and he was arrested on suspicion of possession of a Class A drug with intent to supply on a large scale. The man has been named as Mr David Roberts, of Brooke Street and he is expected to be remanded in police custody upon his release from hospital. Two other people at the premises, a woman and a child, were not implicated in any criminal activity."

Oh but she's just as guilty, I thought, of being criminally fucking up herself!

I dropped the wooden spoon I was using to stir the bolognaise mixture and clapped a hand over my mouth but I was unable to stop the burst of laughter from came from deep down inside. Oh, this was just brilliant! Not only had they suffered the indignity of having the police batter down their door in the early hours, but Dave had stupidly tried to make a run for it, and had broken his ankle in the process. Now he was in a police cell, waiting to have the charges brought against him AND he was publicly named in the news broadcast, meaning it was highly likely he would lose his job over this as well. Serves him right. It couldn't have gone any better if I'd planned it. I did a little victory dance in my kitchen, stopping now and again to shout with laughter once more.

Pictures of Dave, hopping along on crutches and wearing a giant blue plaster boot on his right ankle dominated the front pages of the local paper for days. He was bailed pending trial and allowed to return home after what must have been a couple of very uncomfortable few days in the police cells. I wondered if it had brought back any memories of the first time he went to prison, and also wondered if they would use his previous conviction against him this time. His trial wouldn't come to court for a few months I supposed, but he would almost certainly receive a jail sentence, given the sheer amount of coke that was found at his house. It was even more than I thought.

Funnily enough, nothing appeared on Vicki's pages for a couple of days, no photos of her anyway – just a couple of bullshit inspirational quotes about being together, for better for worse, and a post about the new Game of Thrones series starting that week.
On the day Dave was released on bail he sent me one text.

> **I know you were behind this. You will regret that you ever made that call.**

I fired back.

> **The only thing I regret is meeting you in the first place. Enjoy your incarceration. I guess you won't be able to run too fast with that plaster on your leg, so enjoy making some new special friends.**

A cheap shot, I know, but I had no reason to pull my punches now.

Dave
May

That absolute fucking bitch.

She's put us through hell these last few months. There was what she did to our car. I called the police about that again but, not surprisingly, I wasn't high up on their list of priorities at the moment. I thought that the box of my stuff she sent to Vicki might have been the end of it, but when I saw what she'd done —the copies of the private things I had written to her, the pages and pages of text messages in which I said I loved her, with all the dates on them and everything, the story I'd given Vicki blatantly didn't add up, and so I had to come clean. We sat down and I told her everything, about how left out I'd felt with Joshie was born, about how she never included me in her life unless she needed a plus one for a night out. She sat there quite calmly, did Vicki, until I'd got to the end of my sob story, and then she let rip. The thing that bothered her the most wasn't that I'd been dipping my wick somewhere else, it was the fact that I'd spent money on Katie. I'd bought her jewellery, including the white gold ring which was an exact copy of her eternity ring, and expensive underwear, not to mention paying for a romantic weekend for two in Rome, when obviously, that money would have been better spent on her. And Josh, she added belatedly.

The altercation in between Vicki and Katie in town was the final straw for Vick. She had lost face and she knew it but there was something else bothering her, she told me. Ever since she'd seen that email ping back into my account as undelivered, she'd recognised the name, Katie Fernley, from somewhere else. Going back through her own emails, she'd pulled up the one she had received from Recruit Unique ages ago, the one where they'd really laid into her about her social media profiles. She had been really keen on that job as well, was more than qualified for it and it would have been much better money than being a private nanny brought in. But because of Katie, she never even got the chance to put in an application for it. Scanning the email, I realised I had total gold in my hands. There was no doubt that Katie would be in so much trouble if this email were to come to light. You can bet that she would have hidden her tracks well, but there was nowhere she could hide if the original email was forwarded on to the right people.

When I heard that she'd lost her job a few days later I laughed so hard I got a stitch in my side. She would have to go back to being a till monkey at the book shop if they'd even have her back. I wanted so bad to gloat at her I almost sent her a 'hey, how'ya doing now?' text. There was nothing more she could do to me, to us. Vicki knew the whole story now and, while I was still nowhere near to being forgiven, her frosty knickers approach was thawing out day by day, as

I settled down to prove what a good boy I could be when I put my mind to it.

The next thing I know I'm being woken up at stupid o'clock in the morning by someone arsehole battering down my door. I'm never very good in the mornings, especially when I'm woken up before it's even daylight, so I never had time to think properly. I had hidden the gear in a temporary place when I got back from Poland, intending to find somewhere safer for it later, which I never got around to doing, so it was still hidden but in plain sight if you know what I mean. Yeah, a black holdall under my sons' bed wasn't the best place to keep it, when you think about it retrospectively. They found it within minutes, they obviously had been tipped off that it was there, they knew exactly what they were looking for, had dogs and everything with them. Josh was screaming blue bloody murder when they tried to read me my rights, and the thought of going to prison, at being forced to be apart from my boy, was enough to make me panic, and react with sheer desperation. I wasn't really thinking when I dodged the arresting officer and ran for the window in our bedroom across the hall. It was open a little bit, enough to open fully when I leapt at it and I swung both my legs over the ledge and jumped. Straight onto the concrete below. I don't know if I was thinking I was in one of those cop shows where the bad guys just landed, rolled and bounced back up, sprinting away to freedom and safety, while the bumbling cops looked in disbelief from the open window above.

Anyhow, it didn't exactly happen like that. I dropped, landed sideways on my ankle, heard a massive crack and then I don't remember anything until they got me to hospital and gave me some morphine for the pain. I came to with my left hand handcuffed to the trolley bed and the lead officer looking down at me.

'Well, that was stupid.' He laughed and took a photo of me with his phone which I'm pretty sure they're not supposed to do. 'This is definitely one for our intranet — we've got a wall of dumbest things people have done to avoid arrest, and you just went straight to the top.'

When I got all plastered up and had spent a couple of nights in the cells being 'processed, very slowly I might add, they let me go home until I was called for trial. My father-in-law had put up the bail money, so now there was another reason he had me by the balls. My boss called to put me on indefinite suspension without pay, because apparently it was all over the news what I had done. We both knew I would be looking at going back to prison, because of my previous form I was looking at up to sixteen years, so being suspended was just a formality really. I had lost my job as well. Vicki's dad was going to be livid. He had put up most of the money when Alan was just a start-up and could only offer to pay me peanuts through the government work scheme. Obviously, my father-in-law felt that I needed to be able to support my wife and son financially so he injected a whole heap of cash to get the business afloat, and we were doing really well now, finally in a position to be able to give him some return on his investment. Only I wouldn't be employed there for much longer, and Vicki's part time wage wouldn't cover the mortgage repayments, let alone the amount of make-up and new clothes she treated herself to every week. She would have to move back in with her mum and dad in Scotland, taking Josh with her. It would be too far for them to visit me, wherever I was sent. I would miss the rest of my son's childhood years because of that fucking bitch, Katie. I sent her a text.

I know you were behind this. You will regret that you ever made that call.

She sent back, quick as anything.

The only thing I regret is meeting you in the first place. Enjoy your incarceration. I guess you won't be able to run too fast with that plaster on your leg, so enjoy making some new special friends.

I nearly puked. I hadn't thought of that.

CHAPTER THIRTY
Katie
May

Things were definitely looking up. It wasn't just that we were having the most glorious heatwave, the universe had decided I'd dealt with enough bad karma shit and started showering me with positive vibes and lucky breaks. I managed to get a part time job, purely by chance, selling colourful beads and clothes on one of the market stalls. I was browsing through the piles of Batik sarongs when I fell into conversation with the owner. He wanted to be free to spend more time travelling the globe in search of new stock and had ended up offering me a job, almost full time hours for the rest of the summer. The pay wasn't great, but I got by, and I still had my nest egg from my payoff last month.

Weirdly, Adam, my ex-husband had been in touch. He was still in Thailand and was fully embracing and immersing himself in the Buddhist religion. He had never been particularly spiritual before but his email was full of detail about this massive life change he was undergoing, and how, in order to move his soul forward, he needed to make amends for the bad things he had done in his life so far. He was sorry for taking the money from our joint savings account, he wrote, and would be wiring me my half of the cash soon so that the black stain on his aura could be cleansed and washed away. I didn't care how black his aura was, but I had never expected him to pay me back the money he had stolen. Happy days! The money wasn't in my account yet so I wasn't holding my breath but there was a certain amount of satisfaction in having him admit that he had been in the wrong.

Even better, I had been playing with some of the beads we had for sale on the stall, having a go at creating my own jewellery designs, and they were proving very popular with the younger, more fashion forward market shoppers. Bob, the stall owner had handed me a thick catalogue of beads and jewellery fixings, telling me to order whatever I wanted, giving me a generous budget to work with. I spent happy afternoons coming up with new design ideas, and the punters loved that they were getting a bespoke piece of jewellery, actually made for them in front of their eyes. I took my case of bits and bobs home with me in the evenings as well, spreading the beads out over the floor, dividing them up into textures and colours and playing around with different effects.

It was a simple, happy existence. The other stall holders were like a big motley family, nobody asking too many questions but all were willing to keep an eye on your stall if you needed the loo. It was useful too, in that at the end of the market day there was lots of leftover foods going cheap, and I dined like a queen on street food from all four corners of the world, for next to nothing or even for free sometimes. Harry, who had the greengrocers stall, was kind enough to put aside some bruised vegetables and cauliflower leaves for Monkey and Rocket, meaning I saved a fortune on food for them as well. I brought them both down to the market one day in their smart travel cage to say thank you to Harry in person as it were. They were the stars of the show, being passed around and cuddled by half the market, and drew in an appreciative crowd of children, all wanting to stroke their soft hair. Harry was pleased as well, as the parents often stopped to buy something at his stall while their kids were busy petting the guinea pigs.

'Eh, maybe we've got summat here!' Exclaimed Harry, delightedly filling a paper bag with sweet smelling oranges for one lady. 'One of them ESP's - you know, unique selling points. We could have them little beauties here every day, build them a special cage like.' I laughed.

'I doubt they'd put up with so much fussing every day Harry, but they've been ever so good today.' I kissed the top of Monkey's head proudly and she head butted me back, which means 'fuck off' in guinea pig language.

I checked the papers each day for news of Dave's trial but there was nothing mentioned for ages. I knew it could take some time for a crime of this seriousness come to court, both sides gathering evidence and so on. There was a flurry of activity on her Instagram account and she posted a rare picture of Josh, beaming at the camera and kicking a football in the park.

Vicki Campbell-Roberts@luckyladysoblessed
My little football star! He's getting so good he'll be in the Premier league soon XX #football #talentofthefuture #groweveryday #skills #justlikehisdad #familyiseverything #workhard #playharder #mysonthechampion #getsitfromhismama #minicityfan #grindhardstayhumble #ladyhaveitall #blessed

I guess Dave was still laid up with his broken ankle, so she now had to take Josh to Soccer Stars on a Saturday morning. I hadn't seen either of them in town again, which was a relief as I had no idea how Dave would react if he saw me this time. I had beaten him at his own game, he was facing a custodial sentence or a hefty fine at least, and he would now know how it feels to lose your security like I had. The war was over as far as I was concerned. There was nothing he could do to me now; he'd cost me my job but I'd found a new one which I was enjoying even more. I had money in the bank and the company of the other market traders, I didn't need him, want him or miss him. He could rot in prison for all I cared.

228

Dave
May

I sat, and stewed and stewed on it. Vick had all but given up on me and I overheard her on her phone to her dad, planning on taking Josh to Scotland with her as soon as possible. They were even talking about schools there for him so I could safely assume she wasn't intending to stick by me and come back when I got out. That's even if I did get time - my brief seemed to think my previous conviction was a misdemeanour seeing as I was so young at the time, and hadn't warranted such a harsh sentence. My exemplary record since then would hold in my favour, I had a family, held down a responsible job and was the major contributor to the household. The fact that I hadn't made any move to actively sell the coke, and also that I was just looking after it for some other people would also prove to the judge that I was not a menace to society. We were asking for a fine, some community service and probably I would have to attend some kind of drugs rehabilitation course. I could handle all of that if it would keep me out of prison.

I couldn't do much with my ankle in plaster. It had broken in a weird place and I would be at least three months on crutches, dragging the heavy boot around with me. I couldn't drive anywhere which annoyed Vicki as she now had to fit in all of Josh's activities around her hair appointments and shopping trips.

I got around OK on the crutches but couldn't go far without my leg paining me. They had given me some decent painkillers at the hospital, but they made me feel sleepy so I spent most of the day sitting on the couch at home, smoking weed and thinking of how I could make Katie pay. She had lost her job at the recruitment agency and I was happy about that. Someone had seen her working at the market selling hippy clothes and beads and shit, so I had gone down there one day and spied on her, staying out of sight behind the stall awnings. She looked good, she was laughing at something the person in the stall next door had said and she was all lit up with a glow, the way she used to be like with me. She'd had her hair cut shorter and it suited her, and for a brief moment I felt a pang of something like regret, like loss, for how we had ended, but then I remembered what she had done to me and my family and my heart turned to cold hard stone. I had plenty of time to think about how I would make her suffer, but the trouble was - all my ideas were slightly, well, criminal. I knew plenty of people who do anything for a decent wad of cash but I think even they'd draw the line at maiming a pretty girl for life. The more I thought about it, the more it dawned on me exactly what the answer was. I had taken away her job but that wasn't enough to ruin her like she ruined me, so now I would take away everything else she held dear, starting with those two rat like things she loved so very much.

What Katie had completely forgotten in all this, was that I still had a key to her flat.

I got the bus to the end of her road, then hid at the end of the alley leading to her front door. There were a couple of run down old sheds there where I could perch quite comfortably without being seen, but where I had a good view of her gate and the lane leading to the road. I watched her leave, trailing hippy scarves and carrying a big wooden case. I waited for another ten minutes so I could be sure she wouldn't come rushing back, having forgotten her purse or something. Letting myself in, I breathed in the familiar smell of her perfume and the memories of the many nights we spent here together came flooding back. Ah Katie, why did you have to go and make things so complicated? I thought, completely and conveniently forgetting that it had been my mistake with the email address that had resulted in us getting busted. There was a rustle and a muted squeak from the cage in the corner, and a small patchy white face peeked out at me from the wooden log house. They both knew me; I had been here on so many occasions so they weren't hiding like they would do if it was a stranger. Remembering the day I had brought Josh here, and how much he loved playing with them, I faltered for a second but then Josh was the reason I was here doing this. I was about to lose custody of my precious boy, and nothing, nothing would ever make me forgive Katie for that.

'Here piggy, piggy.' I crooned softly, reaching down into the cage and picking up the first bundle of fluff. Monkey, or Rocket, I didn't know which was which, I never really liked them as much as I pretended I did when it seemed important to Katie.

It turned my stomach to actually do it, but I made sure it was quick for both of them. I'm not that much of a bastard. They wouldn't have known a thing about it; just a short, hard whack against the corner of the kitchen worktop and it was done, simple really, easy even. I laid their broken bodies back on the hay in their cage. They looked peaceful enough. It crossed my mind that maybe I had just committed a despicable act of cruelty and for a moment I wondered if I had gone too far. Oh well, too late now. That'll teach her. Play on says the referee.

Later I threw her key back through the letterbox where I knew she'd find it as soon as she got home. I 'fessed up to Vicki when I got in because she was bugging me so much about where I'd been. She found it quite funny, not surprisingly as she never was an animal lover, she even found a hilarious, but sick, dead pet meme to post on her page, without any captions or hashtags, but she would know. If she was still following Vicki's Instagram, Katie would know.

CHAPTER THIRTY-ONE
Katie
May

I was humming as I walked in the door.

'I'm home, babies!' I sang my usual greeting to the guinea pigs, waiting to hear their excited 'wheek wheek wheek', as they heard me come in and shouted for their dinner. Stopping in my tracks, I felt a chill prickle down my back. Something was terribly, terribly wrong here. It was so still, so quiet and there was a strong metallic smell that was familiar, yet I couldn't quite put my finger on what it was. I crept silently up to the cage in the corner. There, lying still and stiff, with blood pooling around both their heads, were my two precious, precious girls. Monkey's eyes were open and glazed over, Rocket had just the hint of a snarl, baring her teeth at the moment of death. She had always been the dominant one, sheltering and protecting Monkey who was more gentle, sweet and trusting. Oh my poor, poor babies what happened to you? I sank to the floor, keening with grief, and howling out my rage and pain to the ceiling. I screamed so loud that, worried I was being attacked, my neighbours tried to get in, and when I didn't answer the door, they called Jackie, who broke her golden rule of giving her tenants twenty-four hours' notice before a visit and rushed round, taking in the smell of death and blood and the state of me on my knees on the floor. My next of kin on the tenancy agreement was Mel, as she was the closest thing I had to family in this town, so Jackie called the emergency contact number and Mel was by my side within minutes. She rocked me in her bony arms and cried with me, being so fond of them herself. My neighbours formed a small but quiet work party, and laid the two bodies gently on towels, wrapping them up in their shrouds so they were just two small humps in the material.

'Was it a cat, do you think?' I heard one of them whisper. 'Or a rat got in maybe.' But I knew it was neither. I had seen the key lying on the mat when I opened the door, but had not given any thought to its significance until now. I knew exactly what had happened here today. I could see how it played out, my mind unable to switch off from replaying the moment when he had hit them against a hard surface, the moment when their tiny bodies had given up and they had succumbed to the premature deaths he had decided for them. How could he have been so cruel? They were innocent little animals who never hurt anyone, who only gave unconditional love and affection, their only aim in life being to find the next treat, to look forward to the next bowl full of food.

'He did it, Mel.' I choked the words out, my face a mess of tears. 'Dave did this.' She nodded, unable to speak herself, but I felt her spine stiffen with anger and she was shaking with the effort of not tearing around to his place armed with my biggest, sharpest knife. Slowly, I quietened, my crazed wailing turning to steady weeping. I longed to cuddle them one last time but Mel shook her head.

'It's best you don't, love. They're gone now and he can't hurt them anymore.' She helped me onto the couch and bustled about tiding up, thanking my neighbours for coming to my aid and seeing them out. 'I'll drape something over the cage so you don't have to look at it tonight. Do you have anywhere you'd like to bury them?' She asked gently. I didn't have any garden of my own so I shrugged miserably.

'I can't think about that now.' She hugged my shoulders.

'No need to make any decisions tonight, we'll sort it all out in the morning,' With a quick kiss and a promise to call me first thing, she reluctantly left me alone, having first extracted a promise that I would take a sleeping pill and go

234

straight to bed. I followed orders but sleep was elusive. I kept listening out for a rustle of hay or the squeak of complaint from Rocket when Monkey took up too much room in the sleeping house. My beautiful girls, gone. No more seeing their happy faces greeting me in the morning, no more of the clean hay smell of them, no more warm furry bodies cuddling into my neck when I picked them up.

I lay awake watching the room turn from black to grey in the dawn light. I was too devastated to even ponder on what Dave had been thinking, how he could come up with such a disgusting act. It was beyond belief how I had ever laid my soul bare for that man, how I had trusted him and put my faith in him. I had thought I knew him inside out, it never occurred to me he would be capable of such a heinous act of deliberate, barbaric savagery. Just goes to show, we can never really know anyone, even those who are closest to us.

The next morning, I was sitting on the couch, my heart twisting in agony each time I caught sight of the empty cage. A soft knock at my door made me get up. Expecting to see Mel, I was overwhelmed to see several of my fellow market stall holders, gathered together in a small knot on my doorstep, sadness etched on their faces.

'We heard what happened' Harry was the first to speak. 'Just despicable it is, murdering an innocent creature like that.' He was all worked up, they all were. One by one they filtered into my tiny flat, holding out the small gifts they had thoughtfully brought with them.

'We thought we'd give them a good send off.' Rachel, the florist, held out a beautiful spray of meadow flowers and ornamental grasses. 'They were part of the life and heart of the market, after all.'

Harry had fashioned a tiny coffin from the orange boxes he stocked, and Marnie, the face painter, had drawn flower and hearts along with Monkey and Rocket's names down its sides.

'We thought they'd be happier together' Harry said, opening up the coffin to show me the lining of fleecy material scraps given to the cause by Preeta, who owned the sewing goods stall. Tears ran down my face unchecked as I took in the detail on the orange box coffin. These big hearted people, who barely knew me, had collectively made a concerted effort to help me through this unbearable nightmare.

'We found a good place to bury them,' Harry went on, his eyes welling up a little bit as well. 'That's if you don't mind them being on market land. There's a nice little corner, with an old apple tree. I reckon they'd like that, being under the apple tree. We'll mark it out all nice for them, put up a plaque or something.' I was sobbing by now, touched beyond belief at the generosity of this group of salt-of-the-earth folk. They had opened up their hearts and accepted me without question or judgement.

'And if we see that bastard in the market, we'll give him the hiding of his life' Andy said darkly. Andy spent his days lifting heavy crates and boxes for his porter job, and the muscles stood out from his arms and thick neck like steel cables. I wouldn't want to be Dave if Andy ever caught up with him.

'How did you all find out?' I stammered, wiping the tears from my face with the clean handkerchief Harry had pulled from his coat pocket.

'Your friend Mel came to see us, first light this morning. We couldn't let you face this kind of thing alone. I'll miss the little blighters, fond of them I was.' Harry sniffed and blinked rapidly.

'Thank you. All of you. I think Monkey and Rocket would love to be laid to rest by the apple tree Harry. It would make me feel like they're always with me too.' I gave a wobbly smile. With time and the support of my friends, I would heal. The shock of finding my girls dead would never leave me, but the compassion and dignity my market family were showing them would go a long way to helping me come to terms with the senseless loss.

I went to work later that day, and was propped up by the many small kindnesses the stall holders showed me - a cup of tea brought over to my stall, a sympathetic pat on my shoulder when they passed by. Harry and Andy kept close to me, their eyes roaming the crowds for a sight of Dave, hoping they would get their chance to come good on their promise of actual bodily harm. I didn't think he would dare show his face anywhere near me, ever again. If he did, I wouldn't be held responsible for my actions.

We held the burial ceremony when the market closed for the day. A bottle of brandy was passed from person to person and Granny Muir, who had held a stall in this very market for more than forty years, surprised us all by singing a sweet version of 'All Things Bright and Beautiful, All Creatures Great and Small' in a clear and charming voice. It was a lovely way to say goodbye to two of the most lovable animals I had ever known and there were more tears shed by us all as the sun gently set on the pitifully small grave.

CHAPTER THIRTY-TWO
Katie
June

I got by. It was hard coming home to a lifeless flat again and it was a long time before I stopped listening for the rustle of straw from the empty cage in the corner. I had meant to pack everything up and re-donate it back to the animal shelter but it was so hard to get out of this depressive slump. I stopped designing jewellery, finding no joy in the creative process now. I'd had an earworm for weeks now, you know when a song gets into your head and just won't go away, and you find yourself singing it over and over. Mine was a bit random, a mediocre hit from a random nineties' Indie band.

> *This is how it feels to be lonely,*
> *This is how it feels to be small,*
> *This is how it feels when your word means nothing at all.*

Sitting alone, night after night, drinking far too much, I would belt out this song finding a certain solace in the words. The summer was rolling on without me. I should have been out, re-kindling my friendships with the people I'd let go back when Dave was all I needed. I should have been at the beach, or taking long walks with Mel and Maxie. I loved swimming and had been really good at it when I was younger, competing in several inter-school competitions, but I had no motivation to get out and do something. I preferred spending all my spare time in my own company, barely leaving the flat, and letting my thoughts spiral down dangerously into a dark despondency.

I was numb. I wanted to die sometimes. I wanted Dave and his bitch of a wife to die all of the time. No, that wasn't strictly true; I wanted them to suffer first. I wanted them to feel what I was feeling, to have everything they loved and cared about ripped from them, and to know what it was like to live in my world of permanent bleakness, where there was no hope, no point in it all.

Whether it was the result of all that alcohol I consumed every day leeching into my brain and causing it to fire vindictive thoughts into the creative bit, I don't know, but slowly, the fog lifted and my thoughts became clearer and more focused, before sharpening into an almost painful realisation. It was laughably simple really, when I thought about it. The only thing that Dave and Vicki had in common was their son, so therefore it stood to reason, take their child away and I would take their world away.

I had nothing left to lose, no reason to stick around anymore so the consequences were of no importance to me. I had no ties now, my flat was only rented, my job only transient – I would easily be replaced. I could disappear tomorrow and it wouldn't cause so much as a ripple in the world. The disappearance of their child however, was something that Dave and Vicki would never recover from, they would never be able to forget the moment when they took their eye off the ball and lost the most important thing in the world.

See, laughingly simple.

I would take Josh.

The half-formed plan in my head began to take shape. There was so much to consider, every aspect of my final project had to be thought through. There were many pitfalls, timings would be crucial and I would have to rely on good old fashioned luck for some of the more unreliable elements, but it could be done. I could see that. Providing I did my research, covered all the bases and prepared for the ultimate outcome, it would succeed.

There was a wealth of information on her Instagram profile. I had avoided looking at it since that picture she had put up, the one poking fun at people with dead pets, the one that had had me reeling and hunching over the toilet, throwing up bitter bile.

Catching up with what she'd put up since, there were plenty of posts about her gym routine, her latest diet, her hair, her fashion advice, her hair again, her summer days out with her family.

Vicki Campbell-Roberts@luckyladysoblessed
Another Sunday funday at the beach, ending with this beautiful sunset XX
#sunset #happiness #sea #sky #redskyatnight #view #homeiswheretheheartis #grindhardstayhumble #paradise #dreamscometrue #weekendvibes #waterbaby #home #staytruetoyourself #marriedlife #besthusband #familyfirst #familyforever #lifestylegoals #beauty #majesty #blessed

I scrolled through them all until I found what I was looking for. There, the picture she had posted, the one showing her hair flowing down her back.

Vicki Campbell-Roberts@luckyladysoblessed
So glad to be going back to blonde on Saturday. Can't wait until Marco @ Mirror Mirror hair salon works his magic!
#hairgoals #frizz #goodhairday #transformation #blondehairdontcare #blondeisback #splitendsbegone #lorealpro #tigiprofessional #kerastase #chopchop #summercolour #olaplex #smartbond #shinefordays #healthyhair #stronghair #layers #nomoreroots #grindhardstayhumble #blessed

Saturday. I had to get everything done and in place for Saturday. It was only a few days away and I had so much to work out yet.

CHAPTER THIRTY-TWO
Katie

Looking around my little flat, I heaved a sigh of relief. Everything was packed up nicely, and organised well so that whoever came in to deal with my stuff after Saturday would know what to do with it all. The redundant guinea pig cage was packed down, all the remaining food and bowls stacked neatly inside it. I had put post-its' on everything with clear instructions on where everything would go. The cage was going to the animal shelter and I hoped it wouldn't take its hideous memories of violent death with it. I had several large piles of boxes and bags grouped in different places – most of the furniture belonged to the flat so the only things that would be going were the knick-knacks, pictures and cushions I had collected, back when I was trying to create a cosy home. These I would give to Mel, with directions to keep what she wanted and give the rest to charity. There were several large boxes of kitchen equipment, practical things like plates and glasses. I wanted these to go to the Salvation Army, in the hopes that they would help someone like me, someone who had nothing and struggled to be able to afford the basic furnishings in their first flat.

All of my clothes were also willed to the Salvation Army, I wouldn't be needing them anymore, not where I was going. I had left letters to be found afterwards. There was one to Jackie, apologising for not giving notice and including a cheque for the next month's rent so she wouldn't be out of pocket, and one for Mel, just apologising in general and thanking her for being such a rock, regardless of what I had done, and what I was about to do.

So that side of things had been taken care of at least. I pictured the horror and disbelief on everybody's faces when they learned of what I had done. Would they think me a coward, for not staying to face the music? Or would they realise just how desperate I had become, put it down to mental illness and think of it as a cry for help gone horribly wrong? I know it wasn't fair leaving people like Jackie and Mel behind to clear up my mess but I'd made it as easy for them as I could. The flat could be emptied of all of my belongings within an hour, leaving behind only a dancing pattern of dust motes as testament to me ever living there. Mentally checking off the list in my head, I looked around me, noting what was left to do. The fridge had been emptied and cleaned out, leaving just a few bits like milk, just enough to see me through until the weekend. Likewise, the bathroom cabinets were bare and I had scrubbed the whole place until it was sterile, getting rid of all traces of me. The next person to move in here would never know there had ever been anyone else here.

Right, I had some shopping to do.

I thought sleep would have evaded me on that last night, Friday night. I spent hours going through everything in my head, picturing how it would pan out, but I slept like the dead and woke on Saturday morning to a dreary, overcast day, rain beating down on the roof above my head. That was one thing I could count on – this British summer. I needed rain and windy conditions in order to make the last part of my plan work better, and the English summertime had obliged.

Packing up the sleeping bag I had slept in last night, I put that and several heavy woollen blankets in my car. I was too keyed up to eat and it was a struggle to manage keeping down a cup of tea as my stomach tied itself up into tight knots of anxiety and excitement. It was time to put the plan into action, my final day was here.

Stalking someone through their social media is easy. I now knew that Vicki had a hair appointment to get her minging brown-but-going-ginger locks dyed back to blonde again.

She'd even, very helpfully, given me the name of the hair salon she was going to and it was easy to find the number in the phone book.

'Hello, yes, I have an appointment with Marco this morning? The name is Vicki Campbell-Roberts' I spoke coolly to the receptionist who had answered the phone, wondering if I should have attempted to put on a screechy Scottish accent for more authenticity, but she didn't seem to pick up on it at all.

'Yes, Ms Campbell-Roberts!' The girl fawned. 'So looking forward to seeing you today, how can we help you?'

'I'm not sure what time we had agreed for my appointment this morning.'

'Let me have a look.' The line went quiet for a moment. 'Ah, here we are. Ten fifteen.' The girl sounded like she expected a round of applause for working that out.

'Yes, well, would it be possible to move it back a little bit, say by an hour? I have a number of things to do today and I can't possibly fit them all in before my hair appointment this morning.' I went on pompously, thinking that was exactly how Vicki would have said it. The receptionist sounded unsure.

'I'll need to check with Marco.' She said hesitantly as if unwilling to risk the wrath of either Vicki or the legendary Marco. She put the phone on hold and the tinny notes of 'All You Need is Love' floated down the line. I snorted. It was love that got me into this mess, and pure hatred that would get me out. Eventually the girl came back on the line.

'I've just had a word with Marco, and that's fine.' She informed me. 'Seeing as it's you.' Smarmy bitch, I thought, but she was still banging on. 'I've changed your appointment time to eleven-fifteen, but bear in mind you will still need the full two and a half hours to make sure the treatment is as perfect as possible.'

'Thank you.' I said. 'You've been very helpful.' And she had.

I already knew that Dave's ankle was still in plaster and he found it impossible to drive. He managed for short distances on his crutches but it was his wife who had taken over delivering Josh to his football club on Saturday mornings. I wasn't sure if they were still doing the classes at Soccer Stars during the summer, seeing as it wasn't football season, but a quick call to the club secretary and posing as a new mother in town confirmed that, yes, Soccer Stars went all through the year and ran from ten o'clock until one o'clock, every Saturday morning. That would have worked in with her hair appointment, she would have dropped Josh off at ten, then been at her hairdressers for ten-fifteen, being done in time to pick Josh up again at one o'clock. She would be in for surprise this morning though when she turned up too early for her appointment and had to wait an hour before Marco was now scheduled to see her. I didn't think she would consider cancelling the appointment, not now she bragged all over social media about being a blonde again.

Josh would still be dropped off on time, but she would not be able to pick him up until much later now. If the football club ended at one, I would have at least an hour before she showed up. No doubt she wouldn't have given poor Josh a thought, having to wait around after his class for ages before his mum showed up to get him.

With everything I needed for Phase Two packed into my car, I drove to the school where the Soccer Stars classes were being held on their playing field. Parking down a quiet side street, I sat in my car and waited until it had gone one o'clock. This part of my plan completely hinged on getting the timing exactly perfect. Too soon and too many of the other parents would see me; too late and I ran the risk of someone else deciding to give Josh a lift home.

I watched as a dozen excited, muddy children walked out of the school gates, chattering excitedly to the mums or dads holding their hands. Making sure the small plastic bag was still safely tucked into the side pocket of my handbag, I locked my car and walked casually up the street, crossed over the road and entered the grounds of the school, checking all around me that there were no stray grown-ups hanging around, ready to ask if I needed something.

Thud. Thud. Pause. Thud.

The sound of a football hitting a wall was coming from around the side of the sports hall. Peering round the corner, I saw Josh, kicking the ball angrily against the side of the hall as hard as he could. There was no one else in sight.

'Josh.' I called. He didn't hear me and kept on banging the football into the wire mesh that separated the playground from the field. 'JOSH!' I called louder. He looked up, a scowl across his tiny features. It cleared when he saw me and he ran over to me, all excited.

'Mrs Janet!' He jumped up and hugged me. 'Did you come to pick me up? He asked, hope on his face. 'Are we going to your house to see Monkey and Rocket?' I swallowed down the lump of grief that threatened to choke me. What could I say? Was it fair to tell him that no, he couldn't play with Monkey and Rocket again because his father had bashed their heads open on my kitchen units? I changed the subject.

'What are you doing here on your own Josh? Where's your mum?'

He dragged his little football boots in the mud.

'She's late. AGAIN! She's ALWAYS late to pick me up.' The scowl was back on his face, and I leaned down to brush his hair back from his eyes.

246

'Well, you can't stay here alone. It's not safe. Where are the teachers?' He shrugged and pointed over in the direction of buildings beyond the school car park.

'Most of them have gone already. Some of them go in there to eat biscuits after we finish but we never get any.' I presumed he meant they were in the staffroom, safely tucked away out of sight.

'Well, how would you like it if I waited with you – just until your mum gets here?' He nodded. 'Actually, now I've got an even better idea. See that café across the road, the one with the big windows?' He craned his head to look and nodded again. 'Why don't we go in there to wait? We could have a hot chocolate and sit by the window so we can see your mum when she comes up the street.' It was a sound idea. We would be indoors away from the prying eyes of any teachers, and it would be much easier for me to manage him when I needed to get him into my car.

'Yeah!' His eyes lit up and he grinned. He had the cutest gap in his mouth where he had lost his baby teeth and was waiting for his big teeth to grown in. 'Can I have whippy cream again?

'You can have whippy cream AND marshmallows if you want.' I held out my hand and he placed his smaller one in mine, so trustingly, and we walked out of the school grounds together.

It was as easy at that.

The café was quiet. We sat at our table in the window while the man behind the counter made our hot chocolates. Josh had kept up a stream of happy conversation, peppered with plenty of 'Mrs Janet's', which worked out brilliantly. Afterwards, if the police talked to the café staff all they would be able to tell them was that my name was Mrs Janet. The barista indicated that our drinks were ready and I got up to go and fetch them. Sliding the plastic bag out of its hiding place, I pretended to load up the drinks with those little sachets of sugar, tipping several out into my glass. With my other hand I undid the plastic seal of the bag and tipped the white powder into Josh's drink, stirring rapidly and hoping that the combination of chocolate, sugar, cream and marshmallow would hide any trace of its bitterness. It had taken me a long time to work out how many of the sleeping tablets I should give Josh. One was enough for me to have a good night's sleep, and Josh was tiny, with a much smaller body mass than me, but I couldn't run the risk of him waking up later when we got to the harbour so in the end I settled on two pills. I crushed them up and ground them into the finest powder I could make with the end of a rolling pin before scooping the dust into a plastic sandwich bag and sealing it tight.

Smiling brightly, I took both glasses over to our table. Placing the tall glass in front of him, he said 'Wow!' at the sight of so many naughty treats at once and dipped the long spoon into the lump of whipped cream on the top.

'This is the best! Thank you Mrs Janet.'

He was chattering so much it was an effort to get him to finish his hot chocolate. He had just tilted the glass up to catch the very last drops on his tongue and I had to surreptitiously check whether there was any tell-tale trace of the powder left. I couldn't see anything so I guess he got most of both sleeping tablets inside him.

I kept one eye out on the street, looking for that familiar figure of her stalking up the road. My watch told me we had plenty of time, she wouldn't have finished at the hairdressers yet. To entertain Josh, I was showing him pictures and videos of Monkey and Rocket on my phone. Ten minutes later he yawned and slumped into me, his eyes closing then snapping open, then closing again as he fought to stay awake.

'It's OK if you're tired Josh.' I whispered. 'You have a little sleep, you're safe with me.' I pulled him onto my knee and rocked him, feeling his body relax into a deep sleep. When he started letting out little snores, I gathered him up and carried him to the café door.

'Poor thing – he's worn out.' I smiled at the teenage girl who was clearing the tables. She barely gave me a glance and I knew she wouldn't even remember us as soon as we had walked out the door.

Carrying him to my car, I make sure to walk slowly, carefully, so I wouldn't draw any attention to us. I needed for us to look as normal as possible, just a tired, sleepy boy being taken home by his mother. It was hard work. Josh grew heavy in my arms, a dead weight.

Propping him up on my hip, I unlocked the back door and gently laid Josh down on the blankets I had bought especially for this day. He snuffled and turned over, snuggling down into a comfortable position and resuming his snoring. I glanced up and down the street. There was no one to be seen, no one shouting 'Hey, what are you doing with that boy?' at me before calling the police.

Driving to a secluded woodland area a couple of miles away I parked up. I had a couple of hours to wait now but this next bit was the trickiest bit. I couldn't forecast how Dave and Vicki would react when Vicki arrived at Soccer Stars over an hour late, to find her son nowhere to be seen. I imagined her phoning home first, perhaps assuming that Josh had tried to walk home by himself.

'Dave, is Josh with you?' She would say, maybe a little bit annoyed at this inconvenience.

'No. Why? Why isn't he with you?' Dave would be confused, knowing what time the football classes finished and wondering why Vicki was calling him an hour later.

'He's not here.' She would go on helplessly.

'Have you checked with the teachers?' They wouldn't be panicking, not just yet.

'There's no one around.' Maybe just the hint of panic in her voice.

'OK, don't worry. He can't have gone far. Maybe he went home with one of the other kids.' There would be a contingency plan in place, a list of parents' phone numbers for all the children in the class. She would stay at the school, having another look around the sports hall and Dave would start working his way down the list of numbers, phoning each one and asking if they had picked Josh up as well as their own kid, and maybe had forgotten to let him know?

I gave myself two hours. Two hours and they would both be out looking for Josh but would not have thought of phoning the police just yet. It would be in their minds but they would not want to cross that line of imagining the worst, not until they had exhausted all other avenues. I wondered if it would cross Dave's mind that Josh might remember that Mrs Janet lived quite close to Soccer Stars, and Mrs Janet had cool guinea pigs, and think it was possible Josh might have found his own way back to my little flat. It wasn't very likely – Josh had been too upset about his bloodied knee to take too much notice of where I lived, and the side gate wasn't easy to find, a five-year-old wouldn't be able to recognise it. I dismissed this thought almost instantly. I doubt I would have even entered Dave's mind.

CHAPTER THIRTY-THREE

Josh is with me

I sent the text to Dave's phone when the two hours was up. Josh was still snoring peacefully on the back seat; he hadn't stirred since I laid him down there. I checked his breathing a couple of times, suddenly afraid that the dose I had given him had been too high, but it was steady and regular.

My phone jangled its ring tone loudly, jarring my thoughts. Dave must have seen my text, why else would he be calling? I let it go to voicemail, as I did with the next five, six, seven calls he tried to make. Another number I didn't recognise tried calling me too. A mobile, it had to be Vicki, swallowing her pride in order to call me, probably thinking I would relate better to another woman. God, she really was thick, wasn't she?

I waited until the phone went quiet then dialled into my message service. The first ones from Dave were angry, bordering on threatening.

'Where is he, you fucking bitch? Where is my son?' Then they became panicked. I could hear him trying to keep calm and reasonable. 'Katie. Just let us know where you are. I'm not angry. I just need to know Josh is safe.' Yeah, right, you're not angry Dave.

'Katie, if you don't pick up then we will call the police. Just let us know where you are and we will come and get Josh. No questions asked OK?' He was pleading now. Then a message in a different voice.

'Katie, this is Vicki. Josh's mum. I don't know how Josh ended up with you. I mean, I know I was a little bit late going to get him but he knows not to go away with anyone but us. Katie, please, as a mother, I'm begging you to let us know where Josh is.' The last words broke on a sob and the message ended.

I sent through another text to Dave.

Remember what you did to my guinea pigs?

The phone rang almost immediately. Oh Dave, do you really think I'm going to pick up? If you want to communicate it will be by text only. I didn't have long to wait.

That was a mistake and I'm sorry. Please don't do anything to hurt him.

Oh it was a mistake, was it? An accident? You didn't mean to pick them up and bash their poor little heads in as a way of getting back at me?

Do not inform the police. I will text you directions soon.

I left it at that, and switched off my phone. Knowing they couldn't reach me would make their wait seem ten times longer. Humming, I started the car and drove to our final destination.

I had discovered this place last year. A few miles out of town, on the way to the airport, was a small harbour. Built in Victorian times it had a stone breakwater which jutted out more than 500 metres into the sea. It was originally intended for use as a Royal Navy harbour when the threat of French invasion was always possible, but it was soon discovered that the harbour was too shallow for the large Navy vessels, and the harbour was left to the smaller fishing boats, and more recently, the many pleasure boats which moored there.

There was an open parking area which allowed cars to park right up close to the harbour railings, giving the drivers an excellent view of the entire sweep of the bay, with the breakwater to their left. It was perfect for what I had in mind. I pulled up next to a red hire car and sent Dave a screenshot of Google Maps. It would take them a little while to figure out where I meant but I was reliant on them getting here within the next half hour. The weather had stayed dull but the rain had stopped. The heavy clouds reflected in the silver sea and the many boats bobbed merrily up and down on the slight swell.

'This is where it all ends Josh' I told him softly, but there was no reply.

I left it as long as I dared. When I thought they would be on their way to the little known road that lead to the harbour I got out of the car. Leaving my phone and handbag, I opened the door to the back seat.

'Time to go, little man.'

I left the car as it was, unlocked and with the doors open wide. Picking up the heavy bundle, the black hair so like his dads flopping down, I carried the heavy blanket covered shape awkwardly down the slip road to where the water gently lapped at my feet. Wading in, fully clothed, the water was fucking freezing, and by the time it had hit my midriff I was shivering. This might be harder to do than I thought. I should have done a dummy run, but I just didn't have the time. The sandy sea bed dropped away and I was swimming then. The water had soaked into the woollen blankets quickly and the precious parcel they contained got heavier and heavier. I had anticipated this though, had wrapped nylon rope around and around the blankets, looping it into handles which I could use to drag the water logged bundle behind me as I swam. Aiming for one of the furthest boats, I ploughed through the water, doing a sort of sideways crawl. My clothing, deliberately chosen for this, was feeling heavy too, and by the time I reached the side of the boat my arms were aching and my legs felt like numb blocks of concrete. Pulling the blankets towards me, I hid behind the yacht so we couldn't be seen from the land. I didn't want them to see us, not just yet. Gripping one of the ropes that dangling off the side of the boat, my teeth chattered and my hands were stiff as I tried to uncover the blankets enough so the dark hair was poking out and would be instantly recognisable from the shore.

Where were they? I didn't know how long I could stay afloat in that cold sea, and the timing was critical, they needed to be able to see us from the shore, but we would be too far away for them to do anything quickly.

Finally, over the sound of the waves and the gulls, I heard the sound of a car speeding into the car park.

'JOSH. JOOOOSSSHH!' Dave's voice carried out clearly over the water. 'JOSH' he shouted over and over. I peeked around the side of the yacht and saw Dave climb awkwardly out of his car from the passenger side, the bright blue plaster boot slowing him down. He had spotted my car and he limped over to look inside, hoping against hope that we would both be in there, warm and dry.

'JOSH!' A woman's voice screamed, the same voice that had left a message on my voicemail not long ago. 'JOSH, WHERE ARE YOU?'

She got out of the driver's seat and ran to railings in the front of my car, frantically scanning the water below. She walked up and down a few paces, hand to her eyes as she concentrated on the boats and the sea within the harbour walls.

'JOSH! KATIE!' Dave tried calling my name, cupping his hands to his mouth to make the sound travel further. I watched from my hiding place as they came to stand together just next to my car, right by the hire car and scoured the water in front of them. It was time for the final show. Taking a deep breath and letting go of the boat's rope, I swam out into view, pushing the sinking blankets in front of me. Treading water, I waited until I was sure they had seen me.

'Dave!' Vicki spotted me first and pointed to where we were in the water. Using all my strength to lift my arm, I waved and I made sure they were both watching, the horror of what they were seeing making gargoyles of their faces. Never once taking my eyes off them, I turned and kissed the soft dark hair for one last time, before pushing the bunch of blankets and rope away from me. Without me to keep it afloat, it sank quickly, tilting up slightly on its end and slipping beneath the waves forever, the black fronds of hair floating delicately in the water like seaweed. There was no sound. It sank down and was lost from sight almost in an instant, drifting gently down to lie on the sea bed and rest undisturbed. My strength had all but gone now. I had done what I came here to do. The last thing I heard before letting the waves wash over my head was the sound of her screaming.

SIX MONTHS LATER

Katherine

The hot sun burned down on my bare head as I climbed the last few steps of the hill.

'Come on, slow arse!' I crowed, waving my water bottle at the two figures further down the path. I sat on a jutting rock and breathed in the fresh air. All I could see, all the way up the coast and all the way down the coast, was golden sandy beaches and the most brilliant coloured turquoise sea.

The last six months had been the best of my life. Life now was a far cry from the miserable existence I had left behind in England.

The rest of that last day went like a dream, I couldn't have planned it any better. When I dunked my head under the waves in that freezing cold, slate grey sea, her screams had carried underwater for a while. Sinking down almost to the bottom, I used a rock to push off and swam, quickly and silently, underwater to the end of the breakwater wall. It was a fair distance from the boat where I had hidden but all that swim training when I was younger paid off, and I surfaced close to the end of the wall a minute later, gasping for air. I couldn't be seen unless there happened to be someone right at the end of the harbour, looking directly down into the water, but a quick scan showed I was alone, and safe for now. Breaking into a breast stroke I circled around to the other side of the wall, where the sea was rougher and opened out onto an endless expanse of cold choppy waves.

Using the wall to keep me going, I half swam, half dragged myself along to the rusted spikes that used to be a ladder. Praying they would hold, they'd been there at the mercy of the seas and salt spray for a hundred and fifty years, I climbed up the wall using the sleeves of my lightweight jumper to cushion my hands which were soft and wrinkly from being in the water for so long.

The top of the breakwater wall was nearly three-foot-wide in some places and I crawled along the top, keeping low down so Dave and Vicki wouldn't see me. As I had predicted, Vicki was running to the end of the breakwater, desperate to be closer to the spot where we had disappeared under the waves, and for a moment I couldn't see Dave anywhere, but then I spotted a figure thrashing about in the water and knew he had gone in to try and save Josh. They had no reason to turn around and face the car park so they didn't see me jump off the wall where it joined the tarmac and run to crouch behind the other parked vehicles. In seconds I was behind the hire car and I reached into the crevice above the front tyre to where I had hidden the keys. Yesterday I had driven the car here, straight from the car hire place near the airport where I had left my own car in the airport car park, and walked the two miles back to the terminal, before driving safely home. The hire car would be safe enough left there overnight, locked and with the keys hidden.

I got in, all fingers and thumbs from the cold water, and checked that the camera was still running from when I set it before going into the water. The reason I had hired this model was for the dash cam it came with as standard. A quick tutorial on YouTube and I knew how both how to set it running, and how to download the footage onto my laptop, using the built in memory card reader. I switched off the camera, hoping I would have what I wanted but I could waste no more time checking it now. Starting the hire car, I reversed out of the car park and drove quickly away passing several police cars on the narrow road racing towards the harbour, lights flashing and sirens blaring. The service vehicle for the inshore rescue crew was following close behind, towing a small RIB on a trailer behind them. I steered the car around the steep twists and turns before joining up with the main road, and turned in the direction of the motorway and beyond, driving all the way through to London's Heathrow airport.

As I drove, I pictured the looks on all their faces, as they dived down to the bottom of the sea, searching and searching for any sign of Josh's body. What would they think when they brought the small figure to the surface? What would they make of the empty bundle of blankets, tied with rope, and sporting a plastic football head with a cheap, nylon, black wig superglued onto it?

I was sure Josh would be found safe and well that same day, snug and warm in the sleeping bag I had wrapped him in when I left him to sleep in the small copse of trees, the place I had killed time before driving on down to the harbour alone. It was dry under the trees, and sheltered, the tree roots making a natural cradle just perfect for a sleeping five-year-old. There was a small hotel just across the road from the trees, so when Josh woke up he could walk over there for help. He was an intelligent child; he would know what to do.

They would be searching for my body for quite some time, sending the police to check my flat for clues and finding only an empty room with piles of post-it noted possessions, clearly indicating that I never had any intention of returning. I would never be found, bodies often aren't along that stretch of coast, and the search would be called off in a matter of days. Life would go on as usual. Dave and Vicki would realise just how close they had been to losing their son for real. Josh would have no memory of what had happened that day, only that the lovely Mrs Janet had taken him for a hot chocolate and then he went to sleep and when he woke up he didn't know where he was. He was scared for a tiny bit but then it was OK because the nice ladies at the hotel had given him some chips while he was waiting for his mum and dad to come and get him. Riding in the police car with the lights and sirens and everything was a brilliant adventure and he couldn't wait to tell his friends at Soccer Stars all about it.

I didn't mind leaving my car at the harbour, it was a piece of shit anyway and I would buy a new one as soon as I got to Australia, along with a new phone with an Australian SIM card. Adam had come good on the money he owed me, so I asked him to wire it to my new account. If he was surprised it was an Australian account he didn't question it. I got the feeling that this payment was his way of washing his hands of me for good.

It was easy to set up a bank account with Westpac Bank in Australia; I just opened one online, and when I got there all I had to do was go into any city branch and show my ID to get the account active and a debit card issued. My pay off from Recruit Unique was more than enough to get me on a Malaysia Airlines flight to Brisbane, leaving Heathrow late in the evening on Saturday, so I booked a ticket last minute and called my Auntie Noleen who lived on Brisbane's Sunshine Coast on Friday, asking if they minded having me to stay for a little while, just until I could find a job. My Auntie Noleen is married to my dad's brother, Uncle Frank, and they're minted, living in a great big house just outside of Mooloolaba. She almost blubbed with happiness when I said I'd be there in less than forty-eight hours' time. It just so happened that she and Uncle Frank had recently bought a huge Winnebago camper, and were dying to try it out, but they couldn't take their elderly dog with them or leave their cat behind so they were at a loss for what to do. If I was there, I could house-sit for them and look after their pets while they went on a good long jaunt, travelling the length and breadth of Australia for as long as they wanted. I was the answer to their prayers, she said, their guardian angel. No Auntie Noleen, you are mine, I wanted to say.

After I'd handed the hire car back at their Heathrow depot, I lugged my newly purchased backpack into the departures hall of Terminal Three. Juggling that and my laptop bag, I checked in with five minutes to spare, and passed through Border Control with not a glance from the immigration officer or the armed police officers patrolling the terminals. I doubt anyone would notice my passport was missing when they emptied my flat, I had left an old expired one in the handbag I abandoned in my old car. Hopefully they would not look too closely into it, presuming me dead and gone. I had planned to go back to using my maiden name anyway, as soon as I was safely in Australia, so if anyone came looking for Katie Fernley, they wouldn't be led to Katherine Barrett.

Waiting for the flight, I took advantage of the airports twenty minutes free Wi-Fi offer and downloaded the footage from the hire car's Dash-cam onto my laptop. Rushing through the first hour when nothing happened, I stopped when the lens first caught the panicked faces of Dave and Vicki, leaning over the railings and searching the water. The sound was good, very clear considering that I had only left the hire car's windows open a fraction, and the camera had perfectly captured the moment they realised that I had taken 'Josh' into the open sea. What it had recorded next was social media gold.

'Dave, he's in the water! Vicki pointed out in the direction of the boat I had hid behind. 'You have to go and get him! He's drowning!' She screamed.

'I can't with this fucking thing on my leg, can I?' Dave tapped his heavy plaster cast. 'You stupid cow. You go, quickly! I'll call for help' Dave took out his phone and dialled the emergency services.

'I can't go in there!' Vicki's voice rose into a disbelieving screech.

'Our fucking son is fucking well fucking drowning!! Dave roared into her face and gave her a shove towards to water. 'Get in there NOW!'

'But MY HAIR!' She tugged on her newly golden locks. 'I just paid four hundred quid for my hair, and the SALT WATER WILL RUIN IT!'

Dave stared at her for a second in total silent disbelief, before shoving her aside with an almighty bellow and diving into the water himself, phone and all. He tried his best to swim but the cast was dragging him down and he had to stop at the first boat and hold onto the side to stop himself from going under. I couldn't see his face in detail, he was too far away from the camera by then, but I could have sworn he was crying.

CHAPTER THIRTY-FIVE
Katherine

Landing at Brisbane International Airport some twenty-eight hours later, I checked into the nearest backpacker's hostel I could find. There was an information desk at the airport and the young attendant had plenty of suggestions, even helpfully circling the ones who offered a free shuttle transfer from the airport. Somewhere in the city suburbs later, I paid twenty bucks extra for a private, single room so I wouldn't have to share in the dorms. I was by far the oldest person in the hostel but it was fine for a couple of nights until I figured out how to get to Auntie Noleen and Uncle Frank's house. While I was at the hostel I gave fifty bucks to one of the other, younger backpackers to upload the camera footage onto his Facebook page, and share it with as many people as he could. He watched the drama unfolding and turned me.

'So this chick's kid was drowning?'

'Yep.'

'And her fella had a broken leg and couldn't swim?'

'Yep.'

'And she wouldn't jump into the water to save her son because of her fuckin' HAIR DO?'

'Spot on,' I told him.

'Jeez...' He drawled, shaking his head and hissing through his teeth before playing the footage back again. 'What a cunt!'

'Couldn't have put it better myself, mate. 'I said.

She was absolutely crucified.

Within days the video had gone viral, was shared millions of times. OK, I may have given it a helping hand by publicising the name of her Instagram account, and tagging her as Vicki Campbell-Roberts in the video and when my young IT coach had shown me some of the comments people had posted and shared, for a minute I actually felt sorry for her. It was all anyone on Twitter could talk about and had been tweeted and retweeted thousands of times.

+Joe Weston @Joeweston   June 24
Is this for real?

+Natalie Brown @natserb   June 24
Replying to @Joeweston
Yes, it's real. This woman, this person who calls herself a mother, wouldn't jump in the water to save her baby.

+Mommy2Five @bloopers   June 24
I hope she got her baby taken off her. She don't deserve to be a mom.

+Priya @Priyapasanda   June 24
I hope she end up drowning herself. She should be shot.

+Sarah Novak @NovakSarah June 25
Have you SEEN her Insta account? Never seen anyone so self-obsessed in my life!

+Natalie Brown @natserb June 25
Replying to @NovakSarah
OMG! Just looking now. Vain is not the word.

And so on and so on.
Thinking back on it, with the benefit of hindsight when I watched the video again after a few months, I could see she was in total shock. She just couldn't get her head around the fact that her little boy was in the water and she wasn't thinking straight, so she just said the first thing that popped

into her head. The trouble was, the first thing to pop into her head also happened to be the dumbest.

For days after the video was uploaded, the backpacker's hostel rang with shrieks of 'MY HAIR!' in a falsetto screech, followed by bellows of laughter. Vicki had got what she wanted all along.

She was a worldwide sensation.

The next time I tried to look at her Instagram page it had been taken down, and her Facebook account had gone too. I kept up to date with the news from home online, reading the local papers for any coverage about me and my disappearance but aside from a small paragraph stating that the search for my body had been called off there was nothing. I wasn't wanted by Interpol for kidnapping and child endangerment after all. The texts I had sent to Dave when I took Josh had been carefully crafted to look completely innocent. 'Josh is with me' could have simply meant that as a trusted friend I had picked him up from football, there was nothing in them to prove I was intending to hurt Josh in any way.

Dave's court case was up in August. It made the second page headline in our evening paper. He pleaded guilty and his lawyer cited the extreme stress he had been under recently as a reason for leniency. He had lost his job, they told the court, his only son had gone missing and had been feared drowned before being found safe a few hours later. His family had been on the receiving end of all sorts of abuse, even death threats. He had recently split with his wife and was a broken man, struggling to adapt to life as a single father relying on state benefits, his counsel claimed. Dave got an eighteen-month sentence, suspended for two years, was fined £1500, and had to attend a six-week rehabilitation course. Lucky really. It could have been so much worse.

When I think about Dave now I feel nothing. I don't hate him, not anymore, I don't care enough to hate him. He's just like a million other men who thought they could play away without getting caught – and yet when they did, they inevitably blamed everyone else but themselves. He made the mistake of thinking that, because I was vulnerable, I was also weak and stupid. But I am neither.

I phoned Mum and Dad from Auntie Noleen's house in case the British authorities had contacted them to declare me dead, convincing them it was a case of mistaken identity. A hastily constructed story about my car being stolen, my handbag and passport unfortunately in the car too, earned a lecture about responsibility from my dad and being called a silly girl by my mum. I could handle that though, take it on the chin, if it meant that all the loose ends had been tied up, and I could finally breathe again. I could stop looking over my shoulder, stop waiting for that hand of the law to clamp down on me.

Living at Auntie Noleen's was a dream. I had a huge house to myself, only minutes from the sea, and the company of Bonny, the golden retriever, and Pooky the cat. There was a lively beach town scene and I was offered plenty of cash in hand work if I wanted it, allowing me to stay under the radar. I only had to worry about buying food as I was living rent free for at least the next six months, in exchange for looking after the pets and keeping the house clean, so earning money wasn't such a priority. I worked just enough hours needed to keep me fed, with a bit of extra cash for nights out and keep my car on the road.

Auntie Noleen and Uncle Frank had a gardener in to mow the lawns once a week and keep the section tidy, so all I had to do was offer him a cold drink now and again. The first time he turned up I was lying on the deck in my bikini, soaking up the Brisbane sun.

'You do realise it's the middle of bloody winter?' A loud voice with a broad accent startled me out of my semi-slumber.

'It's twenty-two degrees!' I replied, sitting up and hoisting the straps on my bikini up my shoulders. I shaded my eyes from the glare as I took in the figure in front of me. He was wearing shorts, and a woolly jumper. The traditional Australian Akubra hat sat on his head, framing his bright blue eyes and wide twinkling smile. To say he was fit was a massive understatement.

'You're wearing a jumper!' I accused him.

'You're wearing, er, not very much at all.' He shot back, grinning even wider. 'It's bloody freezing!'
I looked up at the broad expanse of blue, blue sky. There was one solitary cloud drifting by, doing no damage at all.

'Where I come from, we would be saying "What a lovely day!" I got up and stepped inside the open sliding glass doors to the open plan kitchen and living space. Bonny heaved herself up from where she had been lying beside me and padded in silently after me. 'Drink?' I called over my shoulder.
He had followed me indoors, stopping to ruffle Bonny's fur gently.

'Don't s'pose you've got any hot chocolate?'

It just got better from there. Jack, my gardener friend, started finding excuses to spend more and more time at Auntie Noleen's, claiming he needed to cut back some of the trees or that the lawn needed feeding. When he cheekily offered to trim my bush, I laughed, and said 'When are you going to ask me out?' He did, then and there, and we've been together ever since. On our first proper date I asked him outright if there was a Mrs Jack and he looked seriously affronted and said 'what d'ya bloody take me for? I never cheated on anyone in me life!'

'Just making sure.' I smiled. 'I just needed to know you're not running home to the wife and kiddies every night.'

'Nah. Fuck that.'

Bonny and Pooky both adore him, and there's something to be said about a man who loves and respects animals and nature. It makes me feel I can trust him. We go hiking on the weekends, taking Bonny with us and roaming the glorious Australian countryside. Jack showed me the many species of native flora, and laughed his head off when I went into raptures over seeing my first ever wild kangaroo.

'They're bloody pests!' He told me. 'Just big rodents.'

'I happen to love rodents.' I replied, airily.

So here we are now. Sitting on top of this big hill, Jack's arm around my waist and Bonny panting at our feet, I'm on top of the world. I feel so happy with how my life turned out that I can even understand now why some people feel the need to share their every feeling, emotion and occurrence on social media. If I was ever to sell out and join modern world, my first post would look something like this:

Katherine Barrett @wanteddownunder
Another day in paradise with my two best friends' #blessed

I'd draw the line at posting pictures of my food though. That's just dumb.

Victoria Campbell @ladygotstyle
Me and my new man, crazy in love! I'm not one to brag but so pleased with my make up in this one XX #lovehim #newlove #newlife #sogood #special #treatmelikeaprincess #iamaprincess #brunette #luxelife #longhair #greeneyes #beauty #MAC #contours #cheekbones #somucheyeliner #grindhardstayhumble #ladyhaveitall #datenight #kissme #Scotland #home #blessed

THE END

Dear Reader

Thank you for reading #Blessed! I would love to know what you thought of it so, if you have a minute to spare, please post a review on any of the following sites:

- Amazon.co.uk
- Amazon.com
- Amazon.com.au
- Goodreads

Reviews help us budding authors tremendously! Not only do they help us recognise where we could improve in our writing but they help other readers decide on their next great read.

Best wishes
T M Creedy

ACKNOWLEDGEMENTS

A big thank you to the following people:

To my sister, Tracey, who nagged and nagged me to read this – my first novel, and who genuinely loved it and told me so. To Jeannette and Bronwen, who were the first to read it, and who supported and encouraged me unfailingly. Bronwen – you were supposed to proof it; you weren't supposed to get so caught up in the story that you couldn't wait to read the end!
To Georgia, for her non-judgemental support and advice on how to get my book noticed in this young person's digital age!
And to Plop. For never doubting me.

Printed in Great Britain
by Amazon

30966145R00153